The Colors of Eliza Gray

A NOVEL

J. Willis Sanders

ISBN-13: 978-1-954763-01-2 (paperback)
ISBN-13: 978-1-954763-05-0 (hardcover)
ISBN-13: 978-1-954763-00-5 (ebook)

BUGGS ISLAND BOOKS

Printed in the United States of America
Cover art by MiblArt

DEDICATION

To my wife: Thank you for understanding my passion for writing and always encouraging me to never, ever give up.

To my daughter: You'll never know how much you encouraged me when you said the ending of my first novel left you "in a puddle of tears." Then again, I'm sure you do.

To my sister: Thank you for your keen eye while reading so many of my stories, and thanks for saying how much you enjoyed them because you really did.

Another very special thanks to my parents, passed on now. Without you instilling the love of books within me, this adventure would've never been possible.

The best and most beautiful things in the world cannot be seen
or even touched—they must be felt with the heart.
Helen Keller

Chapter 1

Holmes County, Ohio

Of all the times the boy across the table had mocked Eliza, she had never wanted to hurt him.

He was sneaky about it, too. He would stop eating, make sure no one was looking, cover his ears, roll his eyes, and go back to his food, smirking.

But this was different. This was worse.

He had elbowed his fork to the floor, crawled under the table, shoved his hand up her dress to her thigh, and had scrambled back to his chair before she could make sense of what had happened.

She probably could hurt him now, and she didn't even care about the beginning of a beard on his chin.

At the other end of the table, Mama and Papa spoke silent words to the boy's mama and papa. To Eliza's left, Tess and Ethan ate roasted chicken and cabbage soup. Beside the mocking boy, his younger brother drank milk.

Eliza tilted her head to one side, considering the three black bonnets and two wide-brimmed straw hats on pegs by the door. If someone made the mocking boy wear a white kapp, one of the bonnets, a white apron, and a black dress, he might understand how it felt to be her.

She straightened her head. No, that wouldn't work. Not

unless he'd lost his hearing as a child. Time to think about something sweet and precious instead of him.

Behind Mama, in one of the boy's old cribs, Ivy pushed her lips in and out as if she were nursing. Similar to the color of Papa's beard, dark red hair covered her head. Ethan and Tess shared the same hair color, but Mama's hair gleamed in shiny black waves down to her waist when, at bedtime, she removed the white kapp and unpinned her hair. Compared to the women on the magazines at the store in town, Mama was as beautiful as they were. Eliza could've been her sister, except a younger, taller version, with a slender waist, black instead of green eyes, and a sharp nose instead of an upturned one. Mama also had crow's feet, a hint of gray at her temples, and a few wrinkles on her forehead from furrowing her brow. That's what she got for being mean. So much for thinking about something sweet and precious.

Across the table, the boy darted his dark eyes around in preparation for more mocking. Eliza drew her feet back and lowered her head to watch for the fork.

During these meals, when his mocking had begun, back when she was a little girl with curls to her shoulders, she lowered her head to hide like a meek little rabbit in its den of briars, except her den of briars was a kapp sewn from stiff, white cloth. Tears in bed followed. They sometimes followed now, but not as often. Teary nights were never good, when she wished someone would place her in a wooden box and lower her into a hole in the ground.

She counted time in several hesitant breaths. No fork fell, so she raised her head. The boy elbowed his younger brother, who touched one ear and went back to his apple pie.

Being unable to hear meant Eliza had to study people's actions to understand what they meant. In this case, since the boy had only touched one ear, he didn't like mocking her. Eliza managed a smile. Unless he loved apple pie as much as Ethan loved apple pie.

Tess placed a slice before Eliza. Ignoring the mocking boy, she enjoyed the tart apples and flaky crust, washed down with cold swallows of milk.

Plate and glass empty, she leaned back against the wooden chair's hard slats.

The few words she could remember from long ago, "tree, water, and river," sometimes peeked above the nest of her memories like baby birds stretching their necks for a worm. No matter how hard she tried, no more words revealed themselves, as if the mama bird had pushed them from the nest.

The idea made her teary, but she'd rather do that later in bed.

When she tried saying those words now, people looked at her with widened eyes before turning away, which is why she'd stopped trying to speak as a child. She was grown now, as tall as the adults, and she hated it when they treated her like this. Even worse was when children and older boys and girls treated her like this.

Then there was the boy across the table. One day she'd prove she was no meek little rabbit, and he wouldn't dare touch or mock her again.

Plates cleaned, glasses emptied, the adults exchanged waves on the porch. The boy's mama and papa even included Eliza, giving her a warm feeling in her chest. As they went inside, her family left for the dirt road that led toward home.

The late autumn sun pressed searing rays into the land. On one side of the road, stalks of corn—green at the bottom, dusky brown at the top—filled a huge field. No breeze stirred the slender leaves nor the golden tassels hanging from the plump ears. On the other side of the road, heat waves hovered a shimmering mirage over a pasture, blurring a brown and white milk cow cropping grass in the shade of an oak. The aroma of manure and dark, rich earth filled the air, intensified by the heat.

Eliza lagged behind her family, preferring to walk by herself. What chores would Mama have for her this afternoon? Pump water from the well and tote it inside? Hoe the withering weeds in the garden? Peel potatoes for—

A hot breeze blew against the nape of her neck, carrying the sour warning that someone was behind her. She turned to peek from beneath the black bonnet.

And there they were, the two boys chasing the meek little rabbit. They carried fishing poles over their shoulders, so maybe they just wanted to see what was biting in the river.

She turned around. No, the oldest boy probably wanted to mock her again instead of fishing—or worse.

Eliza increased her stride to catch her family. Their shoes puffed dust into the air, now dry and still. The sun bore down on their black clothing. Sweat smudged shirts and dresses, darkened underarms and collars.

The oppressive heat surrounded her, concentrated beneath her black bonnet, settled into the hollow between her shoulder blades.

Something lifted her dress. She looked back in time to see the oldest boy jerk his fishing pole away, a grinning smirk twisting his face.

She felt teary again, like the little girl from long ago.

A flash of light caught her eye. To the right, beyond the rolling hills behind her home, the black belly of a cloud bulged and wallowed like a hog covered with mud.

A storm coming.

A cool gust of wind blew the ties of the bonnet around her face. Lightning flashed again, and she turned to see the boys running home, leaving a trail of dust in their wake.

She never expected the boy to touch her leg or raise her

dress, but she should have.

Although she resembled Mama, when Papa shopped in town, she compared her reflection in a sunglass display mirror to the women on those magazines, too. Yes, she looked as nice as they did. Young men in the area certainly thought so, because she drew their glances like an apple drew a horse. Regardless, even though the brushes and paste that Papa took home had brightened her teeth, no young man ever approached her with kindness in his eyes.

In the road ahead, another gust of wind swirled dirt and wisps of dried grass. Papa clamped his hand to his hat and walked faster. Beside him, Mama lowered her head over Ivy. Behind Mama, Tess hurried along, black dress swirling about her ankles. Between Tess and Eliza, holding his hat to his head with both hands, Ethan took long, stilted strides. Papa needed to give him a haircut soon. Why would a man or boy want his hair to look like a bowl turned upside-down? The men in the magazines at the store were quite handsome, with thick hair cut either close or curly. How might it be to finger a man's curly hair, especially if it were brown like soil in the garden?

Papa and Mama turned toward the two-story white house, Tess and Ethan close behind. Knees rose and fell. Pants legs and dresses flapped in the wind. Eliza imagined a family of crows in a pasture, all rising and falling and flapping after a grasshopper, whose veined wings fluttered for its life.

From the swirling clouds, lightning flicked a snake's tongue, forked and brilliant, into the trees hiding the river. Papa broke into a trot. The trees swayed and bowed with the wind. Eliza wiped a huge warm raindrop from her cheek. In the dirt road leading to the house, more raindrops fell, evidenced by puffs of dust. The gray aroma of water filled the cooling air.

Everyone piled onto the porch to wipe their shoes on the mat at the door and enter one by one. Papa removed his straw hat to hang on one of the pegs by the door, followed by Ethan. Mama did the same with her black bonnet. Tess climbed the stairs and Eliza followed.

In the dark corner at the far end of their room, she sat on her bed. Shoes, black stockings, bonnet, and apron put away, she sat again to place her hand on the cool window. Huge raindrops struck the glass, sharing tiny kisses with her palm. The grass in the back yard swirled as if caught in the grip of Mama's spoon stirring cake batter. From the swollen clouds, lightning slashed the sky again and again.

Eliza waited. It always came. Always. Like one violent beat of her heart, a huge vibration buffeted her chest, then faded into gentle caresses.

She imagined a gentle man—not some cruel boy who mocked her because she couldn't hear—holding his hand to her heart—a man who enjoyed the outdoors, long walks beneath the trees, and nothing more than the simple pleasure of being together.

Across the room, Tess lit a lamp. Black smoke fluttered sooty fingertips toward the low, plank ceiling. She lowered the wick and replaced the glass chimney, lay her head on the pillow and opened a book from the nightstand.

Eliza took her hand from the window. She needed more paper for her projects. Maybe Papa would visit a store soon, and she could buy some with the few coins that Mama let her keep from making baskets.

First things first: allow the storm to end and gather mud at the river.

If that mocking boy left her alone.

Lightning flashed again, illuminating the rusted well pump at the end of the backyard, beyond the barn and chicken coop to the right, and the woodshed and basketmaking shop to the left.

Eliza reached into her mind for the first page of her memories, when Mama had slapped her as child because she only knew to get water from the river instead of the well. Chin trembling, Eliza had nodded as a single tear rolled down the four streaks of pain burning her cheek. A confused child did not deserve such treatment. If she ever found a way to tell Mama how deep the scars of that day had cut into her heart, she would.

Shaking the memory from her mind, Eliza went to the back porch. The final drops of rain were trailing from the sky in silver sprinkles of light. The trees stood tall as the wind died. She ran through the cool, wet grass toward the barn for an old bucket. Found in the hay loft seasons ago, it made the perfect container for gathering leaves, berries, mud, or any other color a project required.

Along the path to the river, the earthy aroma of mold greeted her as she purposefully shuffled through last fall's wet leaves with her bare feet. In the branches, where green leaves were turning orange, red, and gold, a gray squirrel sat up while nibbling an acorn, furred tail curled over its back. Further on, to the side of the path, a partially eaten ear of corn marked a raccoon's supper, taken from the garden last night. Droplets of green-smelling water fell from the leaves, almost like daytime lightning bugs with crystalline beacons flashing, gathering, and dispersing the sunshine pouring from the clearing sky.

Eliza stopped at the river. The rolling water, tinted green from the leaves overhead, reflected swirls of sunlight sparkling into her eyes.

Around the bend to the left, the end of the boy's rowboat barely stuck out. He was probably at home, disappointed because he wasn't here to mock her.

Eliza left the bucket on the bank and gathered her dress to her knees. The current, slow and steady, kissed bare legs with cool lips. Raising the dress higher, she continued into the water to mid-thigh. Toes wiggling in the mud, eyes closed, she breathed in the spicy aroma of the leaves yet to fall in the woods behind her. The current swirled. She slipped in the mud, almost fell, and stepped back to ankle deep.

Something brushed her calf. Not looking, she swatted the fly away. It lit again and she swatted again. It lit on her thigh between her legs. She looked down to swat it accurately and realized the fly was the tip of the mocking boy's fishing pole, rising to touch where he shouldn't.

She whirled around. He dropped the pole and elbowed his younger brother beside him, then reared back and laughed like a rooster announcing sunrise. The younger brother took a step backward, fear in his widening eyes.

The time for tears was over.

Holding the dress up with one hand, Eliza went to the boy and jerked his hand to her thigh. He squeezed it, slowly licked his lips, and turned to wave his brother away, who ran into the path. The mocking boy faced Eliza again.

His dark eyes denied the shame of his brother's judgement, the desire to take instead of give, the willingness to hurt instead of understand. Swirling within the flecks of green around the black centers, which reflected her face and the river she loved so well, those things revealed something worse than mocking.

Yes, she could hurt him now.

She placed her hands on his shoulders, leaned in as if to kiss him, and drove her knee into his crotch. He grabbed his belly and fell on his side in the mud. She kicked him to his back and clenched her fist. Not his mouth. Why cut her knuckles on his teeth? She drew back her hand, tightened the work-hardened muscles in her shoulder, bicep, and forearm, and with every ounce of strength she could manage, drove her fist into his nose, resulting in a spectacular gush of blood from his nostrils.

She leaned over the boy to wait for his attention. His eyes opened and he jerked away. Blood ran down his chin and neck and into his collar, similar to a male hummingbird hovering near a honeysuckle bloom. Tears squeezed from his eyes, closed again, but that wasn't enough.

Eliza sucked in air until her lungs ached and screamed into his face, demanding that he never bother her again.

She stepped over him as he continued to grimace in pain. He wouldn't dare tell anyone what she'd done. Other boys would mock him like he'd mocked her, so his explanation to his family had better be an interesting one when he finally limped his bleeding self home. Still, now that she'd hurt him, he might hurt her back. Whatever he might plan, she'd be ready.

She grabbed the bucket's wire handle and left for home.

No man nearby would ever care for her, but one somewhere else might. Did he live in town? Far away? Was he sitting by a lake or a river?

Doubt replaced hope, making her teary. Like her, even if he existed, he might know sadness and heartache as well.

Smiling up at the sunshine in the leaves, she wiped her eyes. The only way to find out was to meet him.

Chapter 2

Clarksville, Virginia

In the shade of the blue funeral home tent, Denver touched the polished surface of an oak coffin, smooth and cool beneath his fingertips. He turned to a second oak coffin beside this one, hardly believing his parents were gone, and touched it also.

Although he'd cried more in the last two days of his life than all the other times put together, his eyes burned with threatening tears.

A mound of roses, deep red to almost black, nearly covered Dad's coffin. Mom's flowers carried hints of spring, with white daisies, a rainbow of wildflowers blended in, and brilliant yellow daffodils scattered about.

Life was entirely too short. One minute they were driving to the grocery store, the next a drunk driver had plowed into them. The resulting fireball of exploding gas and mangled metal had killed them instantly.

Willow, his sister, left a group of black-clad mourners and walked over, a tissue knotted in her hand. "It's so hard to believe they're gone, Den."

Denver slipped his hand around her shoulders and pulled her close. Her auburn curls caressed his cheek. Thank God Willow hadn't been in the car. If so, he'd be all alone. "I know what you mean. I keep thinking they'll walk up and ask who the funeral is for."

Willow pulled away to face him. "I got a text from Dad's

attorney a minute ago. Did you?"

"I left my phone at home. Was it about the will?"

Willow nodded slowly. "Mom donated to her favorite charities for the Deaf. Dad donated to his favorite charities to provide pro-bono attorneys for non-violent crime, along with donations to a wounded veterans association."

"They were great parents," Denver said. "Dad and I were talking the other day. He said some people don't think much of lawyers, but he said all his clients thought a lot of him."

"You've heard Mom talk about how her patients loved her."

"They never said, but I think working with people in a small town like Clarksville had something to do with how people liked them. You know, sort of laid back and friendly."

"I like it here, too," Willow said. "I wouldn't have wanted to grow up anywhere else." She faced the coffins.

"Did the attorney text anything else?" Denver guessed the answer, but making sure never hurt, especially since Willow was in her second year of nursing school and he'd graduated from college this spring, which meant neither of them had paying jobs yet.

Willow faced Denver again. "Did you say something?"

He looked down into her eyes. No doubt about it, the last resting place of their parents would stay in their heads for a long time. "I asked if the attorney said anything else."

"They left us their retirement accounts and their savings and the house. I didn't know about it, but they had seven-figure life insurance policies, too." Willow's chest expanded with a deep sigh. "I hate talking about money. Do you mind if I use some to take time off from school? I'll start again next September."

"You know I don't mind." Denver glanced at coffins. Willow didn't know he'd heard her crying in the bedroom every night since the accident, so he understood how she needed time to get over losing Mom and Dad. Still, with it being the first week in

December, with Christmas just around the corner, the holidays would be difficult, likely with sad faces and more tears. As far as what Mom and Dad had left them, including the life insurance policies, it hadn't surprised him because it showed how much they cared.

"What about you?" Willow asked. "After you graduated, all you talked about is teaching sign language for a year before you apply for a job in solar engineering. Since you haven't gotten a job yet, I thought you were going to look into that."

Grass shuffled nearby. Jan, the woman Denver had been dating for a few months, came over and slipped her arm under his. "How are you two holding up? Have you heard from the attorney about the will yet?"

Jan had asked about the will before, and Denver didn't know what to make of it. Regardless, Mom and Dad had left them with enough funds to last several years if he and Willow wanted, including the gorgeous house on Buggs Island lake, plenty of room for all the privacy a brother and sister might need, and a dock with a pontoon boat, not to mention his canoe, which he paddled on the lake when the notion struck.

A breeze kicked up, sending a cool hint of winter through the church cemetery. Red and gold leaves from maples and oaks scuttled through the frostbitten grass.

"Did you hear me?" Jan said, pulling his arm. "What about the attorney?"

Willow's blue eyes cut toward Denver. His sister's temper concerning his pick of girlfriends never failed to convey her opinion when they were alone, and he hoped she'd keep it to herself now. Her eyes darted to Jan. "You do realize the will is none of your business, Jan. After all, you do well enough with your job at that museum in Raleigh to keep you in new shoes and matching purses. Who knew folk-art made so much money?"

Jan crossed her arms. "Jealous?"

"C'mon," Denver said. "This isn't the time or place for an argument."

Willow offered her hand to Jan. "Den's right. Even though you fooled him into asking you out on the last week of college, I'll let bygones be bygones."

Ignoring the hand, Jan faced Denver. "Ready to go home? I'll make dinner while we wait to hear from your dad's attorney."

"Dinner?" Willow blurted. "People have left enough food to feed us for a week."

"I didn't mean dinner for *you,* Willow. Denver needs some comfort food and my shoulder to lean on while we watch a movie to get his mind off things."

Between the funeral and the sadness tugging at Denver's heart, he'd rather have some quiet time at home with Willow. Still, he enjoyed being with Jan—going out to eat, taking the pontoon boat out on the lake, walking Clarksville's downhome streets on Saturdays. "You better drive home before it gets dark, Jan. You know how the deer are this time of year, and it's a long way to Raleigh."

"That's true," she said, her tone solemn. "Thank you for thinking of me."

Denver kissed her cheek. "I'll call you in a few days and we can make plans."

"You're so sweet." she returned the kiss, started away and stopped. "Make sure to let me know what the attorney says, bye."

Shaking her head, Willow faced Denver. "What in the world do you see in Jan beside her looks? I guess she's great in the sack, but still …"

"I wouldn't know, Willybeans. One thing I like about her is how she wants to wait for marriage before sex. That's not too common these days, and I think it's a good idea."

Willow's mouth fell open. "You mean you and she haven't …?"

"Nope."

"Have you ever been with a woman that way?"

"Have you ever been with a man that way?"

Willow twisted her mouth into a sly grin. "I think it's time to end this conversation and go home and eat some of that buffet we've got."

During the short drive, Denver noted Willow's silence. She might give Jan a hard time and joke with him, but she did that mostly to ease her angst about the loss of Mom and Dad. Adjusting to their absence was going to be as difficult as anything they'd ever done.

At home, he changed into cargo shorts, a sweatshirt and sandals, and joined Willow in the kitchen. "You're not changing out of your dress?"

She spread her hands above the wrapped bowls and plates. "See all this stuff? Whatever we don't eat soon better go into the freezer in the basement."

Denver took a plastic container from a cabinet. "Let's put what we don't want in these containers so people can get their plates and bowls. What do you want before it goes bad?"

Willow took another container from a cabinet. "Den?"

Denver recognized her serious tone. "What?"

"I haven't been with a man that way either."

"Huh, aren't we the old-fashioned brother and sister."

"I'm sorry about what I said about Jan. Maybe I'm jealous because she could pass for a model. You know, all blond and thin and tall."

"What's wrong with a shortish redhead like you?"

"I'd rather be tall like you, but I like my hair. At least it isn't mousy brown like yours."

"Thanks, I think."

"Jan must think you're handsome, or she wouldn't date you. Do you think you'll get serious about her?"

Denver opened the plastic container and took a spoon from a drawer. "If you mean marriage, I never thought about it."

"Has she said she loves you yet?"

"Nope."

"Have you said you love her yet?"

Denver tapped Willow's head with the container lid. "I'd think the obvious answer is no."

"Good. Maybe you'll meet someone you like better." Willow tugged the pockets of his shorts. "Like someone who wears cargo shorts and sandals all winter."

"I don't wear them all winter, and you know it."

"You know what I mean, someone who loves the outdoors like you do. Jan's a city girl, and you know *that.*"

"Nothing wrong with that." Denver spooned some kind of casserole into the container and snapped the lid.

Willow did the same with her container and got another from the cabinet. In the middle of filling it, she sniffled, wiped her eyes, and left for her bedroom, likely for another cry brought on by memories of her and Mom cooking together, especially at Thanksgiving and Christmas.

Denver filled her container, took both to the basement freezer, and walked down the gravel path to the dock. Taking a seat on one of the wooden benches, he sniffled, too, from memories of everyone swimming here or taking the pontoon boat out on the lake.

He wiped his nose. Mom and Dad would want him to remember them with happiness instead of sadness, but it would be a long time before those memories wouldn't include regret.

He glanced at the house. As much as he appreciated having a sister like Willow, one honest to a fault, he didn't care to be forced to question his choice of dating Jan. Still, what Willow had said about him and Jan not being a good match was true. Well, it *seemed* to be true. More time dating her might show if they were good for each other or not.

He rested a foot on one knee and tugged the Velcro of his sandal strap—*rip-rip, rip-rip.* Normally he'd sit on the dock and hang his bare feet in the water, but a recent cold snap had brought the nighttime temperatures down to the upper teens. Cold for the first week of December in southern Virginia, the frigid air chilled the water past even *his* barefooted standards.

The Velcro ripped again. If dusk wasn't darkening the lake, he could drag his battered aluminum canoe down from beneath the deck and work out his frustrations by paddling the four miles up the lake to the Highway 58 bridge. There, the arching span bypassed the lakeside town of Clarksville, stretching from one side of the mile-wide lake to the other. Beyond, the barely visible spans of both the original bridge and the railroad bridge, including two high-voltage towers, also crossed the same width of lake.

If his frustrations weren't gone by then, he could paddle south, where the lake, actually the combined remnants of the Roanoke and Dan rivers, turned left at what local fishermen called Junkman's Curve. After the curve, the lake horseshoed left, toward John H. Kerr dam. Non-locals usually called the lake Kerr Reservoir, but Denver preferred Buggs Island Lake to the non-local name.

The Velcro ripped once more. Who was he fooling? Between losing Mom and Dad and questioning his feelings about Jan, he could paddle the twenty miles plus, from the mouth of Dan River to the dam, and not feel any better. Maybe he should pack some snacks and water and paddle to his favorite sandy spot across the lake and watch the stars come out to get his mind off everything, but he didn't want to leave Willow alone.

Over the mirrored lake, in the blackening sky to the east, the first star winked into view.

Solar engineering, as they said in the south, cranked his engine, but sign language *really* cranked his engine. No, seeing the documentary of deaf kids in Africa who didn't have access to sign language learning their first sign at a new sign language school was what *really* cranked his engine, which had led him to getting a minor in sign in college. Seeing that in person, while being the teacher who taught that to a student, was something he absolutely had to do before he entered the working world of solar engineering.

On the way back up the walkway, gravel crunching beneath his sandals, the thought lightened his step. Mom and Dad and Willow understood his desire to help the Deaf, even if only for a year. Jan didn't care for the idea much, but that was too bad, because if he got the chance, he'd make it happen whatever it took.

Chapter 3

Absalom Gray took a seat on the porch steps. Eliza was probably at the river, but she didn't usually stay so long. Maybe she'd gotten another idea for a painting and had taken the bucket to gather more supplies.

The screened door squeaked open. Oneita came out and set her hands on her hips. "Where's Eliza?"

"At the river, I think."

"Gathering garbage for her pictures again, no doubt. I could store canning supplies in the corner by her bed if it weren't for that stack of them she's smeared with mud from the river and other stuff from the woods."

Absalom ignored her. His allowing Eliza a few hours a day to enjoy her passion rubbed Oneita like sandpaper rubbed the oak he would use to make rocking chairs, if he ever got around to it. Unlike the usual Amish wife, she didn't mind expressing her feelings either. She might be happier if she weren't Amish because she could argue more.

She shook his shoulder. "Did you hear me?"

"Do you need her for something?"

"I want her to bathe Ivy while I fetch more water to heat. Ethan got it dirty with his filthy self."

"You want Eliza to bathe Ivy in dirty water?"

"I bathe Ivy in a small tub instead of the big tub. You never pay attention to anything I do."

"Get Tess to bathe Ivy."

"She's studying for school tomorrow."

"What about Ethan?"

"He shouldn't bathe a girl. Besides, he's studying, too."

The door squeaked again, and Tess came out. "I can hear you inside, Mama. I can bathe Ivy."

"I told you to keep to your books."

"But—"

"Do like your mama says," Absalom said. So much for being the head of the household. He might as well leave the Amish order, as much as his family acted like the English.

"I'm done studying, Papa."

Absalom admired Oneita's dedication to their children's schoolwork, but he'd give all he had if Eliza could learn to communicate. The English spoke of sign language, and the concept of talking with one's hands intrigued him.

"Papa?"

"Go ahead, bathe your sister."

Tess left, Oneita went in behind her, and Absalom cringed at the slamming screen door. What a storm his family could be, similar to the black clouds that had surrendered to the sunshine sparkling on the wet grass in the back yard. Maybe such a peace could envelope Eliza one day. With all she dealt with—work instead of school, teasing from many of the children in the neighborhood—she deserved it.

Grass swished to his left. Eliza stopped at the bottom step and nodded. He nodded back, their familiar greeting she'd taught her family. She raised the bucket and pointed in the general direction of the barn, fluttered her hand as if it were a leaf falling from a tree, and nodded again. This was her sign to tell someone when she intended to walk somewhere, this time to put away the bucket. She'd taught her family many self-made signs. Raising her fluttering hand meant a rising sun and morning. Lowering her fluttering hand meant the sun setting and night. Brushing her eyelids down with her fingertips, like when someone closed the eyes of a dead person, meant bedtime.

Absalom nodded. Eliza left for the barn, still fluttering her hand while swaying side to side as she walked. The sight made him smile at the memory of the day she'd first walked that way, at a livestock show.

Despite how most Amish didn't travel far from their communities, he hitched the horse to the buggy well before sunrise, lit two lanterns and hung them on one side so any vehicles behind him wouldn't mistake the buggy for a car, and took Eliza to the county fair, about two hours away. Oneita, of course, refused to go. Tess and Ethan rolled over in bed when he reminded them.

Several animals caught his eye. The dairy cows chewed their cuds, while twin jets of haze left their nostrils in the cold morning air. Some mooed and plopped steaming piles of manure to the ground. Eliza wrinkled her nose at the grassy odor.

Black Angus beef steers made his mouth water at the idea of a steak seared over an open fire. He could afford such an animal, but the Amish avoided luxuries.

In their muddy pens, huge hogs grunted and squealed in their fight for a place at the trough.

The animals that intrigued them the most, which gave Eliza the idea to walk side to side, were two enormous Brahma bulls. Talk about beefsteak!

The hump above their shoulders stood as tall as Absalom; the huge beasts could weigh over 2000 pounds. The particular bull that intrigued him and Eliza snorted slobber and lumbered over as if to say hello. Mostly gray except for its shoulders and hump, which darkened to black, the bull's neck hung with a flap of skin like a sheet hanging from a clothesline. It waggled its low-hanging ears, snorted again, and walked off, swaying side to side.

Eliza grinned at Absalom, held her hands out to her sides while fluttering them in the air, and mimicked the bull's lumbering gate. Ever since that day, when she intended to go somewhere, she said so by pointing, fluttering her hands in the air, and mimicking the huge bull's walk.

Absalom grinned. At least she hadn't mimicked the bull's slobbering.

The innocence with which she lived—taking joy in simple things, including her passion for her art—made Eliza his favorite among his children, although he'd never admit it to anyone. She never frowned when Oneita pointed at any task, and performed her daily chores to the same perfection as her art.

From time to time, when community children teased her about her deafness, harsh words of discipline tempted his tongue. Without fail she turned away, which pleased Absalom as well as relieving him. Being an Amish man required keeping peace amongst his brethren, and harsh words might cause bad feelings.

Eliza ran to him from the barn, and Absalom decided on a test. He cradled his arms as if holding Ivy and rubbed his face. Eliza nodded and went inside, obviously understanding his improvised signs for her to bathe Ivy.

Inside the kitchen, where the flickering orange glow of several lamps lit the large area that also served as the family room and the area where everyone took turns bathing, Eliza joined Tess. She nodded at Eliza, gave her a bar of soap and a wet washcloth, and held Ivy's legs out of the water so Eliza could wash her feet.

A hand grasped Eliza's arm. Fingers squeezed as if to strip the muscle from her bones. She faced Mama. What had she done wrong? Mama jerked the soap away, took another bar from the counter beside the tub Ivy sat in, and shoved it near Eliza's nose. She sniffed the aroma, somewhat like the roses Mama grew. Papa bought this soap to bathe with, and Tess had given Eliza the bar of dishwashing soap by mistake. Still, she didn't deserve to have her arm squeezed to the point of pain.

Continuing to squeeze Eliza's arm, Mama gave Tess the soap.

Enough.

Eliza shot out her right hand to grip Mama's forearm and squeezed with muscles capable of lifting and carrying two buckets of water with ease. Mama winced and let go. Eliza stepped to Mama and looked down into her eyes.

Mama whirled away. Tess's eyes widened. Eliza snatched two buckets from beside the wood stove and left for more water.

Outside, Papa was gone, likely to the barn for some chore. Eliza set a bucket beneath the well and pumped the metal handle.

Mama had treated her more like a worker than a daughter for longer than she could remember, and this was the first time she'd fought back. Maybe she did so because of the boy at the river. Regardless, enough was enough.

Buckets full, she returned to the kitchen. Baths done, she peeled potatoes for supper. Supper done, she readied herself for bed, blew out the lamp on her nightstand, and knelt by her bed.

Except for Papa, the community held no hope for a happy life. What would happen when his life ended? Ethan would leave before then, followed by Tess and Ivy. Mama would grow old and cruel, to force all the work on the only other person in the house. Then she'd die, to leave Eliza alone and without anyone who cared for her.

She refused that fate. The Creator of the woods and the animals and all that was good and kind and gentle would intervene.

Chapter 4

Absalom hefted a basket of corn from the buggy. Tess climbed out behind him.

On his neighbor's porch, he knocked on the door. Abigail, Vernon's wife, opened it, dishtowel in hand. "Good day, Absalom. Vernon's in the barn."

Absalom pointed at the corn beside the door. "I brought some corn."

"Thank you. I'll have the boys shuck it before supper."

"I'll see what Vernon's doing."

"Tess, would you like something to drink? It's hot out this afternoon."

"Thank you, Mrs. Miller. I'm not thirsty."

Absalom found Vernon in the barn, the horse's hoof between his knees while he cleaned inside the shoe. Vernon raised his head. "What has you and Tess out and about, Absalom? I thought you'd be busy in the garden."

"I brought a basket of corn. I recall how your family loved it on our last visit."

Vernon lowered the horse's hoof to the barn's dirt floor. "I'm glad I bought more salt in town yesterday to go with the butter. Plain sweet corn tastes fine, but I prefer salt and butter with it."

"Anything new in town?"

"As usual, the English in a hurry."

"Like your boys leaving when that storm came the other day. The dust flew from their feet, they ran so fast. Then again, we ran, too. Either that or walk and risk getting struck by lightning."

"They went fishing after." Vernon stroked his long beard and grinned. "Then again, maybe not."

Tess sat on a hay bale. Absalom leaned against one of the barn's supporting poles. "Did something amusing happen?"

"I shouldn't criticize Hannes, but he thinks he can boss Timothy around. They came back not long after they left."

"What's amusing about that?"

"Hannes was walking funny and holding his nose. It was bleeding terribly."

"That's not particularly amusing either, Vernon."

Hannes said he was chasing a raccoon and ran into a tree. If I'm to believe him, not only did he break his nose when he hit the tree, he" —Vernon turned away from Tess and waved his hand over his crotch— "hit down there, too."

Absalom cringed. "That'll make any boy walk funny."

"You know how Hannes teases Eliza. Along with the bossing, he does the same to Timothy, and they may have argued."

"You think Timothy did all that to Hannes?"

"I wouldn't doubt it. I've spoken with Hannes about how he treats Timothy and how he teased Eliza during our last meal together. If he does it again, I may give him more than a conversation. He may not bother Timothy anymore. Maybe Eliza needs to punch his nose, too."

Absalom took his pocketknife out and opened it to scrape dirt from under his nails. "She seems to handle the teasing well. Still, I would give anything if she weren't deaf."

"You remind me of something I heard in town," Vernon said. "A Mennonite who lives near the county seat has built a school for the deaf. Hannes said you should take Eliza there."

"Is this Mennonite anyone I know?" Since the Mennonite had built the school in the same area where Absalom had taken

Eliza to the fair, he might've entered livestock in the competition. Some Mennonite's did such things. Depending on their specific Ordnung, they even drove vehicles, powered their homes with electricity, and used tractors for farm work.

"I heard he's a successful artist," Vernon said. "His daughter is deaf."

"It's nice how he's giving back to the community. Who will teach at the school?"

"He's searching for teachers now."

"Where will the students from far away stay? It wouldn't make sense to make that buggy ride twice a day if I took Eliza."

"If I understood correctly," Vernon said, "those from far away will stay in the school."

"What about food?" Absalom said.

"He's adding a second gas stove to his home so his wife can help with that." Vernon patted his rounded belly. "Good thing I'm not going, eh?"

"I'm not sure I could go myself, with all the work at home. I couldn't send Eliza by herself either."

Vernon neared Absalom and looked him in the eye. "Was I not the first friend you made when you moved here?"

"Yes, but I don't see—"

"I may need to end our friendship" —Vernon patted Absalom's shoulder— "if you don't think me and my boys wouldn't help Oneita and Tess and Ethan while you're away. Besides, you need to learn sign language so you can teach them."

"I agree," Tess said to Absalom. "I'd like to learn how to talk to Eliza instead of pointing."

Absalom faced the usually quiet Tess. Regardless of her calm ways, her interest in Eliza meant she cared about her older sister. Where had the time gone? His twelve-year-old was on the cusp of becoming a woman. He went to the hay bale and pulled one of her ears through the kapp. "If I didn't know any better, I'd say those ears of yours had grown as big as the horse's ears.

Tess touched her ear. "I don't think so, Papa."

"I'm teasing, all right?"

"I'm teasing like you are, except for the part about Eliza learning sign language. What exactly is it?"

"We'll talk about it on the way home." Absalom faced Vernon. "How long before the school is ready?"

Vernon stroked his beard again. "You know, the older I get the less I remember things. He's already found one teacher. The school is almost finished, and all he needs is another teacher."

"I need to— Tess, go check on the horse. I'll be there in a minute." Tess left.

Vernon leaned conspiratorially toward Absalom. "My sneaky friend doesn't want his daughter to tell his wife how we make phone calls at the feed store in town."

"Got that right," Absalom said. "I'm not going to limit myself to buying livestock locally when I can save money by looking for better prices with some of the New Order farmers."

"Bishop Marley won't like it if he finds out."

"Not at all," Absalom said. "He uses the phone, too. All I need now is this Mennonite's phone number."

"How do you know he has a phone?" Vernon said, tilting his head to one side.

"I know because he's a Mennonite who uses more technology than our Ordnung allows." Absalom shook his head. "Come now, Vernon, as the young English like to tell each other, 'duh.'"

"Duh yourself." Vernon took his hat off. "More forgetfulness on my part." He took a slip of paper from inside the black lining. "Hannes made me write the phone number down."

Absalom read the note and slipped it into his pocket. "Too

bad we can't fix your memory. Enjoy the corn."

Tess sat in the buggy, reins in her hands. "Don't think I didn't know you wanted to get rid of me so you could talk to Mr. Miller alone."

Absalom climbed in beside her. "Since you're so smart, young lady, drive us home."

Tess snapped the reins. "I *am* smart. I even think I know what sign language is. It's like when Eliza says it's bedtime by closing her eyes with her fingers."

"An excellent guess."

"I think she's smarter than me. I've never seen a basket that starts out large at the bottom and narrows at the top. The English buy more of those than any of the others me or Mama make." Tess tugged the reins to stop the buggy, looked both ways at the road, and steered them to the right. "She's smart with her paintings, too. Do you ever wonder why Mama won't let her sell them at our stand with the baskets?"

"I never thought about it. Maybe it's because the things Eliza gets from the woods to make her colors dries and comes off if she handles them too much."

"My favorite is the mama raccoon in the fork of a tree with its babies all around her."

"My favorite is the one she did of you when you were about ten and had fallen asleep in the hay loft."

"No, Papa, I looked a mess. My kapp was off and straw was in my hair."

"That's why I like it."

Tess grew quiet. Absalom bumped her shoulder with his. "Are you thinking about the sign language school?"

"On the day of the storm, when Mama wanted Eliza to bathe Ivy, I gave Eliza the wrong soap by mistake. Mama squeezed Eliza's arm before I could tell her it was my fault."

"Did you tell your mama anyway?"

"I didn't have to. Eliza grabbed Mama's arm and squeezed it hard enough to make Mama let go."

"You still should've told her."

"I did."

"Good. Maybe your mama will think twice before blaming Eliza for something again."

"What do you think Mama will say about the sign language school?"

"It doesn't matter what she says. I'm taking Eliza anyway."

"I think Mama should let Eliza sell her paintings. She could make as much money as that Mennonite artist."

"We'll see, but if she ever does, I don't intend to buy a second stove. Or a gas one."

"Good, cooking's not my thing." Tess elbowed Absalom's ribs. "See? I know how to tease, too."

"*See* if you know how to turn us into our road before you pass it, Miss Teasing Girl."

Tess hauled back on the reins, steered the horse to the right, and continued down their road. "Will you talk to Mama now?"

Absalom sat up straighter to look over the horse's head, to the garden to the right of the barn. "Eliza and Ethan are still picking corn. Leave the buggy in the barn and help them. I'll talk to Mama and unhitch the horse."

"I can unhitch the horse."

"You do that. I just want you to stay out of the house while I talk to your mama."

"You mean in case she fusses."

"I won't hear any fussing."

Bishop Marley said wives are supposed to do whatever their husbands tell them."

"I don't mind hearing your mama's ideas. A peaceful marriage needs communication."

"But she fusses sometimes."

"She won't fuss about this if I have anything to do with it, and I do."

Absalom hopped from the buggy as it passed the back door and went inside. Sitting in a rocker, nursing Ivy, Oneita faced him. "You were gone long enough. And you men think only women gossip."

Ignoring the jibe, Absalom sat in a rocker across from her. "Vernon said a Mennonite has built a school for the deaf. I'm taking Eliza when it opens."

"Is it so far she can't walk?"

"It's at the county seat. That's too far to go by herself."

"Four hours is a lot of buggy riding every day. How will you keep up with your work? Oh, and her work as well?"

"I expect you to do it all, Oneita. That's what you get for insisting we become Swartzentruber Amish."

Oneita's jaw worked, a sign that she knew she'd crossed a line between them.

Absalom placed his elbows on his knees. "Do you ever regret being Amish?"

"What kind of question is that?"

"One I'd like an answer to. As much as you force Ethan and Tess to study, it seems you'd want them to do more with their lives than to follow in our footsteps. If that's true, why did you want to join the strictest Amish order there is?"

Oneita shifted Ivy to her other breast. "Do you ever regret it?"

"I don't regret our connection to God through the simple life with nature and our friends."

"I don't regret that either, but I enjoy the discipline of this life."

Absalom held in a grin. Her idea of discipline wasn't very disciplined when she disagreed with him.

"Why's your mouth twitching?"

"It itches. Your turn to answer."

"Honestly," Oneita said, "I sometimes wish for more of a life than ours for our children. They could still lead a simple life and worship God and do something other than being Amish."

Oneita's admission surprised Absalom. "Better not let Bishop Marley hear you say that."

"I agree. I'd hate for him to gossip about me on the phone at the feed store."

"How do—"

"All the wives know you men use that phone, Absalom. We see a lot more than you men think we do."

"Do any of the wives use the phone?"

"That's not for me to say. I don't, and that's all I care about."

"Since you think about our children doing something other than living the Amish lifestyle, you won't mind if I stay with Eliza at the school all week. The Mennonite is letting the students sleep and eat there. Like you said, it's too far away to take the buggy every day."

"You'd leave the rest of your family here to fend for ourselves?"

"I might take Ethan and Tess, too. That leaves only *you* to fend for *your*self." Oneita's mouth fell open, and Absalom added, "Vernon says he and Hannes and Timothy will help."

"Will you come home on the weekends?"

"I need to see what this class is all about before I decide that."

Oneita lay Ivy over her shoulder and patted her back. "When do you leave and how long does the class last?"

"I'm going to town tomorrow and call the Mennonite. Vernon gave me the number."

Absalom stood, and Oneita looked up at him. "Do what you think is best, but I don't know how sign language is going to change Eliza's life—*or* ours."

Chapter 5

After supper, Denver helped Willow take all but three days of food to the basement freezer. During the meal, she'd mentioned his interest in sign language and said she was going to research some lessons online, teasing him by saying he might meet some hot sign language student he liked better than Jan, which, as his loving sister—sarcasm included—meant she needed to learn sign language so she could tell the student how ticklish he was. A quiet hour of TV included a phone call from Dad's attorney, saying to meet him at the county courthouse Monday morning to handle the will, and Denver told Willow goodnight.

In bed, he opened his laptop on his stomach and signed in to look for sign language teaching opportunities. He considered Africa, but when several results popped up saying it required a general education degree, he closed the laptop, biting back a curse word before he let loose.

Knock-knock. "Can I come in, Den?"

"Sure."

Willow took his chair from his desk, sat, and touched the closed laptop. "Looking for a sign language job?"

"Sort of, but not seriously."

"You wouldn't go off to Africa right after Mom and Dad … you know." Willow lowered her head, then raised it. "I wouldn't mind if you taught where I could call you, but I bet a smart phone wouldn't work in one of those remote villages. Besides, Jan would miss you."

Denver set the laptop on the bed. "I guess she would. Her job keeps her busy."

Willow turned away for a second, probably in advance of a question about Jan. "When we were talking about her before," she said, "I wondered if y'all are exclusive."

"No," Denver said, "but I doubt she'd step out on me."

"But you haven't said it? Like implicitly said it?"

"No, but if she dates someone now, after we've been dating since before we graduated, that means she doesn't care about me as much as she acts like she does."

"You could test her by saying you're going off somewhere to teach sign language."

"I'm not worried about it."

"Well, I know how serious you are about it. If you decide to do it, I'll be okay. Besides, some of my high school friends are still around. We can hang out while you're gone."

"Durn, Willybeans, you're ready to kick your old brother to the curb already?"

"Shut up, you bonehead, you know what I mean."

"I do, and I appreciate it."

"You better, we're all each other has now." Willow went to the door. "Better hope Jan doesn't call to find out what Mom and Dad left us. She'll propose if she finds out." Willow closed the door. Her footsteps thudded softly across the floor toward her bedroom, where the door closed with a slight thump.

Denver reached for the lamp. On the nightstand, his phone vibrated. He huffed a summer-dog sigh when he read the text, not a call, from Jan.

You still up?

Another sigh. No way did he feel like talking about the will.

I've got a client coming for a show. We'll do something next Saturday.

This wasn't the first time Jan had changed their plans.

I'm really sorry about your mom and dad.

It was nice of her to say that, but she'd probably ask about the will anytime now.

I think you'll be interested in my client.

Denver dialed her number. If she brought up the will, he'd steer her away from it with questions about her client.

"Hey," he said when she answered, "I was almost sleep."

"Hey, yourself, my thumbs were getting numb."

"What's this about your client?"

"Remember when you told me how you were getting a degree in sign language because of the documentary about deaf kids in Africa? His daughter is deaf."

"What interested me about that documentary were the kids. They lived in villages that were so isolated, they'd never heard of sign language." Denver faked a yawn so he could get off the phone before she brought up the will.

"Another reason I texted you," Jan continued, "is because I've been entirely too selfish. All the time it's me, me, me and that's wrong. When my client—his name's Mr. Raber—mentioned his daughter, it reminded me of how that documentary affected you. You have such a good heart, Denver. I admire you for wanting to work with deaf kids before you enter the working world."

Denver pulled away from the phone to shake his head at the screen. Where did Jan's new attitude about him teaching sign language come from?

"You there, sweetie? Didn't expect that, did you?"

Denver decided to sidestep the question. No need to remind Jan of her former negative attitude about sign language, and she sounded extremely sincere. "Hey, I appreciate that, I think you're sweet for saying it."

"Thank you. Next time you come over, I'll cook a romantic late-night dinner."

"Yeah?" Visions of Jan's exquisite body, in a bikini while out on the pontoon boat, crept into Denver's mind. Many a night after making out on her sofa, he'd gone to his dorm in frustration because she didn't believe in pre-marital sex. Sure, it was a trait to admire, but not when they were nearly naked on the sofa and she stopped all of a sudden.

Jan laughed. "That's an interesting 'yeah.' Sounds like you're looking forward to it."

"Sure, why not. You can tell me more about your client when I see you. Willow and I were talking about my interest in teaching sign language, but the jobs I've been looking at require education degrees. Looks like I'm out of luck."

"Too bad a solar engineering degree doesn't count for anything." Jan yawned.

"Ain't that the truth," Denver said. "I should let you get to bed. Thanks for calling and understanding about my interest in sign language. It means a lot."

"You're very welcome. I know I haven't said it lately, but you're the sweetest guy I've ever known. Goodnight."

Denver placed the phone on the nightstand and turned the lamp off. His window faced the lake, and the full moon reflecting off the water rippled his walls with squiggles of light, similar to nightcrawlers wriggling in the yard after a rain. What a phone call. Jan had really turned a 180 concerning him teaching sign language.

Now, if he could only to get to Africa, or to wherever someone needed a sign language teacher without a teaching degree. Barring that, time to look for a tentative solar engineering job.

Chapter 6

At home, after the meeting with the attorney, Denver followed Willow inside. "I'm glad that's over."

"Me too." Willow hung her coat on the rack by the door. "I didn't realize Mom and Dad had so much retirement along with their life insurance. It'll make affording med school instead of nursing a lot easier."

"Cool," Denver said. "You'll follow in Mom's footsteps."

Willow started coffee, then faced Denver. "How did the job search go yesterday?"

Denver took a bottle of Mom's french vanilla creamer from the fridge. "I'm trying to figure out if I regret putting in those applications or not. I really don't want to work right now."

"I get it," Willow said. "It's not like we need the money. Still, Mom and Dad taught us the value of a job, so I don't want to sit on my butt forever."

The aroma of coffee filled the room as the coffee maker dribbled its last drops into the carafe. Denver made a sandwich with some of the leftover food and took his coffee to his room. He sipped, started to bite the sandwich, and Jan's call tone, which she'd put on his phone—violins playing a classical piece—made him put the sandwich down and swipe the screen. "You get any art that resembles real trees, people, or animals lately?"

Jan made a growling sound in her throat. "I'll never teach you to appreciate abstract art."

"I'd like to recognize what I'm supposed to appreciate. Does your client paint abstracts?"

"Yes, and he does it well enough to earn my commissions."

"What's up?"

"Mr. Raber had a few more shows in some other galleries and is flying back home Saturday morning. If you meet him at the Raleigh-Durham airport at eight, he'll have a ticket for you to go back with him."

"To do what?"

"To teach sign language for a year."

"Uh-huh. What's the punch line?"

"What's a girl got to do to get her man to pay attention? This is no joke."

A surge of adrenaline hit Denver. Dizzy, he left his desk chair, dropped to the bed, and flopped backward to the mattress. "Whaaat?"

"When you come back after the first three months, I expect a big night out on the town. If you're genuinely appreciative, I might cook dinner. You know what happens on the sofa after that."

The dizziness faded. Denver sat up. "Slow down and tell me what's going on."

"Mr. Raber lives in Ohio, in a Mennonite community not too far from an Amish community. I told you about his daughter. He's interested in helping the deaf with—"

"What's the difference between Mennonite and Amish?"

"Don't interrupt. All I'm concerned with is his art and my commissions."

"What's that about the first three months? Oh, why don't the kids there have sign language in school?"

"They have their own schools, but don't have any sign language teachers. Mr. Raber built a school specifically for the Deaf in the surrounding community."

"That's great of him."

"It's also great because you won't need an education degree, since it's not a state operated school."

"I just show up at the airport Saturday morning?"

"That's it."

"What about clothes? Just pack a bag and go? How about toothpaste? Soap? All that?"

"You'd never get through airport security." Jan's tone turned serious. "Now you get to see what I have to deal with when I fly. Airlines—and the TSA—take security seriously." Her laughter lilted from the phone. "If they take a full body scan, ask them to print a copy for me."

"As long as you do the same for me the next time you fly."

"I know you love your cargo shorts, but you better take jeans since it's three weeks until Christmas. Don't forget a heavy coat—maybe some boots if it snows. If you need anything else, the other teacher can take you when he picks you and Mr. Raber up at the airport in Columbus."

"I don't know what to say, Jan, this is unbelievable."

"Just remember our dinner when you get back."

"You still haven't told me about the three-month deal."

"Two teachers teach for three months. Then two more take over while you come home for three months."

"Can I stay at your place Friday night?" Denver hated to ask, but anything to not drive in the morning rush to RDU. "I'll leave my pickup there and you can take me to the airport. How about it, please?"

"How do I know you don't really need a ride as much as you need to see me?"

"It depends on what we're having for dinner. I could sample your favorite recipe."

"Rinse the dishes and load the washer, you've got a deal."

"Sounds like you're trying to domesticate me already. As you know, I'm a man of the woods—I can't be tamed."

"You'll be a man of the woods in Ohio. Holmes County, where you'll be teaching, is out in the country."

"Cool. I'll tell Willow in a minute."

"Is she okay with you leaving so soon after the funeral?"

"We talked about it. You know, just if it were to happen, and she's okay with it. Said some of her friends from high school can keep her company. She said she's gonna learn sign language on the internet, too."

"Good. You'll have some time together before you leave Friday."

"We've already started getting Mom and Dad's clothes together to donate to the thrift shop in town. That's what they'd want, I'm sure."

"Okay, sweetie. See you Friday, bye."

Denver dropped the phone on the bed. Teaching sign language to kids in Ohio—what a break, and a break he needed.

At the kitchen counter, Willow looked up from a laptop. "I heard you talking. Was that Jan asking about the will?"

"No, she—" Denver joined Willow to point at the laptop. "What are you up to?"

"I'm looking for dessert recipes for Christmas. Mom always made the holidays special with her great cooking."

"I hope you won't be mad at me, Willybeans, but I'll be out of town for Christmas."

Willow's complexion reddened. "You better not spend Christmas with Jan instead of me."

"I'd never do that to you and you know it. How does me leaving for Ohio Saturday morning to teach sign language sound?"

Willow's complexion lightened. "Dang, Den, how'd you swing that?"

"Jan 'swung it' with an artist who had a show Saturday. His daughter's deaf. He built a sign language school where he lives."

Willow closed the laptop. "What county in Ohio?"

"Holmes."

"That's where a lot of the Old Order Amish live. I looked them up on the internet after reading an Amish novel. It's gonna suck not having a bathroom."

"Mr. Raber's a Mennonite. He's using the airlines, so maybe they use more technology."

"You've never flown. Better pick up a bottle of motion sickness pills."

"Thanks for reminding me."

"How long will you be gone?"

"Three months on and three months off. Two more teachers take over then."

"You won't be back until March. I guess you know I'll miss you."

Denver noted a hint of sincerity in his sister's voice. "Hey," he said, placing an arm around her shoulders, "You know I'll miss you, too."

Willow shrugged the arm off. "I'll be okay. You better get up early for that drive to Raleigh."

"Jan's taking me to RDU Saturday morning. I'll leave my pickup at her place while I'm gone."

"How romantic." Willow's face muscles tightened into a frown. "You're gonna get a final fool-around before you fly to Ohio."

"Oh, hush. You're the one who wouldn't answer me when I asked if you'd been with a man."

Willow opened the laptop. "*You* hush, I answered later. You're the one who's gonna miss all those great deserts I'll make for Christmas."

Denver left for his room, intending to refresh some of the more obscure signs, when violins played on his phone. He swiped the screen. "How's my miracle worker?"

"You'll kill her when she tells you what's wrong."

"What's that?"

"My sister in Nags Head called. Mike—did I ever tell you her husband's name is Mike?"

"Maybe, go ahead."

"He's going out of town to a dentist's convention Friday morning until late Sunday. She's getting some of our high school girlfriends together for a beach weekend. I haven't seen some of them in years."

"No problem, I'll drive myself Saturday morning. What're your plans for the beach in December?"

"Eat out. Shop the outlet stores. Stroll on the beach and look for shells if the weather's nice. Ride over to Manteo, maybe down to Cape Hatteras. We might even—"

"Okay, okay, I get it."

"I can still cook that dinner I promised you when you get back."

"I'll take you up on that."

"Sounds like a plan, sweetie. Gotta run, I want to do some shopping for a few beachy outfits."

Jan ended the call before Denver could say goodbye. He didn't quite know how to feel about the change in plans. Sure, he'd acted like he was looking forward to a night alone with her, but now that it wasn't going to happen, it didn't bother him as much as he thought it would.

Chapter 7

On the grass beside the porch, glittering frost sparkled rainbow hues in the hard morning sun. Eliza, snug in her coat, waited while Papa hugged Tess. He left her to place his hand on Ethan's shoulder. Their words formed puffs of white between their faces. Holding the squirming Ivy, Mama stood nearby.

None of this made sense. This morning, Papa had packed most of their clothes in two cloth sacks, including a glass jar of water and some sandwiches that Mama had made. He loaded everything into the buggy and went back to the porch, where everyone gathered as if something completely out of the ordinary was about to happen. Until Papa packed her clothes, Eliza guessed he was taking Ethan somewhere, because he also took Ethan and their clothes and stayed overnight when he bought their last milk cow and led it back home, tied behind the buggy. That, along with how he was taking her instead of Ethan, confused her. Still, the chance of an adventure out in the world tingled a tentative line of excitement along the nape of her neck.

Papa spoke to Mama, whose eyes pooled with tears. He kissed Ivy's cheek and spoke to Mama again. She took a few tentative steps to where Eliza waited. A tear ran down one tanned cheek, confusing Eliza further, because Mama had never showed the slightest hint of sadness when it came to her oldest daughter. She placed her hand on Eliza's arm, squeezed gently, and whirled to go inside.

Tess placed her hand within Eliza's. Kind eyes. A slight smile. Dimples in the cold-reddened cheeks. Wherever Papa was going, and whatever they were doing, it made Tess happy. She gave Eliza's hand a quick squeeze and went inside.

Ethan stepped forward stiffly and offered his hand. Eliza took it. He pumped her hand up and down, nodded, and went inside also. The same sincere intention as Tess's, if not as emotional.

Eliza followed Papa to the buggy. Rods of steamy haze shot from the horse's nostrils before dissipating. The crisp air chilled her throat. Good thing she'd worn her gloves, including her black bonnet over her kapp.

Papa steered them onto the main road. The horse increased its gait to a fast walk. Cold slipped inside Eliza's bonnet to nip at her ears, which wouldn't happen if Mama didn't make her wear her hair up.

Eliza loosened the ties on the bonnet. If she got the chance, she'd wear her hair down while she and Papa were away.

She, Tess, and Mama lived a strange life. Why wear black dresses, black stockings and shoes while visiting anyone? Why show no skin ever, not even on their arms in the heat of the summer. Papa and Ethan were no different, wearing black pants, white shirts, and wide-brimmed hats. Why couldn't they live like the people in town? Riding in vehicles looked fun, and the rider wouldn't have to smell the round clods of horse manure when they dropped to the road. Short pants with bare legs might feel cool in summer, too, along with thin, sleeveless shirts.

The buggy rocked back and forth on the road. Vehicles passed, swirling the bitter aroma of their exhaust in the air. Cold seeped inside Eliza's coat, so she wrapped her arms around herself. Papa reached behind the seat for a quilt they kept there when the seasons turned. She took it and covered their legs with it.

Papa's kindness warmed her heart. Ivy's gray eyes staring into hers during baths or diaper changes warmed her heart also. Even Ethan's formal handshake, more amusing than loving, made her feel welcome. Tess, a mix of interested curiosity when Eliza painted, and now, a mix of interested happiness because of this trip, warmed her heart also.

A complete and confusing mystery for as long as she could remember, Mama never showed her a single kindness. No, that wasn't true. One memory, distant and hazy, proved otherwise: Mama holding her in her arms, rocking her in the chair, lips smiling and moving, a soft kiss, a hug. Why wasn't Mama kind to her anymore, like when she'd gently squeezed Eliza's arm, tears in her eyes? That didn't make up for the times when she squeezed her arm for no reason, and it never would.

She appreciated how Mama kept her family fed and clothed: Repairing tears in assorted pants, shirts, dresses, socks. Washing them in a tub on a washboard. Hanging them on a line outside. Tending the garden from spring planting to fall harvest. On occasion, Mama took her and Tess to another wife's home to help make a quilt. During those times, when women gathered around the quilt to move their lips with silent words, sometimes reacting with smiles and crinkling eyes, Eliza grew curious as to what they were saying with those non-stop movements of lips and tongues.

She and Papa passed through town. On the outskirts, he steered the horse to the side of the road and stopped near a stand of trees, thick with a spicy aroma. The needles on these trees never turned red, orange, or yellow and fell like the leaves on other trees. Some of the stores in the town near her community set up trees like this and decorated them with lights and glass balls at this time of the year.

He climbed from the buggy and she followed, wincing at the

sharp pain deep below her navel. Papa tugged at his pants, their signal for relieving themselves. They separated to enter the thick stand of trees. Dress lifted, underclothes lowered, she squatted.

Clothing in place again, she climbed into the buggy beside Papa, who took the sandwiches and jar of water from the paper bag. The roasted chicken and buttered homemade bread melted in her mouth. Mama might be harsh, but her cooking never failed to please. Eliza drank cold water, while Papa took two slices of apple pie from the bag. The flaky crust and cinnamon hint satisfied her taste for something sweet.

Papa returned the wrapping paper and jar to the bag. Reins in hand, he looked behind the buggy for traffic. A car passed. He steered the horse into the road.

The food filled Eliza's stomach, the quilt warmed her legs, and the rising sun heated her black clothing. She leaned against the leather seat. The gentle rocking of the buggy and the crisp aroma of winter in the air combined to make her drowsy enough to close her eyes.

Absalom steered the buggy into a driveway. Gravel crunched beneath the wheels instead of the squish of mud or the silence of dirt like in his own driveway. Jonathan Raber's two-story home, covered in pale green vinyl siding, stood on a hill overlooking the main road. To the right, woods filled with oak, maple, and hickory trees, all ablaze with red, orange, and yellow leaves, stirred in the breeze. Eliza would feel at home if a creek or river ran nearby.

Beside the trees, about a hundred steps from Jonathan's home, the white-sided schoolhouse glared in the mid-morning sun. A man wearing faded blue jeans, a red ball cap, and a dark blue denim jacket came from behind the school. Brown hair trimmed short instead of like Absalom's, which Oneita cut by using a large, deep bowl over his head as a guide, peeked from under the cap. Absalom nudged Eliza with his elbow. She sat up, yawned, and rubbed her eyes. He stopped the buggy beside the man, who shaded his eyes while looking up at them.

"A fine day for a buggy ride, Absalom."

"How did you know it was me?"

"You're the only parent and student I expected today."

"That makes sense, Jonathan."

"Now, now, I told you on the phone to call me Jon."

"Jon it is. This young lady beside me is Eliza."

Jon offered his hand. Eliza took it and climbed from the buggy. Absalom followed. "She's been napping for the last hour."

"The sun must've warmed her black dress to where she felt like an old dog lying in the sun in the winter." Jon waved toward the school. "I was putting toilet paper in the outhouse."

"How many students are coming?"

"Three, unless word of mouth brings more. How old is Eliza? The rest are children."

"She turned eighteen in August."

Absalom considered telling Jon about Eliza's art but thought better of it. His work earned enough money for a fine house and this school. Eliza's art couldn't compare.

"When do we meet your wife and daughter?"

"In a bit. I know I told you on the phone my wife's name is Rebecca, but she prefers Becca."

"What about your daughter? I don't think you can trim Ellie down any more."

"She's just five. She only knows her name by how it appears on our lips, so it's not an issue."

"I was kind of joking, Jon."

"I rarely joke." Jon broke out into a wide smile. "Only about every other sentence."

"Good, I enjoy a laugh now and then myself."

"I'll check on Becca. She's expecting a baby in early March."

"Congratulations."

"Thanks." Jon pointed at another building beyond the schoolhouse. "Leave your buggy in the barn behind my pickup and let your horse in the pasture. There are extra stalls he and other horses can use when it snows. I use them for storing a few things but cleaned them out when I built the school. Go ahead and check out the buildings behind the school. I built one for a shower and a washer and another for an outhouse. The county said my septic system was too small to connect another commode to it. Eliza might like the idea of a shower while she's here. That is, if you bathe in a washtub like many Amish do."

"I might like washing in clean water myself. In the summer, by the time my family's through, it's as brown as our horse."

Jon left for the house. Absalom cleared his throat. "Jon, can we talk about something if you have time?"

Jon returned. "What's on your mind?"

Absalom wiped his hands on his pants, a nervous gesture he often exhibited when an argument with Oneita loomed. "Well, it's difficult to talk about."

"Does it have anything to do with me providing food and a place to sleep for you and Eliza while you're here?"

Absalom stuck his hands in his pockets. "How did you know that?"

"You're clothing and haircut tell me you're Swartzentruber Amish."

"Oneita and me converted before we moved here from Nebraska."

"If you don't mind me asking, what order were you before?"

"We were with a small group from Kalona, Iowa, originally.

We pooled our money and bought a tract of land in Nebraska."

"Really?" Jon's tone was skeptical. "You went from an order who uses anything from tractors to running water, to one who uses none of that?"

Absalom glanced at Eliza, standing by the buggy patiently. "Oneita wanted it."

"Do you mind using electricity and running water while you're here?" Jon asked. "You might or might not know this, but some Mennonites—me included—use whatever technology is available. I have two laptop computers. Becca will have our baby in a hospital instead of being tended by a midwife."

"I don't mind that as much as I mind not paying for food and a place to sleep. It makes me uneasy to talk about it, because it could be considered pride."

"Since when is earning one's own way pride?"

"Do you have something I can do when school's out?"

"Wait for me in the barn after I check on Becca. Don't forget to take a look at the shower."

Absalom motioned Eliza to follow. Behind the school he found a standard wooden outhouse similar to his at home, except this one matched the schoolhouse's white paint. He opened the door, flicked a light switch, and showed Eliza, who nodded. She followed him to the other building. He took her inside to point at the light switch. She clicked it, looked at the lights overhead, and smiled. He led her to the shower stall, which shouldn't be hard to figure out. Eliza knelt to touch the drain, stood to touch the showerhead, and turned one of the knobs. Smiling even larger, she jumped back and rubbed her arms, her signal for bathing. Absalom nodded, turned the knob off, and turned the one with a red H. He gave the flow a few seconds to warm, then placed Eliza's hand beneath it. She nodded again.

Wiping her hand on her dress, she went to the washer, raised the lid, and faced Absalom while tugging her dress. Without the slightest hint, Eliza had guessed the washer's purpose. A clothesline hung beside this building. Having pinned enough clothes in her life to cover his farm, she knew how to do that well enough.

What could she accomplish if she learned sign language? Some young Amish left the order as they aged, but Eliza knew nothing about the order or why they shunned technology. Unlike Jon, most Amish husbands wouldn't tell anyone outside the family if his wife were expecting a baby either.

Except for Eliza's black dress and white apron, including the white kapp and black bonnet that covered her waist-length black hair pinned tight to her head, nothing marked her as Amish, especially Swartzentruber Amish. If it weren't for those things, including Oneita's endless discipline, Eliza might be as free in spirit as her art suggested. Yes indeed, what could she accomplish if she learned sign language?

Eliza raised the washing machine lid, looked inside, and fiddled with the knobs.

Absalom loved the simplicity of the Amish lifestyle, but how might it be to live without being bound by it, almost like Eliza's clothing bound her to its will? God didn't bind people, but customs could. What was wrong with tooth brushes and running water and showers and telling people a family was expecting a new baby to love?

God would lead him through his questions, but he could never leave the order. Maybe he could convince Oneita to lessen her grip on its strict customs, if nowhere else than at home. Shorts in the house in summer—when a person dripped sweat while doing nothing more than sitting—might be a blessing in itself.

Eliza, standing almost to his shoulder, face framed by the

black bonnet, peered into his eyes. Sensitive as always, she'd read his troubled mind. He knelt beside her. She did the same. He folded his hands. She folded hers. She closed her eyes. He closed his.

Dear Lord, please forgive my questioning nature. All I want is the best for my family. Please allow Eliza to reach her potential as she strives forward in our earthly world. I'm so sorry for questioning the order. The simple times within it, including how we live as one within Your creation of nature, and how You provide friends like Vernon and Abigail, is a treasure to the heart and soul. Amen.

Absalom stood and so did Eliza. Her gray eyes questioned him. He nodded, smiled, and took her outside, where he led the horse toward the huge barn behind Jon's home, sided in green vinyl also.

A dual-wheel red pickup filled the area at the far end of the barn, where another set of double doors were open. Absalom unhitched the horse and let it into the pasture to the right of the barn. No horse or cow grazed there, so Jon must not own a buggy or a milk cow. Eliza placed her hands on the buggy and leaned forward as if she were about to push. Intuitive as always, she had figured out Absalom's intentions. She nodded at him for help and he did so, but after the years of steady work that had hardened her muscles, she could easily push the buggy inside by herself if she wanted.

Absalom took their bags of clothes, gave Eliza hers, and headed toward the open barn doors to wait for Jon. She stopped to point at a bucket hanging from a hook. Ever the artist, she wanted to paint. He dropped his bag, raised his hands, and lifted one and then the other as if weighing something: their sign for "maybe."

Jon entered the barn with his wife and daughter. Both wore faded blue jeans. Ellie wore a pink coat, while Becca wore a blue fleece jacket that bulged over her middle. One auburn braid hung over Becca's shoulder. Two barely reached Ellie's shoulders.

Becca offered her hand. "It's nice to meet you and Eliza, Absalom. From what Jon told me, you're as dedicated to Eliza learning sign language as he and I are to Ellie learning it."

Absalom shook her hand. "I can't wait to learn it myself."

"We thought about using the internet to teach, but we think the personal touch will work better. You might not know it, but matching facial expressions to signs is important, too."

"I didn't know that. Eliza picks up names by how they look on the lips when they're spoken. Would you like to introduce her to Jon and Ellie?"

"I'd love to." Becca held out her hand to Eliza, who looked at Absalom, rubbed her stomach, and shook Becca's hand.

"She knows you're expecting," Absalom said.

Jon placed his arm around Becca's shoulders. "And I'm as nervous as a turkey at Thanksgiving about it, too."

"I think all fathers feel that way," Absalom said. "I know I did."

"It's not average nervousness," Jon said. "Becca's family tends toward early births. She had Ellie early, too. That, along with the school and my work, has made me forget something. I wouldn't ask if I didn't trust you, but after our talk on the phone, and after meeting you in person, I need a favor."

"I hope I get to know what it is before I agree." Absalom couldn't imagine what Jon was about to ask, but he appreciated earning the trust of someone so quickly.

"Let me take Eliza inside," Becca said. "I'll show her around and introduce her to Ellie and me, since my tummy sidetracked us." She took Ellie's hand and motioned to Eliza to come with her. Eliza questioned Absalom with raised eyebrows, and he nodded that she could go.

"I have a feeling those three will get along great," Jon said.

Halfway toward the house, Eliza looked over her shoulder at Absalom.

"It wouldn't surprise me one bit," he said. "What's this about a favor?"

"I held an art show in North Carolina Wednesday night. Like an idiot I left yesterday instead of Saturday. I was supposed to meet one of the teachers at the airport and bring him here. I'm flying there this afternoon to meet him in the morning."

"Couldn't he fly here by himself?"

"I gave him my word through the woman who ran the show. I take my word seriously, don't you?"

"You ask an Amish man that?" Absalom smiled to let Jon know he was joking.

Jon didn't return the smile. "Are you saying the Amish take their word more seriously than Mennonites? I didn't expect that from you, Absalom."

"I was joking, Jon, I thought—"

"Gotcha, Ab. You don't mind if I call you Ab, do you?"

"I … well, I …"

"I told you I liked to joke. I'd like you and Eliza to take two bedrooms in the house while you're here. I can't stand the thought of Becca being alone when I leave for more art shows."

"What about when you're here?"

"Why not be comfortable in a bed instead of sleeping on a pallet in the schoolhouse?"

"In all seriousness, Jon, I don't want to intrude on your household."

"Come on, Ab, don't tell me you like running outside in the middle of the night to sit on a cold outhouse seat?"

Absalom couldn't argue with that. "To be honest, it's not one of my favorite things."

"I didn't think so. You can let the bathroom spoil you and Eliza."

"My bishop won't like it if he finds out."

"Hey, whatever happens in my house stays in my house. Besides, Becca will skin me alive if I don't insist."

"What about the work I mentioned? I'd still like to do something to earn our keep."

"Have you ever built furniture?"

"I do some simple woodworking—oak toolboxes, furniture repairs—things like that."

"But not actually making furniture."

"I've always wanted to try. I love a comfortable rocking chair."

"Too bad." Jon leaned against one of the wooden posts supporting the barn's roof.

Absalom didn't know what to make of the man. Was he joking again? "Exactly what kind of furniture do you make?"

"I thought you might cut wood for our stoves while you're here. Cutting wood for furniture is kind of the same thing."

Absalom looked out the barn door. "I don't see any chimneys on your house or the school."

"There's a huge propane tank on the other side of the house. I ran another line to the school."

"Then what's this about cutting wood for stoves?"

Jon left the post to clap Absalom's back. "I should stop messing with you. Becca sometimes threatens to divorce me over my joking. Follow me, I'll show you my rocking chair shop."

"I'm sure you're serious about a few things," Absalom said, keeping pace with Jon in the barn.

"I don't joke about deafness. If one of my teachers changes their minds about teaching, it will *not* be good." Jon passed his pickup and opened a door to the right. "Don't mind the sawdust smell, do you? I think it's great."

Absalom entered the workshop. When he'd let the horse into

the pasture earlier, he only saw few stall doors on the outside of the barn and this explained it—the workshop must be half as long as the entire barn. Sawdust covered the floor like a dusting of yellow snow. Beneath a push broom in a corner, a large mound evidenced plenty of work.

Jon pointed. "Think you can handle a table saw, a band saw, a planer, a drill press, a belt sander, a—"

"Hold on, Jon. I might handle them if you show me, but Oneita would kill me if I went home missing a finger."

At a table, Jon held up a sanding block. "You won't lose any fingers with this." He tossed Absalom the sanding block, and Absalom caught it. Regardless of Jon's joking and his love for the technology that the Amish shied away from, the man sure knew how to make a person feel at ease.

Absalom went to a wooden table and rubbed the curved runner of a rocking chair. The deep brown must be oak. "Show me how to make these runners and we've got a deal. Then we can go inside and see how Eliza's getting along with Becca and Ellie."

Chapter 8

Eliza followed the woman and little girl inside the green house and hung her coat on a rack by the door with theirs. The aroma of coffee and bacon meant this room was a kitchen, but she didn't see a wood cookstove.

The woman picked up a basket of clothes, motioned for Eliza to follow, and left for a door, the little girl at her side. Eliza followed them, still carrying her bag of clothes.

Papa had smiled a lot while talking to these people, so she trusted them. They must be the little girl's mama and papa. Their sky-blue pants looked easier to walk in than a dress in the woods, which snagged on limbs and briars while she searched for colors for her artwork.

Through the door, down a hall, and up a staircase, Eliza followed. At the top of the stairs, the woman continued down another hall, until she opened a door and went in. She put the basket of clothes down, took out a sheet, and offered two ends to Eliza. Eliza dropped her bag to the floor and took the ends of the sheet to help the woman make the bed. That chore done, the woman sat on the bed and patted it, and Eliza sat beside her.

The woman took the little girl into her lap, hugged her, and mouthed a word Eliza didn't catch. She tilted her head to one side to ask the woman to mouth the word again. This time she did it slowly. Eliza pointed at the girl, repeated the movement, and the woman nodded and smiled. The woman pointed at herself and mouthed another word. Eliza repeated the movement. The woman, Becca, smiled and nodded again.

Eliza closed her eyes to thank the Creator of all things for how she could feel words on her lips, tongue, and teeth without hearing a sound. Air flowed across her lips just so when she copied words and names. She'd seen symbols in the books Ethan and Tess stared at and believed they must stand for both words and names. When they were born, Papa showed her how to mouth their names and how he wrote them with the symbols from a book. All this confirmed how the symbols made words and names, and she practiced endlessly in the dark of night by remembering how people talked. She touched her lips while pushing them in and out, felt the way her tongue moved around her teeth, felt combination after combination of so many words and names that she lost sleep until satisfied. Maybe she wasn't putting the symbols together in her mind and in her mouth correctly, but Papa always smiled when she tried, confirming her attempts.

She opened her eyes and touched her chest. Becca moved her lips and tongue to mouth Eliza's name, which Papa must've already told her. Eliza nodded, hesitated, and reached out to touch the sleeve of the shirt Becca was wearing. Dark blue and thick, it looked like it would make a person sweat in the summer.

How wonderful it would be to wear such a shirt, along with the sky-blue pants that Becca and Ellie wore.

Eliza touched Becca's crossed leg and pinched a fold of the cloth, almost as soft as the shirt. She pulled the hem of her black dress up and raised her black-stockinged leg and black shoe beside Becca's leg and foot, which wore a red shoe with a white sole. Her clothes were perfect for walking, running, and going to the woods while searching for her colors. Sticks and acorns sometimes hurt bare feet, as did briars and rocks. The hard shoes Eliza wore hurt worse than briars and rocks.

Becca stood to open a door beside the bedroom door. She pointed at a white thing that resembled the white thing in the other building. Eliza recognized it as a place to sit and relieve herself. Along with beautiful and comfortable clothes, these nice people didn't have to go out in the cold to sit and relieve themselves. Becca held out her hand toward Ellie, who took it. She motioned for Eliza to come with her into the hall. Eliza pointed at the room with the white thing to let Becca know she needed to relieve herself. Becca nodded and closed the door behind her.

Eliza looked through the clothes basket for the pants and shirt she'd seen when Becca took the sheets and quilt out. She raised the shirt to her nose and sniffed a hint of warm spring rain, with a touch of sweetness like flowers. The blue pants smelled the same, but they were worn through at the knees, maybe from when Becca worked in a garden.

Holding the shirt to her shoulders, Eliza admired it. She did the same with the pants. Bonnet and kapp off, she unpinned her hair, which fell to her waist in black waves.

Absalom leaned over a metal box with a glass window, where steam swirled around a rocking chair runner. "That's an interesting contraption, Jon. How long does it take to steam oak so it keeps its shape?"

"About an hour per inch of thickness, Ab." Jon reached under the table for a runner already formed. "I made this by laminating several thin layers of oak. You glue them together before you clamp them."

"Which method is better?"

"Gluing is easier, but I like how the grain in a steamed oak runner pops when you varnish it."

"I'd love to have a shop like this."

"Yeah? I can get you a good deal on a generator to run all the electric tools."

"You and your joking."

"You're hard-core Amish, huh?"

"Well, I see the advantages of working rock-hard oak with electric tools over hand tools."

Jon went to another machine. "Let me show you my new planer. I can take any board I want and cut it down to whatever thickness I want."

Absalom admired Jon's woodworking knowledge, but he wasn't sure about the man's choice of clothes and how the rest of his family wore them, too. Becca was an attractive woman, and the faded jeans fit her to distraction. Thank goodness Oneita, Tess, and Eliza wore black dresses instead of tight jeans, or he'd have a fight on his hands to convince them otherwise. What a mistake to think they might wear English clothes at home.

"Can I see Eliza?" he said. "She might be nervous around strangers."

"I doubt that." Jon went to the door and clicked the lights off. "Becca could make a pig feel comfortable on butchering day."

Absalom laughed while following Jon through the barn. "That's a lot to ask of the pig."

"I agree, Ab, but I bet Eliza feels at home already." Leaving the barn to enter the sunshine, Jon glanced at Absalom. "Are you sure you don't mind if I call you Ab?"

"I doubt it would make a difference if I *did* mind. I also doubt I ever met someone who likes to joke as much as you do."

"Proverbs 17:22, Ab."

"Sure, but all the time?"

"Beats the heck out of a broken spirit and dried bones."

Absalom said nothing. Jon's reference to proverbs 17:22—A merry heart doeth good like a medicine, but a broken spirit drieth the bones—fit many Amish he knew: stoic, stern, and serious. After all, proverbs 17:22 came straight from the Bible, so why question it?

Jon climbed the steps to a porch, wiped his shoes on a mat, and opened the door for Absalom. "After we see what the girls are up to, I need to pack for my flight."

The faint aroma of coffee and bacon greeted Absalom, along with the warmth of the central heating. No cold spots away from a wood stove like at home. At the sink washing dishes, Becca faced him. "Eliza's upstairs. What did you think of the workshop?"

"It's quite a setup."

Ellie, sitting at the large dining table on the far side of the huge kitchen, came over, tugged Absalom's sleeve, and led him to a wall, where she pointed at a painting. "She sure has an eye for colors," Jon said.

Absalom leaned closer to the swirls of green, blue, red, and orange. Brown streaks extended from them to a streak of deeper blue beside a blob of darker green. "What's this supposed to be?"

Jon came over. "You'd think a Mennonite would paint realistic outdoor scenes, but most of mine are abstracts. I tend to look at things from the point of view of the inside instead of the outside."

"Somewhat like the Amish, eh?"

"And the Mennonites. Wants rarely are as important as needs."

"I couldn't agree more," Absalom said, nodding. "Pride takes many forms, mostly in those of flashy appearance and the love of the world."

Ellie returned to the table to thumb through a child's book.

"Especially in the form of anger," Jon said. "I don't have a television because of that. People fuss and fight over the most insignificant things instead of trying to understand each other. Choosing to do that over choosing to listen, regardless of the issue, has worsened many a problem. Too many times, people judge others based on who they think they are before they get to know each other. If they didn't do that, I'd think they'd find they have more in common than they realize."

"Makes sense to me, Jon. You'll never see a TV in my house because of those things."

Absalom turned to the sound of footsteps coming down a hall. A young woman carrying a basket of clothes, shiny black hair hanging over her shoulders, came toward him. She wore faded jeans like Jon, Becca, and Ellie, along with a blue sweatshirt. For some reason she wore no shoes. The young woman beamed a huge smile. Absalom faced Jon. "I didn't know you have another daughter."

Jon's mouth fell open. He looked at Becca. "You didn't ...?"

"I think, uh, maybe Eliza thought ..."

"You *think?*" Heat seared Absalom's cheeks. "Eliza?" What had Becca done to her?

Eliza placed the basket of clothes on the table and turned around as if dancing. Black hair clouded her face. Bare feet on tiptoe twirled in a circle. She stopped and held her hands out as if to say how proud she was of the clothes.

Absalom faced Jon. "Is this your idea of making my daughter feel at home? What about you, Becca? Did you plan this as soon as you got her inside? I didn't bring her here to lose her Amish heritage, I brought her here to learn sign language. If it wasn't for that I'd leave."

"Absalom." Becca took a step toward him. "You don't understand."

"I don't need to understand. It's as obvious as these clothes on Eliza's body. The pants don't even cover her ankles."

"Well, she *is* a lot taller than me."

"That's *not* the point. I don't want her to—"

"Ab," Jon said, "we just got through talking about how anger makes things worse. Let's sit down with a cup of coffee and find out what happened. Besides, Becca wouldn't disrespect your Amish ways by having Eliza change into those clothes. Something else must've—"

"Happened?" Absalom clenched his fists. "How could something else have happened?"

"How do we know until we talk instead of making accusations? Forgive me for saying so, but maybe you're not as Amish as you think you are if you're ready to come to blows over a misunderstanding."

"I'm not ready to come to blows."

"Your red face and fists say you are. Please, let's sit down and discuss this reasonably. You're scaring Ellie, and Eliza, too."

Absalom turned around to see what Jon meant. Ellie had left the table to stand in a corner with Eliza, holding her hand.

"I didn't mean to scare anyone. I just don't want Eliza to lose her Amish roots."

Becca took a small container from a rack, placed it in a strange machine, and pulled a handle down that enclosed the container. "I'll make hot chocolate and give it to the girls while we talk." She placed a mug in the machine and pressed a button. "What flavor coffee would you like, Absalom? I'm having hazelnut after the hot chocolate."

The machine gurgled; a steaming stream of brown liquid dribbled into the mug.

"I suppose that's another of your electric contraptions," Absalom said.

Jon took more mugs from the cabinet over to the machine.

"Fastest coffee and hot chocolate in the west. Makes great tea also. Maybe Oneita would like one."

"You know as well as I do, we don't have electricity."

"You know as well as I do, I'm joking."

"Well, Oneita *does* like hot tea."

Becca took the mug from the machine and replaced it with another. She placed another small container from the rack into the machine, then lowered the handle and pressed the button. "Too bad you don't have electricity."

When the machine finished dribbling, Becca gave Absalom two mugs filled with the aroma of chocolate. "Give these to the girls and sit them at the table by the window. Then they'll know you're not mad anymore."

Absalom did so. At the table, Eliza looked up at him, gray eyes crinkling with her "thank you" expression. There was nothing he wouldn't do for her, including letting her wear Becca's clothes while she was here. What a smile she had smiled when she twirled around. He returned to Becca and Jon.

"Eliza wears a size ten women's shoe. I don't suppose you have—"

"What a coincidence," Jon said. "Becca bigfoot here wears the same size."

"Watch it, Jon," Becca said, "or bigfoot's gonna serve your coffee over your big head."

"Better behave," Absalom said. "Oneita's sensitive about her feet, too."

"He's joking," Becca said. "What flavor coffee would you like?"

"Doesn't that machine need washing so it won't make the coffee taste like chocolate?"

"Not at all."

"What's hazelnut taste like?"

"Jon likes sawdust flavor."

Absalom faced Jon. "She jokes as much as you do."

"We're a pair, huh? I like french vanilla myself. Brew him a cup of that robust blend you bought at the grocery last week, honey. That'll knock his hat right off his head."

Absalom hung his coat and wide-brimmed hat on the coat rack. "Sorry about that. Tell me why Eliza is wearing your clothes while that machine makes the coffee."

The nutty aroma of Becca's coffee steamed from the machine. "It was simple, really, despite how it looked. I took the clothes basket upstairs to make the bed and show Eliza her room. Did Jon tell you we wanted you to stay with us?"

"He mentioned it."

"We made the bed, and I introduced Eliza to Ellie and me by showing her how our names form on our lips."

"She knows our names like that, too."

"Ellie knows mama and daddy like that. Anyway, when Jon's artwork started selling, and when we started thinking about adding on to the house, I insisted on a half-bath for every bedroom. We had an outhouse when we first got married. I'll be darned if I'm going to run outside and sit on a cold wooden seat ever again."

"What's that got to do with Eliza wearing your clothes?"

"I showed her the bathroom and started to come downstairs. I left the clothes basket because I need to make your bed, too. She pointed at the bathroom, so I left without her."

"And she decided to try on your clothes and see what I'd think about them." Absalom glanced at Eliza. "I'm not surprised."

Jon took his coffee from Becca. "Why's that?"

"Whenever I take her to town, I see her looking at magazines with women on the covers. I'm tempted to make her stop at times, because I don't want her to compare herself to those women and their clothes."

Becca dropped another small container into the machine and pulled the handle down. "I don't know of any young woman who doesn't want to fit in. That means clothes, too."

"Well, as I said a minute ago, I don't want her to lose her Amish roots."

"Don't take this the wrong way," Jon said, "but she doesn't have any Amish roots. At least not in the traditional sense."

"What do you mean by that? She was born in Ohio not long after we moved from Nebraska and grew up in an Amish family, so I don't see how—"

"Ab, I like you a lot, but you have a lot to learn concerning how a deaf person lives."

Absalom waved away the offered mug from Becca. "You better explain that, Jon, or I might consider leaving anyway."

"Come on now, we've already talked about how anger makes problems worse instead of better."

Absalom took the mug from Becca. He'd fought anger ever since moving to Ohio and didn't know why, unless it had something do with Oneita's insistence on becoming Swartzentruber Amish, as well as how she made Eliza do more work than Ethan and Tess combined. "All right, tell me what I'm missing about my own daughter."

"To Becca and me," Jon said, "the best way to understand how deafness affects Ellie is to use her perspective, not ours. All she knows about being a Mennonite is what she sees, which means she doesn't understand anything about it. That means all Eliza knows about the Amish is—"

Absalom held up his hand. "Pardon my interruption. I was thinking about this while ago and must've let my temper make me forget it. All she knows about the Amish is the clothes we wear and how we go to a building where some man talks while holding a book."

"That's right," Becca said. "That includes how the other

Amish ways, like driving buggies and not interacting with the English, are different, too. All she knows about the Amish is how the people in her community are different from anyone else, without any reason why."

"I couldn't agree more," Absalom said. "The concept of our religion having anything to do with those differences is completely foreign to her as well." He faced Eliza, who turned the mug up and lowered it to lick hot chocolate from her lips. She rubbed her stomach—a sign that meant she liked it—and nodded at Ellie while smiling. Ellie returned the nod and smile.

Absalom sipped his mug of coffee and licked his lips also. "Not bad. I may have to rethink coffee from a machine."

"Good deal." Jon emptied his mug and placed it in the sink. "I need to pack for my flight and get to the airport for that teacher."

Chapter 9

Denver yawned.

Inside Raleigh-Durham International Airport, travelers moved with, against, and across the general ebb and flow of each other's current. Some darted like baitfish attempting to escape the gaping mouth of a striped bass in Buggs Island Lake. Aggravated expressions, reddened faces, clenched jaws, furrowed foreheads, and barely moving lips, likely mumbling four-letter words, filled the walkway. Shoes scuffed, high heels clicked, sneakers squeaked, perfume wafted. A baby's smelly diaper offended, women frowned, men scowled, antiperspirant failed, underarms reeked. A boy cried, "But I gots ta *pee,* Mama," and every few minutes the roar of one airliner taking off exploded over the roar of the previous one, resulting in a near endless cacophony of mind-shattering noise, sights, sounds, and smells.

Denver cringed. Regardless of his apprehension at flying, it had to be better than sitting in the middle of this mess.

He yawned again, sleepy from tossing and turning most of the night at the thought of all the new experiences—good or bad—on which he was about to embark.

If that weren't enough, he couldn't spot Mr. Raber. Jan took his picture during the show and sent it to Denver's phone yesterday. In the photo, the tanned Mennonite wore faded jeans, a black sport coat, no tie, and preferred his hairstyle similar to Denver's, trimmed shortish. He ran his fingers through his hair. He'd skipped his last haircut, and his brown hair curled at his ears. Mr. Raber's dark brown hair and tanned complexion, along with the black sport coat, should be easy to spot, but no matter how hard Denver peered over the heads of his fellow travelers, his gut tightened with the fear of being left behind. At least the motion sickness pills he'd bought should help, *if* he ever boarded the stupid plane. He slapped his pocket and the pills rattled, muffled by his jeans.

Denver slid his phone from its holder on his belt and checked the time. A hand clapped his shoulder.

"Good morning, Denver. I'd recognize your wild brown hair—Jan's words, not mine—anywhere."

"Mr. Raber." Denver offered his hand. "I can't thank you enough for setting up this trip."

Mr. Raber released Denver's hand. "Let's make it Jon and Denver." He grabbed the handle of a carry-on beside him. "Jan told me about your parents. Are you sure you're ready for this trip away from your sister? I can't imagine losing both parents at the same time."

"It still hurts if I think about it too much, but she understands how important this is."

"That's good of her. I appreciate you both taking such an interest in deaf children. Our flight is at ten, we need to get going. Depending on how many people are traveling, the security check can take a while. That doesn't include waiting in line."

Denver slipped his phone in the holder and followed Jon, who slowed at the end of several lines and stopped at the shortest. "Jan said you've never flown. Are you nervous?"

"I'm doing okay. How many times have you been to North Carolina?"

"This is my fourth trip. Would you believe I forgot about you and had to fly back?"

"I could've driven to Ohio."

"No, sir, when I make a promise, I make a promise. Besides, I'd rather fly an hour and a half instead of driving over eight."

The line moved. Denver followed Jon. "I guess Jan told you about the documentary I saw on deaf children in remote villages in Africa. She told me about your daughter."

"She's a cutie. The Amish tend to keep to themselves, but I thought they might welcome a school built by a Mennonite more so than by outsiders." Jon took a few steps, following the shortening line, and faced Denver again. "We're next. Is your underwear clean?"

"It took long enough. I was— Did you say *underwear?*"

"I'm not wearing any. That really gets their attention when they pull me aside for the full body scan." Jon turned toward the line and turned back. "You know I'm kidding, right?"

"Jan didn't tell me you were such a joker."

"It's better than being a grump."

A TSA agent motioned to Jon. "Place your luggage on the conveyor and remove your shoes. Place them on the same conveyor as your luggage. Empty the contents of your pockets into the plastic box by the metal detector."

Jon did as instructed. The agent patted him down, taking extra care beneath his coat and at his pockets. He asked Jon to step through the full-body metal detector, which remained quiet. Jon winked at Denver. "Your turn."

Denver placed his backpack on the conveyor, jerked his hiking boots off and added them, too. He went through the metal detector. An alarm buzzed; the agent said it was the backpack. He looked through it and scanned it with a hand wand, which beeped, then dumped everything out in a plastic container and faced another agent. "Lisa, scan this guy and his backpack and all his stuff. It's alarming and I don't see anything."

The agent, Lisa, strode over. "Follow me." The other agent gave Denver his boots. In sock feet, he cursed under his breath the entire walk. He checked his watch. 9:45.

He cursed again, louder. The agent whirled around. "What was that?"

"I … uh, I'm sorry. I don't want to be late for my flight."

Lisa led Denver to two opposing panels, where she instructed him to place his smart phone and pocket contents in a plastic container and step between the panels. She disappeared behind one. "Raise your arms over your head." Denver did so, and she added, "Okay." He wasn't sure, but her *okay* carried the same kind of lilting innuendo that Jan used when she wanted to snuggle on the sofa. Denver lowered his hands. "Not yet," Lisa said, "I need one more look." Denver raised his hands. He and Jon needed to get on that plane, like *now* get on that plane.

"All clear." She handed him his pocket contents and his smart phone, then scanned his backpack and handed him that. "All clear, too. You have a *real* nice flight, okay?"

Taking his belongings, Denver eyed her, trying to figure out if her *real* meant more than someone else's *real*, especially with that continued lilt in her voice. She gave him a huge smile, and a laugh erupted from the other side of the inspection area, where Jon waited with his carry-on. Denver shuffled over in his socks and sat in the floor to put his boots on. "Is it me, or was that agent flirting?"

"Did you like her smile?"

"I guess it was okay, why?"

"I might tell Jan when I come back for my next show, that's why." Jon set off at a fast stride, and Denver followed.

"Not if you don't want me to make up something to tell your wife."

"There you go, my stiff Virginia friend. It's about time you made a joke." Jon laughed again.

Denver said nothing. Getting to Ohio took priority, not the agent's possible flirting or Jon's joking.

On the plane, Jon stored his carry-on in the overhead compartment. Denver sat by the window, his stomach fluttering. He should've taken the aisle seat in case he got sick. He took the motion sickness pills from his pocket. "When do we get something to drink?"

"Not until we reach cruising altitude. Do you get motion sickness?"

Denver rattled the pill bottle. "I even get woozy when I'm not driving."

"Too bad, you should've taken those pills a few hours ago."

Loading doors closed, the captain instructed everyone to fasten their seatbelts. The pitch of the jet engines rose. The airliner shuddered slightly, taxiing out to the runway. Denver's gut tightened a notch. The engine's pitch rose again, and the seat vibrated beneath him. He squeezed the armrests and closed his eyes. The engine's roar and the vibrations worsened. The plane angled upward, and the seat leaned back as if it were a recliner. It leveled after several minutes, and Jon patted his hand. "Need a bag?"

Denver opened his eyes. "What kind of bag?"

Jon handed him a blue plastic bag. "For saving your breakfast."

"I'm okay." Denver swallowed to ease the nausea filling his throat. "But I'll be glad when I can get something to drink so I can take these pills."

The announcement came to unfasten the seatbelts. Flight attendants rolled carts of water and soft drinks down the aisle, stopping to ask passengers what they preferred. Denver and Jon took crinkly plastic bottles of water, ice-cold. Denver washed the pills down. "You say the flight is an hour and a half?"

"About that, give or take to Columbus." Jon swallowed water. "I live five minutes north of the Holmes County seat. It's about halfway between there and Holmesville."

"Any rivers or lakes nearby? My family has a waterfront home near a small town on a lake. The town's great, but I like the wooded lot and the water view."

"We have a large creek in the woods behind the school. It's just a short walk."

"How many students do you expect?"

"Five including my daughter. They're all under eight except one."

"Won't it be crowded with the four students and their parents sleeping in the school?"

"It would've been if I put beds in. Think you can a manage a pallet on a neoprene sleeping mat?"

"I'm used to camping with one of those." Denver drank water from the plastic bottle. "Will the lack of privacy bother any of the Amish parents?"

"Did your research, huh? All the students except one are coming from close enough to make the buggy drive every day. My wife's pregnant, so I asked one father and daughter—she's the older student you'll be teaching—to stay in the house while they're there. I'll be busy with my art and a few trips I've got lined up, so I'd like them to keep an eye out." Jon drank more water." Did Jan tell you there'll be two teachers?"

"She did. I guess I was too excited to ask why. What's this about me teaching the older student?"

"I installed a chalkboard in each end of the room. I want one teacher to work with the younger students and one to work with the older."

"Any particular reason?"

"I could be wrong, but I think a woman teacher might work better with the younger students."

"Jan said the other teacher was a man."

"Do you mind sleeping in the same building with a woman? I already asked her and she doesn't care. You can sleep in the cold barn if you mind."

"Why me? Let her sleep in the barn."

"You really mind?"

"Not really."

"She's tough enough to do it. Her name's Akina. She served four years as a Marine before college."

"That's kind of a different name."

"You'll meet her today. She's getting at the airport around the same time."

"What about her name?"

A flight attendant stopped at their seats. "Good morning, gentlemen, I'm Renee. Today we have a turkey or ham sandwich, with a side salad. Which would you like?" Renee beamed a perfect smile at Denver.

"How about both?" Denver patted his stomach. "My breakfast ran out a long time ago."

"Two sandwiches? Are you still a growing boy?"

Jon elbowed Denver. "The TSA agent at the airport thought so."

"Why's that?" Renee said.

"Don't pay any attention to him," Denver said. "I'll take whatever, I'm not picky."

"Two sandwiches for the growing boy." Renee gave Denver the sandwiches. "To drink we have beer, wine, soft drinks, and—"

Jon held up his hand. "While my friend is making up his mind, I'll have the turkey sandwich and ranch dressing for the salad and finish my water with it."

"I believe you've done this before." Renee smiled at Denver again. "Made up your mind, growing boy?"

"Go ahead, growing boy," Jon said. "Tell Renee what you want to drink, I'm hungry."

"I'll have olive oil and balsamic vinegar on my salad and finish my water, too."

Renee handed Denver the salad and two packets of dressing. "There you go, have a *real* nice flight." Denver watched Renee walk away. *More* flirting? With smiles and an innuendo-filled lilt in her voice like the TSA agent? Either that or he was imagining things.

Denver waited until Renee moved a few seats away and faced Jon. "What the heck is going on with these women flirting with me?"

"Did you date much in high school and college?"

"I'm kind of a homebody. I tend to clam up around girls, but if I ever found one who enjoyed the outdoors as much as I do, I might be different."

"Jan doesn't like the outdoors?"

"Dirt is her sworn enemy, especially when she's wearing new shoes."

"What I'm trying to ask is if you weren't interested in girls in high school or college? Don't you know you're a nice-looking guy?"

Although Denver saw no need to bring up his past and how it had made him shy around girls, the next comment was true. "I don't think about stuff like that. I go for inner beauty rather than outer." He took a bite of the turkey sandwich and washed it down with a swallow of lukewarm water.

Jon's comment about his looks puzzled him. He never thought about himself as attractive, or even good-looking. Jan, as gorgeous as she was, had asked him out on their first date, so it was possible. Still, it didn't matter. To him, inner beauty, such as being kind, caring, and understanding, was more important, although he couldn't deny that being physically attracted to someone was important, too. Along with those qualities, sharing goals and dreams, as well as having interests in common, was important also. Thank goodness he and Willow had fine parents to pass on those fine values.

He and Jan shared some of those values, but were they enough for something as important as marriage? Regardless, it didn't matter, because they subject had never come up.

Chapter 10

Denver jerked upright in his seat, and Jon stopped shaking his arm. "Buckle up, sleeping beauty. We're landing in a minute."

"Thanks for waking me." Denver snapped the seatbelt. "Hey, you never told me about Akina and her name."

"She's a licensed physical therapist."

"What's that got to do with her name?"

Buckling his seatbelt, Jon cut his eyes at Denver. "I'm getting there. Her great-grandmother inspired her. She was a trained masseuse. Akina learned sign language in college like you did."

"That's an interesting combination. How did her great-grandmother become a masseuse?"

"Her great-grandparents are from Japan, which is why her name is different. Her great-grandmother comes from a long line of respected massage therapists. She worked for the Emperor before World War II."

"Wow, that *is* an interesting background."

"It sure is. As interesting as your solar engineering degree."

"I guess Jan told you about that."

"She did." Jon turned to face Denver as much as the narrow seat allowed. "Your sign language skills are my priority, but I'd like you to make a preliminary design for a solar power grid for my home, if you don't mind. I'll pay you, but teaching the children is what's important. That's why I didn't mention the option of doing the solar work to Jan. If you're interested, take some notes and work everything up when you get home for your three-month vacation."

Denver's luck amazed him. "I never expected to teach sign language and get paid to work as a solar engineer."

Jon straightened in his seat. "I'm hoping some of the surrounding Amish communities will consider having schools for the Deaf, too. Then they won't need to take such long buggy rides, or stay overnight."

"My research said some of the orders don't like using electricity."

"Maybe that'll change if they use solar." Jon elbowed Denver, probably in advance of a joke. "Because electricity comes from the light, get it?"

"I gotcha, Jon, I gotcha."

The plane took a sharp turn. The G-force pulled Denver to one side of his seat. The plane leveled out, engines winding down. The wheels thumped to a smooth landing.

Like in Raleigh-Durham International, bustling travelers flowed toward a TSA checkpoint. Within thirty minutes, Denver and Jon neared the main doors, where a young woman stood from a bench. "It's about time, you two. My flight got here an hour early."

Jon offered his hand. "I recognize you from the photo you sent with your resume."

Akina, with shining-black, shoulder-length hair, and dark, almost black eyes, faced Denver and signed, "Nice to meet you, Denver." She looked at him long enough to make him uncomfortable. "Don't take this the wrong way, but you've got gorgeous eyes."

Denver slung his pack over one shoulder and signed, "Thanks. Just so we're clear, I'm dating someone."

"Just so we're clear, too, my Marine background makes me outspoken, even to strangers."

"Are you trying to say you're a pain in the butt?" Denver signed without thinking. Maybe Jon's joking was rubbing off on him. He didn't mind because the jokes had gotten his mind off losing Mom and Dad.

Akina looked up at him. "Just letting you know, I don't mind shooting the breeze about anything and everything."

"That's not fair," Jon said. "I don't know a sign from my big toe."

"Good," Denver said. "Now I can pay you back for all your joking in Raleigh and on the plane."

"What did he do?" Akina said.

"It wasn't me," Jon said, "it was the woman who scanned him at security, smiling at him."

Akina looked Denver up and down. "Well, you aren't ugly by any stretch of the imagination. Does your girlfriend teach sign language like you do?"

"She works at the museum where Jon had his last art show. She told him about me and that's how I got here."

"Jan's attractive," Jon said to Akina. "Between her and that security agent and a flight attendant who smiled at him, too, you have some tough competition."

"Being a Marine," Akina said, "I'm up for a good fight."

"*Ex*-Marine," Denver said.

"Once a Marine, always a Marine." Akina took her carry-on from beside the bench. "Let's get this show on the road, Jon. I want to see where me and my bunkmate will be sleeping together for the next three months."

Eliza wiped sweat from her brow. After lunch, Papa had taken her to the barn again, to a room filled with strange metal machines and the yellow aroma of sawdust. He gave her a piece of paper, rough as if sand was stuck to it, and showed her how to rub a curved piece of wood until it was smooth. A fine dusting of gold from the wood coated her fingers. Sweat trickled into the small of her back. A bath in the building he showed her yesterday would be wonderful. She stopped rubbing the wood, gathered her hair, and slung the aggravating black mass over her shoulder, where it wouldn't keep falling into her face and on the wood.

Beside her, Papa stopped rubbing his piece of wood and wiped sweat from his forehead, which released a sour odor from beneath his arm. Eliza pointed to one of her underarms and wrinkled her nose at the odor. Papa's shoulders rose with silent chuckles. He motioned her to stay, then left the room. Eliza continued rubbing the wood.

Several strokes later, she yawned. The bed here was as comfortable as her own, but she'd tossed and turned because of the unanswered question of why Papa had brought her here. Yes, everyone was kind, but Papa had never taken her somewhere to stay like this, much less somewhere where the people wore clothes and styled their hair like the people in town instead of the people near their home.

She huffed a few stray hairs out of her eyes and rubbed the wood again. Becca's husband, who wore the same kind of pants as she did, smiled a lot. He and Becca even made Papa smile after his fit of anger yesterday. People who smiled were special, and Eliza liked being with them.

Papa returned with a pair of pants, socks, and a shirt like Becca wore. He motioned for Eliza to follow, then led her inside the building that housed the place to bathe. Smiling a thank you, she took the clothes.

Undressed, she caught a stronger whiff of sour body odor, almost as bad as before her one bath a week at home. Why didn't her family bathe more often? Carrying and heating water was nothing compared to all those sour bodies. Dirty and clean clothing on a hanger on a wall, she took a cloth from a stack on a shelf. Inside the white room, she pulled the curtain closed and turned the shiny metal knobs until the water warmed to suit her.

The calming flow tingled along her shoulders, down her back, legs, and ankles.

The people in the community at home didn't show affection or kiss in public, but some of the people in town did. Once, when she and Papa passed a house, a couple on a porch were locked in an embrace that left nothing to the imagination as to what they would do inside, like when farm animals joined. The man gripped the woman's bottom and pulled her toward him. The difference between people and animals shone in the couple's kiss, his hand that tugged her collar aside, his lips that found her neck when she leaned her head back.

Eliza raised her face to the water and let it run down her breasts. Was this how a man's fingertips might caress her body in the dark of night while doing what that couple would do? She ran her hands over her body and smiled. She'd rather have a kerosene lamp flickering its yellow glow upon the man's muscles, writhing with curve and grace like those of a snake climbing a tree. Contract … advance … release … contract. Another tingle, unlike anything she'd ever experienced, burst into a singular ball of heat below her navel. She shook her head to rid herself of it, and her hair, growing heavy with water, caressed the curve of her bottom.

She opened a bottle on a shelf made into the white material of the bathing place and sniffed. This must be soap, but a bar of soap, similar to the soap at home, sat on another shelf. The soap in the bottle smelled sweet and subtle, like a bottle of liquid she'd sniffed from a shelf in one of the stores she and Papa had visited. The bar of soap here smelled plain. She poured soap from the bottle and lathered her hair. Who wanted their hair to smell plain?

How might it be to always bathe this way instead of in the brown water left over in the metal tub after everyone at home had bathed? She had no idea, but she'd like to discover how that might be, along with flipping a lever for lighting a room.

She soaped the small cloth and scrubbed herself from head to toe. Brown lather flowed from her body and disappeared into the metal thing in the floor. Eliza rubbed her toes across the holes. Where did the water go? No matter. She ran her hands over her skin—clean, smooth, and glowing in the light overhead. She and Papa would likely return home soon, but living here was wonderful. What other miracles might she experience before they left?

She took a large cloth from a stack beside the small ones and dried herself, including her hair, at least enough to stop water from dripping down her back. Dressed in clean clothes, she folded the dirty clothes and placed her hand on the door knob to leave.

Jon pulled his pickup into the driveway, and Denver admired the farm. "Nice place you got here."

"I remodeled the house myself, except for the electric and plumbing."

Jon parked just past the house. "That's the school to the right. You and Akina get settled. I want to see what Becca and Ellie are up to."

Behind Denver, Akina shoved his seat. "You heard the man, move your behind."

"Sheesh, hard case, give me a break." Denver climbed out, Akina behind him.

"Some of my platoonmates called me 'hard case' when I was on active duty. Who knows why."

"It's your outspoken personality you told me about."

Akina gave Denver his backpack. "They called me that because I rode them hard. No slacking off, or I'll ride you hard, too."

"You need a drink to calm down. Wonder where we can get a beer around here?"

"Jon said there's a refrigerator in the school for bottled water." Akina took her carry-on from the pickup and closed the door. "The subject of alcohol never came up, but I doubt he wants it around the kids."

"Good point, Marine."

"Got that right. Alcohol makes people do things they wouldn't do otherwise, like me kicking your butt if you don't do a good job teaching."

"Yeah, right. What are you, five-two?"

Akina took off her jacket and pulled her sleeve up to flex a bulging bicep. "I miss my weights already. I might lift you."

Like her, Denver bared and flexed his bicep. "Not bad, huh? I paddle a canoe on the lake where my parents lived."

Akina's playful expression turned solemn. "I'm sorry about your parents. Jon told me about them."

Denver appreciated her thought. "I'm sort of glad for this trip. Sometimes you need to get away from home after a thing like that."

"Do you have any other family?"

"A sister named Willow, she's twenty. She's going to learn sign from the internet while I'm gone."

Akina left for the school. "I'm about to pee my pants. Jon said the outhouse and a shower's around back."

"An outhouse?" Denver fell in step with Akina.

"He said his septic system wasn't big enough to handle another bathroom, according to the county."

"What about bath water?"

"I guess poo takes priority over water."

"Did he tell you we had a clothes washer?"

"And no dryer. Who cares, they smell great hanging on a line." Behind the school, Akina opened the door to the smallest building and set her carry-on down. "This is it, be right back."

Denver dropped his pack beside the steps to the larger of the two buildings and pulled the doorknob.

Eliza turned the doorknob and started to push. The door opened on its own, and she fell into the arms of a wide-eyed young man with curly brown hair and eyes as blue as a midday sky. She squirmed out of his arms. What made him think he could put his hands on her? He was no better than the boy with the fishing pole.

He smiled and then spoke, but his lips moved too fast to understand the slightest word.

He didn't *seem* like the boy with the fishing pole. He must've pulled the door when she pushed, and him catching her was an accident. Besides, it wasn't right to think something bad about someone before they proved whether they were bad or not. The first step was an introduction. Otherwise, he might think she was as dumb as the boy with the fishing pole. She placed her hands over her ears and shook her head. He nodded, placed his hand on his chest, and mouthed the word that must be his name.

Placing her hand on her chest, she mouthed her name. Men greeted each other with a handshake, so she offered her hand. His hand grasped hers, shaking it up and down slowly.

Those blue eyes and a welcoming smile were nothing like the boy with the fishing pole. Heat gathered between their hands, gathered within her in a sudden burst. She could get lost in his blue eyes and broad smile. He looked toward the building beside this one.

"Took you long enough," Denver said to Akina as she left the outhouse.

She strolled over and gave the girl a quick wave. "Hi, I'm Akina."

"I think she's the oldest student come to take a shower," Denver said. "Her hair's still wet."

"Why do you think she's a student?"

"Introduce yourself. Just remember, she doesn't know sign language."

Akina placed her hand on her chest and said her name, pronouncing each section slowly, slightly exaggerating the movement of lips and jaw.

The girl replied as she had to Denver, also giving her sign of deafness.

"See?" Denver said.

"Lucky you, having an Amish goddess in your class since she's older."

Denver looked around. "I wonder where her parents are?"

"Is something wrong?" A broad-shouldered man wearing black pants, a black coat, and a wide-brimmed straw hat rounded the corner of the school.

"No, sir," Denver said, not wanting this red-headed mountain of an Amish man, possibly the girl's dad, to get the wrong idea. Not only was he broad-shouldered, he was at least six inches taller than Denver's five-eleven height, maybe more. An average-sized man wouldn't stand a chance in a physical confrontation with this guy. "We're just introducing ourselves," Denver said.

"You must be the teachers. I'm Absalom Gray. This is Eliza, my oldest daughter."

"Nice to meet you," Akina said. "My name's Akina and this guy's Denver."

Absalom tipped his hat. "Eliza was helping me in Jon's woodworking shop and got sweaty. I thought she'd enjoy her first shower."

"I think she liked it." Akina glanced at Denver. "I think she liked meeting her teacher, too."

See you Monday," Absalom said. "I can't wait to see what Eliza thinks of sign language." He and Eliza left. At the corner of the school, she looked over her shoulder and smiled.

"That poor, innocent girl," Akina said, picking up her carry-on. "You've gone and ruined her with your sexy blue eyes and pretty smile. You'll have to take her back home and marry her."

"She's too young for me, probably sixteen or seventeen." Denver swung his backpack over his shoulder and left for the front of the school. Akina caught up. He bumped her shoulder with his, knocking her off balance. "You, on the other hand, might make a decent wife, if …"

"*If* what?" Akina returned the bump.

"If you weren't so jealous."

Inside the school, they unpacked their belongings. Denver pointed at two rolled-up neoprene sleeping mats beside a stack of towels and washcloths on a table, where they were placing their clothes. "All the comforts of home except for a pillow. I'll roll up a towel for that."

Akina looked out a rear-facing window on the other side of the table. "Did you know the clothes washer's in the outhouse?"

"No way," Denver said. "You mean we have to smell what's in that hole when we wash our clothes?"

"No, Miss Sensitive-nose, I was trying to get a rise out of you by joking. Jon said the washer's in the building with the shower. Good thing, or he would need to hang a dozen air fresheners in there to keep your pretty little nose from wrinkling." Akina turned away to fold some of her clothes. "If you haven't noticed it already, I'm one of those people who never met a stranger. Might as well get used to it."

"Good grief." Denver dropped the towel with the others. "What has Jon gotten me into?"

Chapter 11

Denver finished laying out his clothes on the table and hung his coat on a hanger beside Akina's near the door. At one of the desks, he opened a drawer. It held plenty of paper and pens and pencils for notes while teaching, perfect for making those notes for the solar plans Jon had mentioned, too. Another drawer held chalk for the chalkboard and an eraser. He took a stick of chalk from the box and placed it and the eraser on the shelf at the bottom of the chalkboard.

Akina walked over. "Staking your claim already?"

"Not if you'd rather use this end of the room."

"I'm messing with you, lighten up."

"I'm trying to get ready to teach Monday. Does everyone in the Marines joke all the time?"

"Okay, Mr. Serious. Got anything special planned?"

"I haven't thought about it much."

Knock-knock.

The door opened. A woman with an auburn braid hanging over her shoulder and a tray of food stepped in. "Who's ready for an early supper?"

She took the tray to Denver's desk. A slightly rounded tummy bulged beneath her fleece jacket. Denver offered his hand. "You must be Becca."

"That's me." Becca shook Denver's hand. "My tummy give me away?"

"Jon said you were expecting," Akina said. "You didn't have to bring our food all the way out here."

"I need the exercise. You must be Akina." Becca offered her hand. "Jon and I appreciate you and Denver coming here to teach sign language." She pointed at the tray. "I hope you like stew and grilled cheese sandwiches with an apple for dessert."

Denver caught the aroma of beef and onions. "Jon said he'll be busy. I guess you'll learn sign language with your daughter."

"He expects me to teach him when he has time." Becca faced Akina. "When do men ever have time to learn anything new from their wives?"

"I wouldn't know, I'm not married."

"Any serious relationships?"

"Being the take-charge type, I'm in no hurry." Akina looked up at Denver. "Denver says he's seeing about a dozen women or so."

"Jon says he's seeing Jan," Becca said. "She handles his shows in North Carolina."

"Don't pay any attention to Akina," Denver said. "She scares guys away with her muscles."

"I see that. Do you know how to operate the heat and the partition?"

"If you mean the propane space heaters on each end of the school," Denver said, "I can handle it. What's this about a partition?"

Becca went to the middle of the room, where a vertically pleated curtain, thick and sturdy, hung folded from the ceiling to the floor. "Jon put this in to separate the older from the younger classes. I kind of hate it because Ellie likes Eliza so much."

"Makes sense." Akina said. "We don't want to distract each other while we're talking to the parents."

"How old is Ellie?" Denver asked Becca. "Jon said all the students except Eliza are under eight."

"Ellie's five, cute as a redbone hound pup."

"By redbone pup, you mean she has red hair like you?"

"That's it." Becca went to the desk for the tray. "I'll take this back for next time. Is the water in the fridge okay to drink?"

"I'm good," Denver said.

"Me too." Akina said. "Do you have something we could drive? We could go to town for bread and sandwich stuff for lunch, and cereal and milk for breakfast. We could save you some work."

"There's another pickup behind the barn. I don't mind, really."

Denver tasted the stew. "This is great."

"Don't make Becca feel guilty," Akina said. "We can handle breakfast and lunch. Besides, I might take you out to eat if you do a decent job of teaching."

"I'd take her up on that if I were you, Denver," Becca said. "Like Jon keeps telling Absalom, what happens at our house stays at our house." At the door, she turned. "Absalom said he and Eliza met you out back. Did you wonder why she's wearing jeans and a sweatshirt?"

"I did," Akina said. "Denver didn't have time because he was checking her out."

Shaking his head, Denver cut his eyes at Akina, and said to Becca, "Jon sure stuck me with a joker for a sign language teacher."

"You don't think Eliza's attractive?"

"I didn't think about it."

"Come on," Akina said. "You couldn't take your eyes off her."

"Can't say I blame you," Becca said. "That's one stunning young woman. Then again, Akina, you're attractive, too. Can you and Denver behave for three months?"

"I can," Denver said.

"He's a man," Akina said. "That makes him completely corruptible."

"What's your middle name?" Becca said. "Because it sounds like it should be Eve."

"Adam was ripe for the corrupting," Akina said, looking at Denver.

"Eve was as ripe for it as he was," Becca said. "As far as Eliza wearing jeans and a sweatshirt, I thought you might wonder why. It's a long story, but the gist of it's how her father gave in to her happiness."

"Makes sense," Akina said. "I could wrap my dad around my pinky when I was little."

"See you later. Whenever you need the pickup, the keys are under the visor." Becca left.

Akina took the spoon from the other bowl of stew and licked it. "You know I plan to take you out and get you drunk and take advantage of you, don't you?"

Denver swallowed stew. "When you said you're the type of person who never met a stranger, did that mean you flirt with everyone?"

"Are you such a stick in the mud you don't like joking around?"

"Well, I'd rather joke than be boring." Denver got two bottles of water from the fridge. Akina scraped her chair to his desk, sat and took a bite of grilled cheese. Denver opened the bottles. "You want that apple?"

"Mom believes an apple a day keeps the doctor away. She overdoses me every chance she gets."

Denver dropped the apples in a desk drawer.

Denver took the empty paper bowls, plates, and the plastic bottles to the trash.

"Lookin' good there," Akina said. "Jan's a lucky woman."

"Becca's right." Denver came back to the desk.

"About?"

"Me putting up with you for the next three months."

"I doubt I stand a chance next to Eliza. That girl could be a model."

"You could too" —Denver dropped the trash in the container— "for junior high girl's fashions."

"Is that your smart-aleck way of telling me I'm short?"

"Short, petite, whatever."

"Good things come in small packages, Mr. Solar Engineer. I guess Jan is Barbie doll tall and Barbie doll blonde."

"Nice guess."

"I think you've got a thing for dark hair. Eliza had you in the palm of her hand when I came out of the outhouse."

Denver sat at the desk and stood again. "Time to get away from you."

"Like where?"

"A shower."

"I told you I never met a stranger. Wait until you start missing your girlfriend. Bet I won't be a stranger then."

Done with the shower, Denver relaxed on his mat while looking through a book of signs for Monday. His minor degree covered two years, which made his skill level decent but not outstanding when it came to speed. During supper, Akina told him she had a four-year degree and a year's experience working with the Deaf, making her a near expert.

She came in, hair still damp from the shower, and unrolled her mat at the wall beside him. Sleeping, they would form a forty-five-degree angle, heads together. She locked the door and fiddled with the heat on their end of the building. "I'm bushed, you done with that book?"

"I guess." Denver dropped the book beside the mat.

By the door, Akina turned out the lights and came back to kick her sneakers off at her mat. Moonlight streamed through a window to illuminate the thin sleep-shirt that fell to her knees. Denver tried to look away but couldn't. No doubt about it, Akina was extremely attractive, and his being a virgin didn't help things. He yawned. "Good night, mini-Marine."

"I'll 'mini-Marine' you." Akina dropped to the mat and pulled the covers to her chin. "Do you snore? I hope you don't snore. I'll strangle you in your sleep if you snore."

Grateful for the warmth in the cool room, Denver pulled the cover up to his chin and rolled onto his side. Because of the propane heaters Jon had installed, he'd also installed a carbon monoxide detector in each end of the room, which somewhat illuminated both areas. Denver's head was about a foot away from Akina's shining, dark eyes. "You're too much, you know that?"

"Eliza thought you were too much, too, staring at you over her shoulder when she left. All jokes aside, you do have gorgeous eyes."

"Well, I think a person's inside shows who they are more than their outside."

Akina slapped her hand to her chest. "Be still my beating heart, you're a poet, too. Let's go to sleep before I'm tempted to make you forget all about Jan."

Denver turned over to face the wall. "Good idea. Monday will be here before we know it."

Chapter 12

A breakfast of scrambled eggs and bacon brought by Becca—with buttery biscuits, homemade strawberry jam, and two mugs of hot coffee—tightened Denver's stomach against his belt.

Akina sipped the last swallow of coffee and set the mug on the desk. "I can't believe I suggested going to town for cereal when we could eat like this every morning."

"That oatmeal we bought yesterday will be good when the weather turns colder." Denver pointed. "Good thing we've got a microwave." He sipped coffee. "You turned Jon down quick when he asked about going to church."

"I've never attended a Mennonite church and didn't want to start now. That's why I said we were going to town when Jon asked."

"And Becca was still good enough to make breakfast for our first day of class." Denver took the paper plates to the trash, rinsed the mugs with a bottle of water, and dumped them in the grass outside the front door. He set them on the table with his clothes and returned to his desk to glance at his watch. "The students should start coming any min—"

The door opened; Becca entered with Ellie. "Some buggies are coming down the driveway. You two ready to show your stuff?"

"As ready as we'll ever be," Akina said.

Becca and Ellie took desks on the other end of the room.

A horse snorted outside. The door opened again, and a

woman dressed in traditional Amish clothing—white kapp, black dress, white apron, black shoes, along with a boy of about six or seven, in black overalls, white shirt, and a wide-brimmed straw hat—hung their coats on the pegs by the door. The woman took the boy's hat, hung it over his coat, and joined Becca and Ellie. Akina closed the partition halfway. She'd already put a sign up that asked for younger students to come to that side of the room.

Two more mothers, one with another boy and one with a girl, entered, followed by Absalom and Eliza.

Denver gestured to two desks. "Morning, Absalom. Y'all might as well sit up front." Denver took a clipboard and pen from the desk and wrote Eliza's name. He looked up from the clipboard. "We're keeping records of the students. How old is Eliza?"

"She turned eighteen in August. She lost her hearing between two and three from the measles." A slight smile, a shake of his head. "What a chatterbox she was." The smile fell away. "She stopped saying full words after a while and went back to sounds. When we didn't know what she was saying, she stopped trying to talk."

Denver wrote her name and age. What a sad story, one he'd heard often while learning sign language in college. At eighteen—well, almost eighteen and a half—Eliza wasn't too young to date in a world without Jan. Denver worked his jaw. Why think that after just considering how sad her story was? Even if they hit it off, he lived in Virginia and she lived in Ohio—in an Amish community at that.

He turned around to set the clipboard and pen on the desk. What an idiot. He'd just considered their distances apart, too. If Absalom wasn't so big, he'd ask him to choke some sense into him.

He took a deep breath and turned around. "What Akina and

I hope to accomplish is to raise everyone's ability to communicate. I'm sure Eliza and her family have come up with simple hand signs and gestures for everyday things. With sign language, you can speak as well as with actual words. When people can't communicate, they can't share their feelings with each other. This is especially important for families, because we want these kids to have the best chance at a full and happy life as possible."

"Eliza's happiest when she's painting her pictures," Absalom said. "I'm thankful she has that talent and enjoys it so much."

"What kind of pictures?"

"She'd like to paint while we're here. You and Akina can go with her into the woods for her supplies and see what she does with them."

"Sounds like a plan." Denver took the two apples from the desk drawer. "Our first lesson is to help the student understand what we're trying to teach. The rest comes easier then."

He gave one apple to Eliza and took a step away. She pointed at the apple and mouthed a perfect approximation of the word apple.

"I see she knows how a person's mouth moves when they say apple."

"She picks up things like that," Absalom said. "She does the same with her painting."

"How do you mean?"

"She can see something one time and paint it, no matter how complicated it is. Isn't there a phrase for that?"

"Really?" Denver said, using the time it took to ask that question to wrap his head around the fact that Eliza apparently had a photographic memory.

"Yes, really." Absalom's tone was sincere. "She's very talented with her paintings. I hope that makes her talented with sign language, too."

"It might. Let's see how well she understands what I'm trying to teach her. I'll use visual aids for her and speak while I sign. That way you'll know what the sign is."

"Denver looked Eliza in the eye. "Eliza." She nodded, and he pointed at the apple in her hand and, with his other hand, made a loose fist, leaving his curled index finger outside the rest of his fingers. Touching the knuckle of his curled index finger to his cheek while swiveling his hand back and forth, he said "Apple."

Eliza touched his apple and made the sign perfectly. Her gray eyes narrowed, as if she were solving a problem in her mind. She gave Absalom the apple and jumped from the desk, pointed at the florescent light overhead and held her hands in the air, waiting. Denver held his hand up and spread his closed fingers, the sign for light. Eliza repeated the sign, ran to the chalkboard, and tapped it with her fingertips. Denver tossed his apple to Absalom. He caught it, grinning like a man watching a miracle. At the chalkboard, Denver rubbed a finger across his forehead, made a square by spreading the thumbs and index fingers of each hand and holding them apart, and squiggled an imaginary line through the air where the square would've been, the sign for chalkboard. Again, Eliza made the sign perfectly. She looked around, maybe for something else to learn the sign for, and faced him instead. The gray eyes filled. Silver tears formed, spilling onto her cheeks. Head down, she covered her face. Huge sobs, low and deep within her throat, shook her shoulders.

Absalom wiped his eyes. "I think she understands." He stood and touched Eliza's shoulder. She raised her head, and he nodded. She hesitated for a second, nodded in return, and threw her arms around Denver's neck.

He peeked through her hair, soft and sweet with the floral

aroma of shampoo, to see Absalom. "I think you're right. She definitely understands."

Eliza pulled away and looked Denver in the eye, touched her forehead to his as if to say *thank you*, and returned to the desk.

Emotion at how the miracle of sign language had affected Eliza—the same as how it had affected the boy in the African documentary—jammed in Denver's throat. He unrolled three paper towels from his and Akina's supplies stacked in the corner, gave one to Absalom and Eliza each, and kept one for himself to wipe his eyes like they were doing.

"All right then," he said, "the hard part's out of the way. Let's see what else Eliza can learn so fast."

Eliza awoke, dressed, and ran downstairs. She grabbed the bucket by the door, where Papa had left it. Five days had passed since she'd met Denver. Papa used his signs last night, simple and slow, to explain how she could take Denver and Akina into the woods to gather her colors. Too bad Akina couldn't find something to do.

At the table, Papa made the sign for "eat." She shuffled to the table, put the bucket on the floor beside her, and forked a bite of warm eggs into her mouth. Papa put two sausages on her plate, followed by a biscuit oozing strawberry jam. Becca left and returned with a glass of milk, sat and stood again to hold her braid and make a question sign. Eliza nodded. Becca must be asking if she could braid her long hair. She went behind Eliza, separated her hair into individual lengths, and started weaving them in and out. Eliza was glad. She loved how her hair streamed down her back, but it would get in the way while she painted, like it did when she rubbed the curved pieces of wood with the rough paper.

Breakfast done, she questioned Papa with raised eyebrows. Smiling, he shooed her away as if she were a fly. She threw on her coat, grabbed the bucket, and ran across the yard that glimmered with frost in the morning sun.

At the school, when she knocked on the door, Akina let her in, signed "Hello," and mouthed Eliza's name.

Eliza stepped inside, returned the "hello," and looked around the building. Akina touched her shoulder, said Denver's name, and signed, "He is in," plus a word Eliza didn't know. She shook her head. Akina tugged her pants as if to lower them, then squatted slightly. Akina meant Denver was in the outhouse. Eliza placed her hand over her grinning mouth while Akina stepped to the far corner, where two green mats lay on the floor. This puzzled Eliza. Were Denver and Akina married? She hoped not. Besides, they hadn't shown any signs of affection during the week of school.

Eliza walked around the room, signing the names of the various items she'd learned. "Backpack. Chalk. Eraser. Paper. Pen." She picked up the— Had she forgotten? No. "Clipboard."

During a lesson, Denver had written his name on the chalkboard. He also taught her his name in more detail than when she fell into his arms after her shower. Repeating it over and over, he waited each time while she copied the motion with her mouth, lips, and tongue.

Eliza hated how she had misjudged Denver when they met. He was nothing like the boy at the river. He was nicer too— *much* nicer—*and* much more handsome. As handsome as the men in the magazines at the store.

Akina stopped by Eliza with an armload of clothes and signed "wash." Holding in a grin because she would be alone with Denver, Eliza signed "okay."

At the desk, she took a pencil and wrote DENVER on the paper clamped to the clipboard. She also had learned the written version of her name that day, and beside his name wrote ELIZA. This didn't quite seem enough to her artist's eye, so she drew a curled line, like a vine connecting two trees in the woods, and connected their names. Still dissatisfied, she drew small leaves on the line and around their names, then added a circle over the drawing with lines coming from it to represent a shining sun.

The door opened, and Denver came in. She turned the clipboard over on the desk.

Saying her name, Denver signed "Hello." She returned the greeting, loving the way his name brushed across her lower lip when she mouthed the V.

Introductions complete, she took the bucket from the desk, showed it to Denver, and signed, "More."

Holding his palms up, he lowered one while raising the other. "Maybe."

He rummaged through several items stacked in a corner and pulled out a large bowl. Containers in hand, they left the school and entered the path that led into the woods behind it.

Eliza knelt for a handful of leaves and sniffed their spicy aroma. She nodded to Denver, who sniffed the leaves and smiled. Could she use the leaves for her project today? Yes, she could, since she hadn't known what to paint until Denver had just smiled at her. She dropped the leaves in the bucket, broke a few twigs from a tree, and continued along the path, Denver beside her.

Summer—the best season because of the shade, the young squirrels playing in the green branches, the roly-poly raccoon kits toddling after their mother, the spotted whitetail deer hiding in honeysuckle thickets, where honeybees wriggled inside yellow and white blooms sweet with nectar. Summer— the season of sultry heat similar to the warmth that emanated from Denver whenever he looked Eliza's way. Yes, summer was magical, with the season of birth and newborn things. But winter in the woods—its stark contrast of bare limbs against either gray overcast, roiling white or, like now, with crystalline sky so blue it might shatter—carried its own special magic, of limbs entwining like the fingers of people who cared for each other, like when Mama and Papa sometimes held hands.

Unfortunately, Denver's hand nearest her held the bowl, so she couldn't slip her fingers into his.

Better get her mind back on her project.

Several wild grapes, dried almost like raisins, hung from a vine up ahead. She pulled what she could reach and dropped them in the bucket. A few steps beneath an oak tree, she stooped for a handful of acorns the squirrels hadn't chewed with their chisel-like teeth and dropped them in the bucket, too.

Denver stopped, and she did also. He peeked in the bucket and signed, "Our lunch?"

Grinning, she shoved his arm and continued down the path. He caught up and pulled her braid, and she skipped away like a week-old colt prancing around its mama. Denver caught up again, bumped her shoulder with his, and smiled.

Like the day of her first shower, heat rushed to her innermost places, the same as when she'd wondered if the water's touch might feel like a lover's hands caressing her body.

She didn't dare return his smile now. If she did, and if he smiled back the same way—huge, warm, and inviting—she'd have to risk a kiss.

No, not now, not when they were breathless from walking. Perhaps in the quiet of night and near water, definitely near water. She wouldn't kiss him in a hurry either. Their first kiss should be as gentle as the breath of spring, a timid touch to let him know how much she cared for him.

She turned her attention back to her project.

Leaves, twigs, grapes, acorns—she needed mud to make

everything stick together. Stopping to sniff the air, she pointed ahead and signed "water?" to Denver.

He nodded. Jon must've told him about a river or stream nearby, because its aroma rode the morning breeze like a gray blanket.

She picked up her pace. Her breath formed a haze in the chilly morning air like with Denver's breath. It seared her nostrils, burned deep in her throat.

A silver sliver of water appeared through the bare limbs of the woods. More quick steps brought her and Denver to the edge of a large creek, where water rippled and sparkled over rounded stones in the sunlight. On the opposite bank, a flash of brown caught Eliza's eye as a deer raised its head. The doe whirled, raised her white flag of a tail, and bounded away, leaving a leafless bush quivering in her wake. Another white flash followed as a huge buck trailed her, muscled hindquarters rippling, mating on his mind like the deer she'd seen by the river at home.

A grinning Denver held his hands over his head and spread his fingers to mimic antlers. Eliza waved his silliness away and knelt to scoop a handful of gritty mud. She put the bucket down and tugged Denver's pants. He knelt and held out the bowl for the mud, which she placed into it. Hands rinsed in the icy water, she wiped them on her pants and stood. Did she need anything else? Yes, she did. Denver's silliness had made her forget how she needed to find something green in this faded and leafless world of winter. She waved at him to follow and ran up the path toward the school.

Eliza's braid tapped her back. Her breath again formed white clouds in the chilly air. Denver ran beside her, taking smiling glances every few steps. She loved his boyish ways, loved his sky-blue eyes, loved the way he made her feel like a little girl, running to her own river at home to gather her colors.

If the Creator allowed it, maybe she could take him there one day.

At the front of the school, where the sun was melting the frost on the grass, she snatched a handful, dropped it in the bucket, and went inside.

Warm air from the tiny blue flames flickering in the heaters at each end of the school welcomed her. She and Denver hung their jackets by the door. Instead of going to his desk, she raised her hand in front of Denver, spread the middle three fingers of her hand, and touched her index finger to her lips. At the refrigerator, he took out two bottles of water and met her at the desk, where they sat. He twisted the top off the plastic bottle and drank, throat working as he swallowed. Instead of opening the bottle he'd brought for her, she took his bottle and drank. The warmth of Denver's lips ignited the now familiar spark of heat deep within her.

Mama and Papa never kissed in front of their children, but Eliza saw them kiss late at night in the kitchen. She drank again, desiring to feel more of Denver's lips upon hers than just their fading warmth on the bottle.

Half the water remained. She set the bottle on the desk, took the twigs from the bucket, and chewed the woody-tasting ends until they resembled toothbrushes. Done with that, she signed to Denver for a piece of paper. Otherwise, he'd never see her surprise on the clipboard.

He took a sheet of paper from the desk drawer, and Eliza held in a frown. Time to take matters into her own hands.

Rubbing her arms to tell him she was cold, she got up to turn the knob on the propane heater.

Denver admired Eliza as she strode toward the propane

heater. Statuesque and stunningly beautiful—how could he *not* admire her? Along with those attributes, he admired her intelligence even more. The combination was more than intriguing. The whole of her was intoxicating—entirely too intoxicating for a guy dating someone.

Eliza returned to the desk and sat. He leaned close to watch her work.

In the woods, at the creek, and in the yard, his curiosity had swelled like whitecapping waves on Buggs Island Lake during a sudden summer storm. Not only had his curiosity swelled each time she chose an item, it swelled at how quickly she could learn. In class this week, she absorbed every sign he threw at her, even holding up her three middle fingers for the W when he wrote "water" on the chalkboard. If she could learn signs this easily, the possibilities with her art, at which she was so completely engrossed, might be endless.

Eliza used the largest of the sticks to spread a thin layer of the sticky, whitish mud on the paper. In the bucket, she crushed the dried leaves into tiny bits and pressed them into the mud on the lower third of the paper.

The fluorescent light above the desk hummed softly, illuminating faint freckles across her nose, highlighting her black hair, fresh with the aroma of the crisp morning air.

She took the grass from the bucket and tore it into tiny bits like the leaves, made a pile on the desk and sprinkled the grass on the part of the picture without the leaves. Then she pressed the bits of grass into the mud and cleared a vertical space about three fingers wide through it, from the leaves to the top of the paper. Turning her head to one side as if trying to make up her mind, she removed more grass, which left the upper third of the paper wiped clean.

She dumped the acorns and shriveled grapes and bits of leaf on the desk, chewed the grapes, sipped water from the bottle, chewed again, and spit the bluish mass into the bucket. Perfect for the sky, the color clung to the bristles of a clean twig, which Eliza used to fill in the white space at the top of the paper.

She poured more water into the bucket and swished it around, left to pour it outside and returned to the desk. The acorns, after she peeled the dark brown hull away with her teeth, received the same chewing, mixing with water, and spitting. This treatment created a yellow mass. Eliza chose another clean twig to paint a yellow circle in the center of the top of the page.

Denver shook his head in amazement. The yellow circle resembled a sun rising on a foggy morning. He got up to turn the temperature down on the propane heater and sat again, to fan himself with the clipboard.

Eliza took another twig, bit most of the bristles off, and used it to make thin, vertical lines, as if they were trees with limbs reaching out and upward on either side of the cleared space that rose to the sun. The cleared space must be a path into a section of woods, similar to the one behind the school.

Denver stopped fanning himself, put the clipboard on the desk, and picked it up again.

Eliza had written their names on a sheet of paper on the clipboard. Small leaves flourished vines that connected their names. A sun, its rays beaming down, rose above their names as well. Eliza— intuitive, sweet, and amazingly artistic—might have a crush on her teacher.

Then again, he might have the beginnings of a crush on her, too. When was the last time he'd felt—and acted—like a boy, by running after her, pulling her braid, and grinning all the time like a teenager with his hormones gone wild? Beginning or not, his crush needed crushing. Their lives only ran together in three-month cycles, so nine months later, after watching her personality bloom from learning sign language, he'd never see her again.

Eliza spat the colors onto the desk. She mixed the rest of the grape and acorn mixture to form a bluish tint, chose another clean twig, and brushed this creamy color onto the top of the paper to create a cloudless sky around the sun. Using a fingertip, she blended the blue into the outer edge of the yellowed circle to create more of the foggy effect, then brought it down into the vertical space between the trees.

Except for the obvious imperfections, Eliza's painting held a magical presence. Almost genuine with its 3-D effect from the viscous paint, the leaves, the grass, and wild grape peelings, the picture was a near-perfect copy of the path into the woods.

She gently lifted the paper, keeping it flat, and offered it to him, mouthing, "Eliza colors."

Denver smiled and nodded. So this, as well as any other paintings she might create, were the Colors of Eliza Gray. "Beautiful," Denver signed, curving his fingers over his face. He took the picture and set it on the desk. "You see this somewhere?"

The door opened. Akina came in and signed, "You two have a nice time while I washed clothes?"

Denver signed and said, "Take a look at this."

Akina came to the desk. "Wow. I'd swear that's the path into the woods behind the outhouse, except in the summer."

Eliza touched the paper. "Needs." Her brow furrowed. "Needs Eliza." Her brow furrowed again. "I need to see." In a flurry of faded blue jeans, red sweatshirt, and black braid flying, she ran out the door, leaving it open.

"What the heck's up with her?" Akina said.

Denver went to the door. "Darned if I know." He waited as Eliza ran to the house. Hardly no time at all passed before she ran back, holding what appeared to be a black dress and a white kapp.

Breathing hard after the run, Eliza came in and offered the clothing to Akina, who faced Denver. "I think she wants to put herself in the painting." She took the dress and kapp, gave them to Denver, and signed to Eliza. "I'm too short. Let Denver wear them."

Eliza's eyes widened, followed by a severe fit of laughter. He took the clothing and told Akina, "You're gonna get it for this."

"Anything to see you in a dress. I'll pay you back for the laughs by taking you out to dinner like I promised you."

Denver slipped the dress over his head and put the kapp on. Grinning hugely, Eliza adjusted the ties to hang down his chest.

Akina snickered, giggled, and finally laughed out loud, bending over double and holding her stomach. Eliza laughed too, her bubbling personality exposing itself to the world, possibly for the first time. Denver couldn't help but laugh himself.

Absalom opened the door. "It sounds like three donkeys have taken over the schoolhouse." He closed the door. "Please sign to Eliza for me, Denver. You too, Akina. I have a lot to learn yet."

"Come on in," Denver said, signing at the same time for Eliza. "Eliza needs a model for her picture."

"And I'm too short for the job," Akina signed.

"This is a picture I have to see." Absalom came to the desk. "I know why she wants to put herself in the picture." He touched Eliza's shoulder and signed, "I remember." He pointed to Akina and then Denver. "You show."

Eliza grabbed Denver by the arm and pulled him to the front of the desk, where she faced him toward the far wall. She raised his arms out to the side and turned his palms down, nudged his feet apart with hers and disappeared behind him.

"I see what's she's doing," Akina signed. "This actually happened, Absalom?"

"It happened when she invented the sign she uses to tell me when she's going somewhere. We were visiting a fair, and this huge Brahma bull came over to see us. He was so big, he swayed side to side. When Eliza wants to go somewhere, she waves her hands slow and steady, like how that bull walked. Then she points toward where she's going."

Denver looked over his shoulder. "What's she doing now?"

"Stop peeking," Akina signed. "She's using a twig to make an outline."

Facing the far wall again, Denver listened to the scratch of the twig on the paper as it stopped and started, until he couldn't wait any longer. "Y'all mind if I come over?"

"What's up with that 'y'all?'" Akina said.

"What can I say? I'm from Virginia."

"No wonder, I'm from D.C. I think she's almost through."

Someone grabbed Denver's hand and turned him around, and that someone was a beaming Eliza. She held the picture flat for him to see, which now included an exact replica of his pose in the black dress and white kapp, as if she were walking along the path.

He took the picture, smiled and nodded to let her know how much he liked it, and offered it back.

Instead of taking it, she clenched her hands into fists, left her index fingers out and curled, and pushed her fists toward him. "Gift."

Denver nodded. Eliza's eyes glistened as she looked into his, possibly searching for an acknowledgment that they meant more to each other than student and teacher.

No. That was wishful thinking on his part.

"You've made Eliza very happy, Denver." Absalom said. "You too, Akina. I can't tell you how much it means to us that you came here to teach sign language."

"Glad to do it." Akina winked at Denver. "That also goes for this hot Amish chick."

Eliza pointed at Denver and laughed again.

"I hear you, Marine." Denver went to the desk and put the picture down. "Now I can get out of this dress."

Chapter 13

Denver swallowed the last bite of sandwich for lunch and took his and Akina's paper plates to the trash. "Willow mentioned Christmas Eve when she called this morning. I hadn't even thought about it being today. The last three weeks went right by."

"I guess it's because we've had teaching on our minds." Akina drank water from a plastic bottle.

Denver came back to the desk. "Did your parents mention Christmas the last time you called them?"

"I told them to not worry about a card or gifts. I'll be there next year anyway."

"Huh."

In the middle of more water, Akina swallowed. "What?"

"I just realized I haven't called Jan since I got here."

"Says a lot about your relationship."

"She hasn't called me either."

"Says even more, doesn't it?"

"She's probably busy with work and getting ready for Christmas with her parents."

"Maybe." Akina's tone was doubtful. "Any plans to celebrate Christmas here?"

Denver snapped his fingers. "I remember a certain sign language teaching Marine promising to take me out for dinner."

"Not a bad idea." She left the desk to look through her clothes stacked on the table in the corner. "Looks like all I have to wear on our date tonight is my best pair of jeans."

"Me too." Denver went to the table. "I wonder if any restaurants are open in town?"

Akina looked up from the jeans. "Why not get one of those disposable charcoal grills and a huge T-bone steak at the grocery and have that here? We can get stuff for a salad, too."

"Now you're talkin'," he said, pumping his fist. "Think Jon will mind if we pick up a six-pack of beer?"

"He's not here, remember?"

Denver couldn't believe his forgetfulness, likely brought on during class when he couldn't keep his eyes off of Eliza. Sometimes she didn't braid her hair, and she'd watch him teach while twisting a long, black strand around her finger, gray eyes focused, sometimes crinkling, full lips pursing in a sensuous half smile, almost as if she knew he was watching her for reasons other than teaching. Becca's jeans only covered part of Eliza's shapely calves, and the muscles tightened when she shifted her legs to cross her ankles. Watching Eliza was like watching a living, breathing sculpture.

Akina snapped her fingers in front of his eyes. "The thought of that steak making you zone out on me?"

"No, I was … what were we talking about? Oh, when Jon said they were visiting Becca's parents and I didn't think about it being for Christmas."

"Why do I get the feeling you were thinking about Eliza?"

"Maybe I was thinking about you." Denver hated to lie, but he couldn't admit what he was thinking about. Not exactly.

"I'll take that as a compliment," Akina said. "Eliza's hot, but I think I'm pretty hot myself. Did Jon say how long they're staying? I guess the students will take the same time off."

"He said all week."

"Think you can go without seeing Eliza that long?"

"Why shouldn't I?"

"Today's Saturday. Wanna bet she makes Absalom bring her back first thing Monday morning?"

Denver emptied his water bottle and threw it in the trash. "I think it's time to get that steak." Sure, Eliza attracted him a million ways, but Akina really knew how to rub salt in his psyche.

Denver patted his stomach. "Geez, I'm stuffed."

"Me too." Akina swallowed beer. "Except you're stuffed from those four beers you drank to my two."

Denver said nothing. Although he'd enjoyed the meal, it reminded him of similar meals at home. Dad had considered himself the "Master Steak Master," proving it often on the grill on the deck. The cold beers had gone down bitter, crisp, and yes, more than he usually drank because of family memories. The four had also left him a bit woozy and unsteady on his feet.

Akina took their trash to the container and came back. "You becoming Amish?"

"Why?"

"The internet says they only take one bath a week."

Denver shot Akina a hard look. Between his intoxicated state and the painful memories, he didn't feel like messing with her. "You trying to say I stink?"

"Just a little."

Taking her hint, he went to the table where their clothes were piled and snatched a towel and a washcloth and a change of clothes from it. As he passed Akina, she grabbed the towel. "No, sir, me first."

Denver went to the desk chair and sat. Good idea. Because of the four beers, if he tried walking to the shower, he might fall on his face.

Akina gathered her clothes. "Care to join me? We'll conserve water."

Denver waved her away. Despite his foul mood and hazy brain, seeing Akina wet and soapy was *not* a good idea.

Akina returned from the shower, toweling her hair. "I miss my blow dryer. Do you miss anything?"

Reading his notes from Eliza's last lessons, Denver raised his head. "I miss a few TV shows. Documentaries and stuff."

"You can't say you miss beer." Akina's dark eyes peeked from beneath the towel as she squeezed water from her hair.

Denver grabbed clean clothes. Good thing she went first. He could walk fairly steady now.

In the stall, he turned the water on as hot as possible, but only a lukewarm stream sprayed from the shower head. Akina sure liked hot water.

In the cooling spray, he washed and rinsed his hair, scrubbed from head to toe, and stopped.

This was exactly where a naked Eliza had stood on the day he met her. Closing his eyes, he leaned under the spray.

Imagine Eliza here or not? Imagine wet hair glistening—hanging down her shoulders, past shoulder blades, ending at the sensual dip at the small of her back—or not? Imagine the rise and fall of thigh and calf—long, lean, and smooth legs beneath his fingertips—or not?

Not, because imagining all that was wrong in every way.

He gave the hot water knob a hard twist, shuddered when the icy spray flowed down his back, and closed his eyes again. Maybe those beers were turning him into a pervert.

Shower done, he toweled off and dressed. Akina turned when he opened the door. "That didn't take long."

"You used all the hot water."

"I bet you thought about Eliza taking a shower in there."

Denver threw his dirty clothes in the corner. "Close your eyes while I put on my pajamas."

"Were you thinking about me in the shower, too?"

"Can you please just turn around? I'm tired and want to go to bed."

"Okay, Mr. Grouchy, I'll turn the lights off while I'm up." Akina did so and crawled beneath the covers on her mat. Denver did the same thing, rolling over to face the wall.

Visions of family dinners with Mom, Dad, and Willow popped into his head, along with Thanksgivings, birthdays, and Christmases. Dad never failed to get a genuine tree, and the spicy evergreen aroma filled the living room. Mom and Willow never failed to fill it with decorations and lights. Then they'd make eggnog, and everyone sipped from mugs while admiring the tree as Christmas music played in the background.

Emotion filled Denver's throat. Those days were gone now. Thank goodness Willow had delayed college. When he flew back home, they could spend some time together. She was family … the only family he had.

His eyes burned as they filled. Despite trying to hold his grief in, a tight sob escaped his throat.

"Denver? Are you okay?" Akina's voice was soft, concerned.

"I—" Denver rubbed his stinging eyes. "Memories, you know."

"About your mom and dad?"

"It's so hard to believe they're gone."

Sheets rustled. Akina sat beside him. "Sit up for me."

"I'll be okay. I didn't mean to keep you awake."

She touched his cheek. "Hey, we're friends, and friends hug each other when they're feeling down. C'mon, I won't bite."

The hint of her familiar humor brought Denver out of the worst of his grief. He sat up and faced her. She wrapped her arms around him. "I'm sorry you had to go through all that. I can't begin to imagine losing my parents." She pulled away and kissed his forehead. In the dim light of the room, her dark eyes focused on his, seemingly searching, asking. It would be so easy to kiss her, maybe even go farther if she wanted to.

How in the world had he made it to twenty-two without sleeping with anyone? Dumb question, he *did* know how.

During a general psychology class in college, he'd realized how, when he was an overweight kid in elementary school, the subsequent teasing had given him trust issues. Even when he'd slimmed down in high school, he rarely dated, not having the confidence to ask girls out. In the years after his confidence had slowly returned from the psychology class epiphany, he'd dated Jan, admiring her ideal of no sex before marriage. Still, teasing him on her sofa with her half-naked self was pure torture.

If Akina's dark, searching eyes meant she wanted him, what about contraception? He dismissed the question. She was a grown woman, who'd been in the Marines and college. She wouldn't take a chance on getting pregnant. Yes, not only was he attracted to her, he enjoyed her teasing and vivacious personality.

Her soft lips kissed his forehead again. She paused, eyes searching his once more.

Would it be so wrong to be with her this way? To take comfort in her arms if she were willing? Some might think so, but right now—right at this very moment—it didn't feel wrong at all.

Taking a chance that she felt the same way, he eased forward until their lips came together. She pulled him to her, and the kiss became firmer, firmer still, until she pressed him down and rolled over on top of him.

Floral aroma of shampoo. The scent of freshly showered skin, soft and firm beneath his hands. Kisses and more kisses. Silky soft hair in his face.

The magnitude of the moment took Denver into another world—a world he'd only imagined with Jan.

And sometimes now, with Eliza.

Chapter 14

Tired and cold from getting up before sunrise to drive the buggy back to Jon's home, Absalom let the horse into the pasture and closed the gate. Eliza had seen Jon give him a key, and all weekend she'd signed "Go back." Lucky thing Jon didn't mind them returning before him, or she would've sprained her wrists. She sure loved sign language.

Wearing her traditional Amish outfit, Eliza darted her hand toward Absalom as if it were a snake striking, which meant she wanted the key so she could change into Becca's clothes. She snatched her bag of belongings from the buggy and ran toward the house. Absalom strode after her. They hadn't eaten breakfast, and his empty stomach argued with him to do something about it.

Hat and coat on the peg by the door, he dropped his bag to put away later. Shivering, he turned the dial on the wall for heat. Something could be said for technology, such as pressing a button to raise the number on a digital readout for heat instead of cutting wood with a crosscut saw for a fire.

In jeans, sweatshirt, and sneakers—black braid over her shoulder—Eliza skipped into the kitchen from the hall and twirled around. Absalom stroked his beard. Sign language or Becca's clothes, which one made Eliza the happiest?

She took her jacket from the peg. Absalom shook his head and signed, "Eat first. No lights in school. Denver and Akina asleep." He rubbed his stomach. "You hungry?"

She tilted her head side to side, which meant in her usual

way, "maybe."

"Eat what?"

She shrugged her shoulders. Then her eyes brightened as she pointed to the coffee machine. Hot chocolate, no doubt. Absalom nodded. "Eggs, toast, bacon?"

Nodding, Eliza licked her lips. Absalom opened the refrigerator for everything her hungry heart desired. Was there anything he wouldn't do for her? Not likely, not likely at all.

Absalom raised his head from the blessing. Eliza sipped hot chocolate, crunched bacon, and forked scrambled eggs. He loved watching her eat—every sense alive, every sense alight, eyes darting with curiosity at the world around her.

He sipped coffee, took warm eggs, swallowed.

And stopped as a tear rolled down Eliza's cheek.

Absalom signed, "What's wrong?"

Her slender hands hung in midair, fingers unsure. "Papa?" she mouthed.

"Yes?"

"Why does Mama …"

"What, Eliza?"

Her fingers faltered like a broken-winged butterfly, confused and alone, unsure where to fly, unsure where to seek shelter. She squeezed her own arm—slapped her own cheek.

A violent hitch hung in Absalom's throat. Eliza thought Oneita—her own mother—hated her, and she wanted to know why.

Shame heated Absalom's face. This was as much his fault as it was Oneita's fault. He'd seen the things that were now making Eliza ask this question, such as how Oneita's attention toward her had changed when her deafness took hold, which changed even more when Ethan and Tess were born. He understood it to a degree, but believed his love could make up for Oneita's lack of showing love. The word "wrong" couldn't describe his opinion on the situation.

He slid his chair facing her, cupped her cheek in his palm, then drew it back to sign, "Mama loves you."

"How do you know?"

"Not know enough signs. One day."

She nodded, continued eating, and so did Absalom.

Thank goodness for Denver and Akina. One day he'd know enough signs to explain his and Oneita's twenty-year-old grief, including why it had left such a long-term scar on their lives. Oneita wouldn't like it, but she must make amends before she could reconnect with Eliza, because the connection should've never been broken to begin with.

Forks clicked in plates. Cups raised and lowered. Toast spread with butter and strawberry jam provoked no satisfied smile nor licked lips from Eliza. She took their plates, cups, and silverware to the sink. Absalom went to her and kissed her cheek, handed her the coat from the peg, and she ran out the door.

Denver awoke to the warmth of Akina's head on his shoulder, one smooth calf draped over his legs, her hand on his chest, her breath feathering heat against his cheek. Beneath her eyelids, darting eyes signaled dreams.

Two days ago, the morning after they'd first slept together, she verified his belief in her by telling him she was on birth control pills for hormone issues and had only slept with a few men, all of which she'd demanded to know their sexual habits. Denver didn't admit to being a virgin, but told her she didn't need to worry about any sexually transmitted diseases. Open discussion concerning sex—the only way to go.

He brushed hair from her cheek and kissed her there. "Hey, ready for oatmeal?"

Long lashes fluttered. Dark eyes opened. "Hey, yourself. What time is it?"

"Not sure, but the sun's up."

Akina said nothing, then, "Do you regret this yet? You know, since you have Jan?"

Denver ignored the "Jan" part. "Do you regret it?"

Pursed lips followed by a sly grin. "Not at all. Don't let it go to your head, but you're really great in the bunk."

"By 'bunk' you mean a Marine bunk."

"Sure, but don't get the wrong idea. Like I already said, I wouldn't do this with just anyone."

"Me neither." Denver paused. "Can I ask where you think this might go?"

Akina's eyes narrowed. "I don't want it to *go* anywhere. You needed me and I needed you, that's it." She got up, dressed, and went to the door. "I need the outhouse. Make us that oatmeal, okay?" She opened the door. Eliza stood there, knuckles raised to knock. She came in and raised her hands.

"I made Papa bring me back early."

"I'm not the least bit surprised," Akina signed. She looked back at Denver. "I told Denver you might." She left for the outhouse.

Eliza's gray eyes darted to Denver beneath his sheets. "Are you—" Her hands stilled. "Are you and Akina married?"

Denver had to make a conscious effort to keep his mouth from falling open. Despite his lack of control by continuing to sleep with Akina after that first night, and yes, while cheating on Jan, now he had to lie to Eliza to keep her from thinking he and Akina were sleeping together. "Akina got up before I did.

She had to go to the outhouse."

Gray eyes bored into his, followed by a slight pursing of her full lips, red from the cold. She tilted her head to one side. As the muscles in her smooth neck tightened, her nostrils flared. Denver didn't know what to make of all that, but it felt as if she were reaching inside him to touch his soul.

He raised his hands. "Please turn around so I can get dressed."

Eliza turned, but he had the strangest feeling that she was watching him. While he buttoned his jeans, she tapped his shoulder and stuck her hands in front of him. "You haven't eaten breakfast. Can I come back for a lesson later?"

Denver pulled on a T-shirt and faced her. "Sure. Akina's going to town for a few things."

Eliza left, and Akina came in. "I told you she'd get Absalom to come back early."

"I'm glad she didn't catch us." Denver nodded toward his neoprene mat.

"Can't have that," Akina said, striding toward the corner. She stopped. "Did she notice the one mat?"

"She asked me if we were married. I told her you got up first."

"Ain't happening. My dream husband is a romantic Marine who's not much taller than me." Akina took a pack of oatmeal from their stash in the corner. "I haven't told you yet, but I like how gentle you are when we have sex. You're very sweet about it."

"What can I say? I'm a sweet guy."

"It's almost like—" Akina tore the oatmeal bag open and dumped it into a bowl. "I shouldn't say, it might embarrass you."

Denver took a bottle of water from the refrigerator. "Like we have any secrets left. I'm cheating on Jan, remember?"

"And you're half in love with Eliza. "Akina took the bottle from Denver and opened it. "I'd almost swear you think about her when we're together." She poured water in the bowl, stirred it, and put it in the microwave. "Denver."

"What?"

"Am I the first woman you've slept with?"

Denver said nothing.

Akina pointed a plastic spoon at him. "Did you know your lips tighten when you don't want to talk about something? Which means the answer is yes."

"Well, I guess everybody has to have a first time. Jan wants to wait until she's married."

The microwaved dinged. Akina took out the steaming oatmeal that smelled of strawberries. "Now I feel even more special. When you and Eliza get married, you'll remember me."

Denver took a pack of oatmeal from the box and ripped it open. Oatmeal flew in the air, similar to a swarm of gnats over the lake at dusk. "Don't say that—there's no way it can work."

"I can tell you're attracted to her, not just physically either. Anyone who can paint like she does is an artist at heart."

"Whatever."

"You think about being with her. I can tell when you look at her."

"What I'm thinking about is trying to eat without making a mess." Denver knelt to brush the oatmeal in a pile. "Think we can do that?"

Someone knocked on the schoolhouse door. Akina answered it while Denver stayed at the desk. Black hair unbraided, Eliza came in. Akina signed "Good luck with your lesson" and left.

Denver placed a chair opposite his. In the African

documentary, children were sometimes mistreated by their families. They rarely smiled, and many were delegated to most of the work in and around the home. Mistreatment such as this sometimes led to unexpressed anger that couldn't be discussed. Along with sign language, facial expressions helped communicate anger, as well as other emotions. Eliza already smiled during happy conversation, raised eyebrows for questions, and slightly narrowed her steel-gray eyes for serious discussion. But she hadn't learned the facial expressions for anger, which she needed to know in order to fully communicate those feelings to others.

Standing almost as tall as Denver—wiry-muscled, especially in her biceps and forearms—Eliza, who likely did a lot of the farm work at her house, could jerk a person around like a feather if she got mad.

Eliza sat. To begin the lesson, he signed, "Was growing up deaf hard for you?"

"Sometimes."

"Did other people make you mad?"

"What is 'mad?'"

Denver signed "red face," made a fist, and punched the air.

Eliza nodded violently, as if something like that had actually happened to her.

"Do you want to tell me about it?"

"No." She grinned.

Denver hadn't expected *that* answer. But then, so much about her was unexpected, including that interesting grin. Better get on with the lesson.

"Act like you're mad at me."

She tried to frown, but a smile burst through. Shaking her head, she said with silent lips, "Not with you." She placed her hand on his cheek and caressed a single small circle below his eye with her thumb.

Sunlight shone in the window, illuminating the space between them. Her breath swirled dust motes toward him and his breath swirled them back. The minuscule bits of fluff joined and parted, like a tornado of heartbreak in the making. Denver pulled away from her hand.

"Have you learned many names of things by moving your lips and mouth?"

Downturned eyes. A single, almost invisible shrug. Raised hands. "Some."

"Do you remember any words from when you were young? Deaf people can learn how to talk if they want to."

Eliza signed tree and said "Eeeee," down deep in her throat. She signed water and said "Waaaa" the same way. She blinked for a moment, signed river, and said "Rrrvvvrrrr." One more blink. She signed dog and followed that by saying "Dawww."

Denver signed, "Good job, Eliza. Very good."

She touched his chest. "Teach me your name."

"You know parts of it," Denver signed. "Say some of dog."

"Daw."

"Not so much."

"Duh."

"That's it."

Denver continued with the rest of his name by using the E from tree and the V from river and asked Eliza to say it all together.

"Deevvvrrr."

"Great job," Denver signed, giving her a huge smile. Instead of smiling as he had expected, she dropped her head, then raised it. "Thank you."

She took sign language so seriously, evidenced by her stoic expression that bordered on sadness. Would it be wrong to hold her to let her know how amazing she was? He stood and held out his arms. Without hesitation she rose from the chair to press against him, soft and warm and firm at the same time. The silky feel of her hair against his cheek and the sinewy strength of her arms around his neck combined to tempt him sexually. But what tempted him more—no, a better word was intrigued— was her connection to nature through her art that must come from a deep love for everything in the natural world, which he loved, too. Taking that into account, she could possibly be a better match for him than Jan ever could.

The revelation jarred Denver. Falling in love with Eliza couldn't happen. He'd leave in two months, come back after another three, and never see her again.

Eliza still clung to him, as if she cared deeply for him, too. His fear at hurting her with his leaving made him rub small circles on her back. Her arms tightened around him. Her head shifted on his shoulder. Those sensual lips kissed the sensitive spot below his ear, which shot an intense tingle from the base of his neck to the base of his spine. She raised her lips to his ear, kissed him there, and said, "Deevrr."

Denver eased away. This couldn't happen. No, *they* couldn't happen. "I'm happy you're happy," he signed. "You didn't need to kiss me."

"Me—" She lowered her hand in that now-familiar expression of hesitation. "Is it wrong?"

"You're happy to learn my name. That's all."

She spun away from him like a woman in love, upset that the person she loved wouldn't return her love. He collapsed into his chair like a hot air balloon at Clarksville's Lakefest, empty on the ground after an afternoon of giving children tethered rides. If her feelings for him were this strong, should he leave? No, that would let her, Absalom, and Jon down. Not come back after his three months at home? That was possible, if Jon could find another teacher, or get whoever would take his place to stay. What if the teacher was a man who would take advantage of her? Or someone Eliza might care for? Denver bit his lower lip. Jealousy wasn't a trait he aspired to, the same with indecision.

He touched Eliza's shoulder. She turned around, and he signed, "I didn't mean to make you sad. Can we talk?"

They returned to the chairs, and she signed, "I'm sorry. My life has been hard. Only Papa has been good to me." Her hands hesitated. "I have feelings for …" Unsigned, the word *you* fell to her lap with her hands. She raised them again. "Where do you live? Is it far away?"

"I live in Virginia. It's a few states away."

"What's a state?"

The simple question from this complicated young woman floored Denver. How could he explain the concept of a state to someone who didn't understand the concept of the miles it took to travel there? He had to try. Nothing else—especially not him—was more important than Eliza.

"How long did it take your papa to bring you here in your buggy?"

"It took from just before sunrise until a lot of cars started passing us. I slept part of it."

Absalom had told Denver it took about two hours to drive the ten or so miles here in his buggy. "If your papa drove to my house in a buggy, it would take about four days. That's without stopping to sleep or eat."

Eliza's eyes widened. "That's very far away. How long did it take in Jon's pickup?"

"I flew here on a plane. I'm sure you've seen those in the sky."

"I will try one day. You will see."

"It almost made me sick the first time."

"Like a sick baby," she signed, grinning.

In spite of how Denver wanted to keep the conversation on

a serious tone, he laughed. "You don't think it would make you sick?"

Eliza flexed her bicep. "I am strong. I will try it one day."

"You know what?" Denver signed. "That wouldn't surprise me one bit."

Chapter 15

Someone shook Denver's shoulder. He sat up, blinking in the glare of the fluorescent lights.

"Sorry to wake you," Jon said. "Becca's water just broke."

"At least she waited until the first of March," Denver said. Thank goodness he and Akina had behaved last night, or someone would need to explain the locked door.

Akina sat up. "What's going on?"

"Becca's in labor," Jon said.

"Uh-oh, and Absalom has gone home for the weekend."

Denver looked around Jon. Yawning, Eliza held a rolled neoprene mat, a quilt, and a pillow. "No problem," Denver said. "Eliza can stay here."

"Thanks," Jon said. "You're welcome to use the stove in the house and whatever's in the fridge until we get back from the hospital. I'm sure you're tired of oatmeal."

"Does Ellie need to stay with us?"

"She'll stay in the waiting room with my folks." At the door, Jon turned. "We're staying however long Becca stays. See you then."

Akina signed to Eliza that she could sleep below her, next to the wall. Eliza unrolled her mat and pulled the quilt to her chin.

The warmth of sunshine on his face woke Denver. Snuggled in her quilts like a child, dark hair scattered about her face, Eliza slept beside him on the mat she'd moved in the night. He tilted his head upward to check on Akina, still asleep.

He raised his hand near Eliza's cheek but stopped. Brushing the hair from her face might wake her, and she might take it as a sign of his affection that he needed to keep hidden. He sure couldn't keep it hidden from Akina, and she'd tell him about it when she woke and found Eliza beside him.

Denver eased from his mat and pulled the partition partially closed. Behind it, he dressed and then went outside.

Snowmelt dripping from the overhang of the schoolhouse plopped cold wetness on his head. In the woods behind him, songbirds warbled their morning lyrics. A gray squirrel hopped from around the corner, tail flagging and arching, and landed in a ball. It spotted Denver and uncoiled back toward the woods.

His hiking boots squished in the spongy yard, crunched through icy patches of snow. The air, crisp but wet, sent a chill into his sinuses, throat, and lungs. Still, it carried the hint of spring, of leaf mold and birth, of the promise of budding leaves, of the sun awakening the world with its sudden burst of life when least expected, when it seemed like winter might last forever.

In Jon and Becca's kitchen, he went straight for the coffeemaker. Instant didn't compare to the real thing. Pan on the stove heating. A carton of eggs on the counter. Coffee dribbling from the maker. Package of sausage sliced into patties.

Akina came in. "Anything you'd like to tell me?"

Denver took the mug from the machine, blew steam away, and sipped. "I like my coffee black."

"You know what I'm talking about."

"You like your coffee with too much sugar."

"Joke all you want, Eliza's falling for you. The question of the day is, as you well know, are you falling for her?"

"Why do that when I've got two girlfriends? One for fun and one for …" Denver's hesitation didn't surprise him, because he wasn't sure why he was with Jan at all. Sleeping with Akina and having feelings for Eliza didn't help matters any.

A yawning Eliza came in and raised her hands, "Hot chocolate, please."

"You heard the girl," Akina signed and said. "She's got you wrapped around her little finger already."

Breakfast passed with signs, smiles, and licked lips. Morning passed with useless sign lessons. In only three months, Eliza knew everything Denver had taught her to perfection, including quite a bit of grammatical structure, and Akina was helping with that after the other students left. Afternoon passed with Denver driving to town to replace the food they'd eaten during breakfast, and to pick up a couple of frozen pizzas for supper. Dusk passed with a pink sunset behind ribbons of cloud over the horizon, ending with hot showers, hair dried with Becca's borrowed dryer, followed by dressing for bed.

Denver closed the partition halfway while everyone changed. Wear a T-shirt with his pajama bottoms? Definitely. He went to the edge of the partition. "Y'all ready over there, Akina?"

"Come on over, lover."

Denver opened the partition. Hiding his mouth, he said, "I hope you didn't say that where Eliza could read it."

"Yes, Denver, I'm not as dumb as you think I am."

"I don't think you're dumb. I just … you know."

"Yeah, I know." Akina raised her hand over her mouth. "You don't want your Amish goddess to get the wrong idea about us."

"You know it's rude to talk around Eliza with your hand over your mouth." Denver went to his mat, sat cross-legged, and opened one of Akina's mystery novels she'd bought in town. What was wrong with him? He was talking around Eliza without signing, too. Whenever she was around, his mind went to mush.

Eliza watched Akina and Denver talk behind their hands. It was almost like they were together, but she didn't care. Whether during classes, during the meals they shared today, or when she took him into the woods to gather her colors, his eyes spoke more than signs or words ever could.

So far, after the day he'd taught her how to say his name, she hadn't kissed his neck again or touched him to show her feelings. She didn't want to upset him with her sadness either. The plan was to bide her time, make him see she was strong enough to handle any trouble that being together might cause, and to let him know with looks and touches how she cared for him as deeply as she believed he cared for her.

She tugged at the collar of her flannel nightgown, which she needed in the cold upstairs at home. Her room in Jon and Becca's house was too warm, so she slept there in nothing but panties and a T-shirt. The weather had changed today, and the warmth made sweat moisten the back of her neck beneath her hair.

Akina offered her a magazine. She and Denver picked up books. Instead of opening the magazine, Eliza touched Akina's leg. "Is your nightgown cool? I'm hot."

Akina put a marker in the book, stood to take another gown from a stack of clothes on a table, and tossed it to Eliza. "Try it on, if you don't mind it being too short."

Eliza watched Denver. Time to see if he liked her body or not. She pulled the flannel gown over her head. A hint of hesitation—he closed his eyes and signed, "How about a warning first?"

"Way to go, girlfriend," Akina signed. "That's as red as I've ever seen his cheeks."

Eliza got to her knees. Denver's hesitation meant he liked her body. She slipped the gown on; the soft, lightweight material felt wonderful against her skin. She signed to Akina that she liked it.

"I'm glad." Akina shoved Denver's shoulder, and he signed, "Can I look already?"

A grinning Eliza signed to Akina, "I think he did."

Denver opened his eyes, signed "polite," and shook his head so Eliza would know undressing like that was *not* polite.

She stuck her tongue out at him, then said his name. His lips twisted into a mix of frown and grin.

Akina signed to Denver, "When did you teach Eliza your name?"

"When you went to town that day."

"How?"

"By using sounds from the words she remembers before she lost her hearing."

"That's right," Akina signed to Eliza. "Denver told me about that. How many do you remember?"

Eliza nodded. "Some."

Denver's eyes roamed from her head to her toes and back again, pausing at her long legs. "Don't you look nice? Just like a Virginia girl."

Eliza raised her hands to sign if he liked her legs as much as a Virginia girl's legs, but didn't because it was obvious he did. "I would like to be a Virginia girl, if my family lived in Virginia near you." She pointed to a book Akina was reading. "What kind of book?"

"Nothing you need to read," Denver signed.

"Why?"

Denver touched Akina's book. "Eliza wants to know what you're reading."

Akina gave her the book, and Eliza touched the cover. "Why are they almost naked?"

"Ask Akina," Denver signed. "It's her book."

Akina signed, "They're hot like you made Denver when you took your nightgown off." Her mouth quirked like someone trying to stop a grin.

"Oh, that's why the people are sweating." Eliza waited for more of an explanation that didn't come. Denver didn't want to talk about these half-naked people, and Akina thought they were funny. They weren't going to get away with not answering questions.

She pointed at the woman's breasts. "Why so big?"

Akina's lips quirked again, revealing more of a grin. "Ask Denver."

Eliza faced Denver, whose cheeks were pink. "Why, Denver?"

"Ask Akina. It's not important to me."

"You're my teacher, tell me." Eliza shoved Denver. He fell onto his back like a turtle, then sat up again.

"Remind me to never get on your bad side."

Eliza looked down at her small breasts. "I'm happy it's not important to you."

Akina touched Eliza's elbow and pointed at her own breasts. "Me too."

"Yours are bigger than mine. Does Denver like bigger or smaller?"

Akina fell back on her mat—eyes closed, mouth wide open,

chest rising up and down—in what Eliza knew to be laughter. Eliza faced Denver, who was shaking his head and frowning at Akina.

Akina sat up and wiped her eyes. "Thank you, Eliza. I haven't laughed that hard in forever."

"I still don't know what was funny."

"Denver's red cheeks were funny, not you. That meant he was embarrassed."

"What's that?"

"It means he felt uncomfortable about us talking about our bodies. Some people are, some aren't. It doesn't mean anything bad."

Denver went to the light switch and turned it off. "I think it's time we got some sleep."

Rain pattered on the tin roof of the schoolhouse. Lightning seared through Denver's eyelids. Thunder rumbled, low and echoing, rattling windows. He opened his eyes. Lightning flashed again, illuminating a sleeping Eliza beside him.

She opened her eyes, took her hand from beneath the quilt, and cupped his cheek, like when he'd taught her his name. Slowly, gently, she caressed a single small circle below his eye with her thumb, and said, "Deevrr."

Roll over? Sign not to do that? He couldn't do either, not with flashes of lightning illuminating Eliza's gray eyes. Lightning flashed again. For a full second the entire room lit as if the lights were on. She turned toward the window and turned back, placed his hand within the curve of her breasts. Thunder rolled long and loud. Eliza released his hand and signed, "I feel it in my heart." She returned his hand to his mat, signed "Goodnight," and closed her eyes.

Denver raised his fingertips near Eliza's cheek. Touch her or not? He pulled his hand away. Their situation was impossible. Not only was he attracted to her, he was attracted to how she looked at him—like she knew he was missing something in his life and that something was her. Some people thought relationships between abled and disabled people were wrong, because the abled person might think they were rescuing the disabled person. In his case, it was like Eliza knew he was the one who needed rescuing. As far as leaving, all he could do was to promise to come back after his first three months at home. Then, when he came back, he'd start acting like a teacher instead of a complete fool.

Chapter 16

Lessons done for the day, Eliza and Absalom left the schoolhouse. Akina's students followed through the gap between the partition and the wall, and Denver went around it. At her desk, Akina looked up. "What's up, lover? Can't wait until tonight to fool around before you go home tomorrow?"

"No, I—"

"Forget it. Are you gonna man up and leave Jan so you can be with Eliza or not?"

"How many times have I told you it won't work between us?"

"Enough to tell me you're a coward."

"Geez, Akina, why can't you let it go?"

"I don't like seeing two people with the chemistry you and Eliza have wasting it." She leaned back in the chair. "Okay, I'm done. What's up?"

"Are you coming back?"

"I'm not leaving."

"You're not going home?"

"I told Jon I'd stay the full year."

"You never told me that."

Akina got up to walk around the desk and lean against it. "Why should I? It's not like we're anything more than sex buddies."

Denver didn't understand her attitude, much different than when she'd comforted him on the first night they'd slept together. "Where's this coming from? You know I appreciate how close we are from when I was upset about losing my parents."

"I know we're more than friends. That's why I'm aggravated about this thing between you and Eliza."

"What about you staying here? You're not going home to see your family?"

"After all the time I spent in the Marines and in college, they're used to me not being around. I'll go home in nine months and it'll be great."

Denver didn't want to ask the next question because Akina would tease him about it. Regardless, he wanted to know the answer. Maybe she wouldn't tease him if he asked like it wasn't important. "You know, I hadn't thought about it. Do you know if my replacement is a man or a—"

"Don't worry, she's a she. No one will take Eliza away from you."

"Here we go again," Denver said, glaring at her. "Didn't I just say it won't work between us?"

"You thought that when you met me, didn't you?"

Denver rubbed his chin, thick with three months of beard. "Good point."

"Then don't think it can't work between you and Eliza. I know love when I see it."

"Maybe it's just a crush."

"C'mon, the entire weekend she stayed with us, she moved her mat next to yours so she could sleep by you like a lovesick puppy. I know you have feelings for her too, I see it when you look at her. If Jan saw you two together, she'd know it right away. How long are you gonna keep that sweet young woman wondering if you care about her or not?"

Denver went to a desk and sat. "Look, she's Amish and so's her family. Absalom would kill me if I tried to take her away from him. And I sure don't want to convert to Amish."

Akina's lips twisted to one side. "Yeah, that's a lot to overcome. Maybe she'd rather marry you and be an artist. As far as I'm concerned, that picture she painted for you—along with everything else she's accomplished with sign language—makes her amazing. There's no telling what she can do if she gets a chance."

"I can't think like that. I'll never see her again after my last three months here and that's that."

"You're giving up? Really giving up?"

"Absalom asked me to explain to her what being Amish means because he doesn't know enough signs. When I do, I also need to explain how she'd never see her family again if she were to leave to be with me."

"What a mess." Akina shook her head. "I never thought about how they shun a family member if they leave."

"Exactly. That means I'll get my stupid heart broken if I give in to my feelings. The main thing is I don't want to hurt her."

"What in the world am I gonna do with you, Denver Andrews?" Akina went to him, dark eyes looking down into his. "You know being all sweet and sensitive makes me want you, right?"

"I hope you know I think more of you than a simple roll in the hay."

Akina pulled his nose. "Whoa, now, don't talk like that. I'm not sure if marriage is my thing."

"I don't know why not. Any guy would be lucky to have you. You could have a cute little boy like Jon and Becca have now. He's even got her auburn hair."

"He's a cutie, that's for sure. He's all Ellie signs about."

"You don't want to have kids one day?"

"The Marines taught me how to depend on myself. Some guy might want me to depend on him. That" —she tapped Denver's chest— "is not gonna happen."

"Unless it's another Marine, huh?" Denver got up and squeezed her bicep. "I remember what you said about that. Maybe you want a Marine with muscles like yours for when you attack him like you attacked me."

Akina punched his arm. "That's not how it happened and you know it."

"Uh-huh. I'm just teasing you."

"Better not. I was gonna give you a massage for our last night together."

"Jon told me about your great-grandmother. Are you good enough to make me feel like an Emperor?"

Akina locked the door and went to their sleeping mats. "Come on over here and we'll see."

Chapter 17

Eliza opened her eyes. Why get out of bed when Denver was leaving today? She'd rather not face him, rather not tell him goodbye, rather not hold in the tears.

A warm droplet rolled from eye to ear lobe, slowed and continued its wet path down her neck.

Waiting for him for three months without knowing how he felt about her would be one of the most difficult things she'd ever done. Even though she'd followed her plans, letting him know her feelings with slight smiles, subtle glances, light touches of fingertips upon his hand as he'd taught her words from a book, he offered no similar assurances.

She jerked upright, grabbed a book from the nightstand, and opened it to search through the words. Fingertip on a letter, she said, "I." Biting her lower lip, she flipped the page. The second word was— There it was. "L … lo … lovvve." One more to go. There it was on the next page. "You. I … love … you." Thank goodness Akina had explained how, when two people wanted to be with each other all the time, it meant they were in love. Now she could tell Denver how she felt about him.

Eliza threw her clothes on and ran downstairs to sit at the table between Papa and Jon. Becca sat in a rocking chair in the far corner, the new baby Samuel in her arms. Ellie stood beside her, stroking the red fuzz on his head.

Eliza grabbed a fork and shoveled eggs into her mouth. Beside her, Papa signed, "Your belly empty?"

Nodding, she chewed and swallowed.

Jon emptied his coffee mug and stood. Denver had told her he was driving Jon's pickup to the airport so the other teacher could drive it back here. He might be leaving soon.

A sip of hot chocolate, a nibble of bacon, another forkful of eggs. Better not choke before Denver left, or she wouldn't be able to tell him she loved him. Meal done, she signed "Thank you" to Becca and ran to the schoolhouse.

At the door, her heart thudded in her chest like thunder in the recent storm. She closed her eyes, took several deep breaths, and knocked. A moment passed. The door opened and Akina signed, "It's that day, isn't it?"

Eliza jerked her hands up. "Can I see Denver?"

"Sure. I'll step around back for a minute."

Eliza closed the door. Denver was sitting at his desk, backpack on the floor beside him. The walk to the chair opposite his was like slogging through ankle deep mud at her river.

He opened the desk drawer, took out the picture she'd given him of her walking along the path in the woods, and placed it on the desk. "Do you mind if I take it with me?"

"I want you to have it," she signed. "It's part of me." She touched her chest. "Part of my colors."

"I don't understand."

"Other than Papa, only my colors have made me happy. Our colors are inside us."

Denver tilted his head to one side. "How do you mean?"

"To me, our colors are what you explained as hope." She pressed her palm to his chest. "Our hope is in here. My first picture gave me hope. You gave me hope. Now you're leaving."

"I told you I'm coming back. Three months won't last long at all."

"Will you miss me?"

"More than I can say."

"Can I ask you something?"

"You can ask me anything."

"What do you feel for me?"

"I feel a lot, Eliza." Denver's hands stopped in mid-air—halting, sad. "But I'll go home after three more months." He blinked several times, fingered moisture from the corner of one eye.

"Can't you stay?" Eliza signed. "Please stay."

Denver's chest rose and fell. His nostrils flared and calmed. Whatever he was going to say, it worried him.

"Do you know why your family wears black clothes? Why they don't have light switches and washing machines? Why they burn wood instead of having heat like Jon and Becca?"

"Those things are nice. I—" Eliza stilled her hands. Admit this to Denver or not? "I think about you when I take a shower. I run my hands over my body and want you to touch me. Is it wrong?"

For a second, Denver's chin jutted to one side, as if he wanted to admit something but knew he shouldn't. His jaw straightened. "Well, you're a young woman. Young women have those thoughts."

"Do you have those thoughts about me?"

The muscles in his neck tightened with a hard swallow, so he *did* have those thoughts about her.

"I need to tell you why your family doesn't live like Jon and Becca. Your papa doesn't know enough signs, and he asked me to explain it."

Eliza reached over the desk to palm his cheek, but he pulled away. Why was he fighting her like this? He loved her. She knew it and so did he.

"Fine. Why is my family different?" Heat warmed her cheeks—she didn't want to talk about that.

Denver leaned back in the chair, relief in his chest rising and falling. "Do you know anything about God?"

"What is God?"

"He's what the Amish and many other people believe created everything."

"You mean like all the animals, and trees, and people? I always thought someone created them and all the colors and painted rainbows in the sky."

"Your idea about God is right. Your family is Amish. They dress simply and live simply because they believe that's how God wants them to live. The Amish have strict rules about outsiders. They call them the English. I'm an outsider, Eliza. Your papa won't let us be together."

"Papa brought me here to learn sign language. Jon and Becca and Ellie don't dress and live like the Amish, and we live with them."

"Your Papa does that because he loves you."

"If it makes me happy to be with you, he might let us be together."

Denver steepled his fingers. His eyes roamed the ceiling. His chest rose and fell again. "I hate to tell you this, but when an Amish person leaves their family for good, the family isn't supposed to ever see them again. I know you don't want that, so we can be friends, okay? I'm sure you don't want to leave your family and your papa and never see them again."

"Maybe my family could leave, too."

"It's not impossible, I guess, but asking them to do that means asking them to give up everything they believe."

"I don't—" Eliza's fingers slowed. "It wouldn't be right to do that."

Denver took a pair of jeans from the backpack, wrapped the picture in them, and put both in the backpack. "You'll be back home teaching your family sign language before you know it." He took the keys from his pocket and picked up the backpack.

Eliza stood, tears threatening. "Will you hug me goodbye?"

He put the keys and backpack on his desk. Eliza held out her arms, and he signed, "We shouldn't hug unless it's a friendly hug."

Her chin trembled. Hot tears streamed down her face. The space between them took on the feeling of a tree, hard and impenetrable. She lowered her hands. Another hard swallow from him, moisture shining in his eyes. He signed "goodbye."

Eliza followed him outside. What could she do to change things for them? She didn't want to never see her family again, and asking Denver to become Amish and never see his sister again was wrong also. Still, she loved him, and he loved her, too. Regardless of everything, if those words were the last things she ever recognized on his lips, she'd fight to see that happen.

Smelly smoke puffed from the pickup. Tires spun gravel.

Waving, Eliza ran after the pickup. Denver waved his hand in the back glass. Eliza snatched a rock from the driveway and threw it at the pickup. The rock missed.

She crumpled to the gravel.

He'd left before she could tell him she loved him.

Chapter 18

In Raleigh, Denver left the plane with the rest of the passengers. At the TSA checkpoint, he glanced at his watch. Saturday morning, 11:14 a.m. He'd told Eliza goodbye only three hours ago, and he missed her already. The TSA line shortened. Forty minutes later he was driving to Jan's house.

During the flight, he'd convinced himself he was either in love with an Amish girl in Ohio, it was lust only—with Akina's influence—or he needed a serious mental evaluation. Regardless, Eliza's happiness was most important, and regardless of their feelings—feelings proven by their tears when he left—he needed to remember that.

He charged his phone before leaving the school, and as the plane was pulling up to the departure gate, he texted Jan, saying he'd stop by. Seeing her might clear his head. Maybe.

When he pulled into the driveway, Jan ran out the door in a skimpy nightgown that showed more than he needed to see and kissed him. "Did you miss me?"

"What's with the nightgown?"

"I just took a shower and threw it on when I heard you drive up."

"Your hair's not wet."

"Typical man, I didn't wash my hair."

"Can I stretch out in your recliner? Those airline seats are terrible on a person's back."

"Are you hungry? I can make veggie omelets for lunch."

Denver started toward the house but stopped. "I need to

grab my backpack. I want to—"

"You brought me a present?" Jan's voice climbed an octave on "present."

 "I got you something at the Columbus airport." He closed the pickup's rear door, backpack in hand.

Inside, Jan took the backpack from him, and he collapsed into the recliner. "What did you get me?" she asked. Instead of pulling out his things individually, she dumped the entire contents on the sofa, scattered them about, and scooped up what the vendor had described as a "handstitched" Amish Kapp. "Ah, you met some hot Amish chick and want me to wear this on our honeymoon."

Denver held in a wince at the word honeymoon. She'd never mentioned marriage before, except in the concept of no sex before marriage. "No, I just thought you'd like to see what Amish women and girls wear."

Jan returned some of the items from the sofa to the backpack. Eliza's painting fell from the jeans. "You could've given me this instead. It's gorgeous, where'd you get it?"

"One of the students did that."

"What did she use for paints?" Jan sniffed the dried mud. "It kind of stinks."

"That's mud from a creek. Everything there came from the woods behind the school. I think it's cool."

"Is this a self-portrait? Even from the back I can tell she's attractive." Jan cocked her head toward Denver, blue eyes visible through stray strands of blonde hair. "I don't have anything to worry about, do I? Maybe I shouldn't let you go back in three months. Afterall, *I'm* the one who set up your trip."

Denver said nothing. The idea of not going back because of his feelings for Eliza tempted him.

"I love how it has a folk-art feel to it," Jan said, picking the picture up. "Still, the emotion of the piece is obvious. Is there a story behind it? Many great artists use their life experiences in their work."

Dried mud fell to the sofa, and Denver pointed. "Careful, okay? I wrapped it in the jeans to protect it." She lay the picture on the sofa, and Denver said, "Her dad said they were at a county fair. A huge Brahma bull walked up and Eliza imitated his walk. After that she came up with a hand sign to tell how she was going somewhere."

Jan nodded. "Are you glad you went?"

"The kids there are like the deaf kids in that African documentary. They dont't even know sign language exists, and then they find out they can learn to communicate like anyone else. I loved their smiles when they learned their first sign."

"How old is Eliza? She's not a child, not by any stretch of the imagination."

Denver couldn't believe it. After everything he'd just told Jan about kids learning sign language, all she could manage was jealousy. "She's eighteen."

He yawned from his last restless night at the school. As much as he wanted to go home, a nap before the hour and a half drive might keep him from falling asleep on the highway. "Mind if a take a nap while you make omelets? I don't want to crash into a tree on the way home."

Jan slinked over and kissed him. The skimpy nightgown fell open, revealing cleavage. She lifted his chin. "Enjoying the scenery, sweetie? We could nap in my bed after breakfast. Then we could lounge around all day, doing whatever pops up. You could even stay the night. Willow can do without seeing you one more day, can't she?"

"I'd ... uh, I'd like to get home. You understand, right?"

Jan's lips took a definite quirk to one side, as always, her sign of impatience. "Take your nap. A good meal might give you enough strength to handle any activities we come up with for later." Hips swaying seductively, she left for the kitchen.

Denver closed his eyes. Omelet or not, the last thing he wanted was sex with Jan.

"Hey, sleeping beauty, ready to eat?"

Denver blinked and shook his head. "Wow, I was gone." He followed Jan to the kitchen. The aroma of sautéed sweet peppers, onions, and mushrooms filled the air. "Smells great." He sniffed. "Coffee? I'm glad I stopped by."

Jan set the plates down. "And I thought you came to see me. Instead, you're lusting after my coffee and not paying attention to my skimpy nighty." She filled two cups and sat beside him. "Don't you like it?"

"You don't usually flirt like that." Denver sipped coffee. "Are you trying to seduce me? What happened to no sex before marriage?"

Jan jabbed a fork at him. "I doubt we'll ever get married."

Denver looked sideways at Jan. Sure, he wanted to give their relationship a chance, but it was time to nip this marriage business in the proverbial bud. "Except for talking about sex, you never said anything about getting married."

Jan's lips pressed into a hard line. "What's wrong with talking about it now?" Tight and clipped, her voice carried a definite edge of anger.

"Don't get mad, okay? We've only been dating six months, and we never said we wouldn't date other people either, so why rush things?"

"I …" Jan turned away and turned back. "You're right about us never talking about seeing anyone else."

"Why do I get the feeling that's not all you were gonna say?"

"I danced with a guy in Nags Head and had drinks with him the next night. It didn't mean anything, but I feel guilty about."

Denver sat back in the chair. After his sleeping with Akina, Jan dancing and having drinks with someone was nothing to complain about. Then again. … "Is that the only time you did anything like that?"

Jan looked away. "I … a movie once. Drinks with another guy once."

"You really got around in Nags Head, didn't you?"

"It was here, with people from work. Just friends."

"Really?" Denver paused to let that sink in, and to let his next sentence sting. Sure, he'd messed up with Akina, but he wasn't the one talking about marriage. "Did you bring any of your *friends* back here to the sofa?"

Jan whirled toward him, panic in her eyes. "No, never, I wouldn't do that, okay? I'm sorry, but I didn't think of them as dates. I really care about you, don't you believe me?"

Denver said nothing. Again, dancing, drinks, and a movie were nothing compared to his philandering, but was she telling the truth about bringing anyone back to the sofa or not? Hard to tell, so all he could do was give her the benefit of the doubt. Afterall, Jan had her good points, and she'd admitted what she'd done, so none of that was a reason to break up, especially since a future with Eliza was impossible.

"I believe you," he said.

She hugged his neck and returned to the chair. "I'm glad." She took a bite of omelet and swallowed. "I guess you were too busy teaching to call."

Guilt started to creep into Denver, until he remembered how she hadn't called him either. More movies, drinks, and dances she hadn't admitted to in the last three months? Each possibility removed some of his guilt about sleeping with Akina. "I had a lot going on."

"Have you thought about my offer of napping with me and lounging around and being lazy? I'll take you out to dinner later, my treat." She slid her bare foot along Denver's calf. "We'll have dessert in bed."

So much for Jan's guilt about those guys. "I've been away from home for three months. I miss my bed because there's no sleep like sleeping in my own bed. I need a haircut and a shave before I go out anywhere, much less a nice restaurant. I'd like to see Willow, too."

She ran her fingers through his hair and tugged his beard. "You almost look like an *Ewok* from *Star Wars.* All right, I'll let you off the hook." She tugged his beard again. "*This* time."

Denver swallowed a bite of omelet. "I owe you, for the omelet and coffee, too."

He stood and so did Jan. She kissed his cheek. "I packed all your stuff while you were asleep."

Denver returned the peck. "Thanks." At the front door he turned around. "I'm glad you like the kapp."

"Thank you for thinking of me." He opened the door, and she grabbed his arm. "You believe me about not bringing anyone here, right?"

"I believe you." Denver noted how she still hadn't said anything about not dating other people in the future.

"I'm glad," she said. "I really do care about you."

Driving along interstate 85, Denver rubbed his forehead. Really give Jan the benefit of the doubt or not? Well, she'd told him about her mistakes, so that meant something, like maybe she really did care about him. Yep, get the sign language teaching out of the way, get back home, and then see where their relationship went.

As far as Akina, he should've never slept with her, and it needed to stop. As far as Eliza, like he'd told her, they needed to be friends.

He slapped the pickup's dash, stinging his fingertips. Yeah, right. Thinking about Eliza as nothing but a friend would be like trying to stop the freakin' sun from rising over Buggs Island Lake every morning.

Chapter 19

At home, Denver found a note on the kitchen counter. Willow was out on the pontoon boat, attempting to catch a striped bass or two for his welcome home supper. A fresh fish dinner, deep-fried to a golden brown, with fries, slaw, and hush puppies. Wow.

In his bedroom, he opened the window and sniffed the warm March air. Springtime in what some of the locals affectionately called "lake country" couldn't be beat, but fall came in at an extremely close second place."

Unpacking, he propped Eliza's painting on the mirror above his dresser. Bits of mud crumbled and fell. Clear urethane spray and a frame should stop that.

In the mirror, his scruffy reflection stared back. He needed to get his mind off his troubles, especially his feelings for Eliza. Steve at the barber shop in Clarksville always offered witty and distracting commentary on various issues. A haircut and a shave would bring his appearance back to normal, so it might bring his perspective back to normal, too. Denver left a note detailing his plans beside Willow's fishing note and hopped in his pickup.

Somewhat quiet for a Saturday afternoon, main street's parking places held few cars. Denver parked at the barber shop and opened the glass door. Steve, reading a magazine, hopped out of the barber chair. "Hey, stranger, where've you been?"

Denver sat in the chair. "Missed my curls on the floor, huh?"

"Your hair does tend to curl when it gets this long. I bet the ladies would like to run their fingers through it." Steve spread a white apron over Denver's chest and legs, then tucked it in at his neck. "Met any lately?"

"Ladies?" Denver glanced over his shoulder at Steve. "Too many, how about that?"

"You say that like it's a problem. Too many pans in the fire?" Steve snipped his scissors a couple of times. "Weren't you seeing a girl over around Raleigh? Jane … Judy …"

"Jan."

"Then who're these other women you're talking about?" Steve snipped hair.

A lock of hair brushed Denver's eyelashes and fell to his chest. Not a good idea bringing up the "other women" subject. "I was pulling your leg about other women. You know how guys talk."

"Sure, but where've you been?"

"Remember that documentary I told you about, and how I got a minor in sign language because of it? I've been to Ohio for three months, teaching sign language in a school for deaf Amish kids."

"Daggone, when you decide to go somewhere to teach, you decide to go somewhere to teach." Steve leaned from behind Denver to look him in the eye. "Going back?"

"It's three months on, three months off, for a year. I'll head back the end of June."

"That means you'll miss Lakefest in July. It's the fortieth anniversary. More fireworks, more hot air balloons. I heard the town's going all out."

"I hate to miss it," Denver said, meaning it. "I usually go out on the pontoon boat with the family to watch the fireworks."

"I haven't seen you since the funeral." Steve circled to Denver's front. "You and Willow doing ok?"

"We're ok until a memory hits." He didn't say anything else, or he might get upset now. Steve had one of those revolving red, white, and blue barber poles mounted to the shop beside the door, and it reminded Denver of when Dad had taken him for his first haircut as a kid. Time to change the subject. "Have you ever gone out on the lake to watch the fireworks?"

"Too many boats out there for me. They look nice with their lights on." Hair continued to fall with the *snip-snip* of the scissors. "I normally park on the backstreets and walk with the family down to the end of the old bridge and watch from there."

"Sounds like you're looking forward to it."

"What I'm looking forward to is when main street is blocked off so the food vendors can line both sides. Whole fried onions, hot dogs, turkey legs, chicken on a stick—it's like being at the county fair." Steve turned on a set of electric clippers and buzzed Denver's neck. "Want me to trim your eyebrows before someone thinks they're two caterpillars?"

"Go ahead."

Steve buzzed Denver's eyebrows. "How about the beard? Dye it white, you could play Santa Claus."

"Come on, it's not that bad."

"I'm just messin' with you."

"I know, whack it off."

Shave done, including the back of Denver's neck with warm shave cream, Steve whipped the apron away and turned Denver toward the mirror. "Look okay?"

Denver stood and took cash from his wallet. "Look's fine." He handed Steve the money and nudged the pile of hair on the floor with his shoe. "By the time I make it back, you'll have to cut that much off again."

"Have a safe trip. Oh, and take care of all those women you deny being a problem."

Denver held a finger to his lips. "Hey, what's said in the barber shop stays in the barber shop, right?"

"Noooo problem." Steve winked. "Just don't let 'em get together and figure out what's goin' on. You'll find yourself in the middle of a mess if that happens."

Denver left the shop shaking his head. Akina would cover up their fling, but Jan would never lay eyes on Eliza, thank goodness. It'd be hard to cover up how she looked at him when they were alone together. And how he looked at her, too.

Instead of climbing into his pickup, he strolled the sidewalk further into Clarksville. The small town, the only one on the lake, held a certain charm that Denver enjoyed. Many of his parent's friends had worked at a huge textile company located only a few miles from home. It closed in 2001, leaving people searching for jobs. Still, campers visiting Occoneechee State Park on the other side of the lake, anglers seeking the many species of fish, and vacationers desiring to stay at one of the two lakeside hotels, helped ease the lost tax income.

As Denver's sandals slapped the sidewalk, he passed a longtime furniture store, a consignment shop, and crossed the street that marked the center of town, where two churches were located to the right, toward the marina. Fresh air filled his nostrils. His stride increased. Next came two of the many realty businesses specializing in lake property, followed by a pizza place, a Chinese restaurant, an indoor mall, the town hall, another realty plus contracting company, and two stores that carried men's and women's clothing. He took a right toward a large thrift shop he visited occasionally. A shopper never knew what they might find in the store, where people donated anything from clothing to golf clubs to furniture to electronics, sold by the store that contributed to the community. Books filled a back room. Since he had to work up the preliminary plans for Jon's solar installation, no time for reading. Denver continued through the parking lot, down an exit ramp, and stopped at the sidewalk. To his right, opposite one of the hotels, was a restaurant where he enjoyed a craft beer now and then.

He picked up his pace. Heart pumping more than it had in a while, he speed-walked to his pickup and climbed in. On the way home, about a block past the barber shop, he drove by a combination bed and breakfast and restaurant that served the best crab dip he'd ever tasted. With the flavor of crab, cheese, and spices slathered on a crusty baguette portion making his mouth water, he headed home to see if fish was on the dinner menu.

Home again, he went to side of the house, where he could see the dock. The pontoon boat tied there and the aroma of hot oil in the deep fryer on the deck hinted at his welcome home meal. He carefully unlocked the front door and slipped inside to sneak up behind Willow at the counter. Busy slicing potatoes into french fries, she jumped when he placed his hands over her eyes. "Guess who?"

She pulled his hands down and turned. "You didn't have a barber near the school?"

"There was one in town, but I just let it grow."

Steve did a great job. "I bet you looked like Tarzan before you got a haircut and a shave."

"Sure did, except with a beard. I smelled the oil heating on the deck."

"Was the other teacher a man or a woman?"

"A woman, why?"

"What's her name and what's she look like?"

"Her name's Akina."

"Never mind that. What's she look like and is she nice?"

"Why?"

"No stalling, answer me."

"Dark hair, dark eyes. Her head comes to my chin. She's pretty tough, she was a Marine."

"How close did you get to her to know her head comes to

your chin? Close enough to get Miss Janna Alexander off your mind while you were away?"

Denver noted Willow's sarcastic use of Jan's full name, which she hadn't done in a while. "Why would you say that, Willybeans?"

"Because Jan's not a good match for you, and I was hoping the teacher would make you forget her."

Denver ignored the comment. When Willow finished the fries, she shoved the bowl over. "The fish is done and keeping warm in the oven. Cook these while I make slaw."

Denver eyed the fries. "You cut up a lot, didn't you?"

"It's enough, okay? Hurry up so they'll get done before the fish gets soggy."

Denver took the fries outside, eased them into the popping oil, and went back inside to lean against the counter as Willow grated a cabbage half. "Did you learn much sign language while I was gone?"

Willow raised her hands and signed, "I met someone the week after you left."

"Oh, really. Something you want to tell me?"

"I just did, Den, his name's Mark." Leaning back over the grater, Willow huffed an auburn curl out of her eyes. "Your tone is like Dad's when I brought my first date home."

Denver took a piece of cabbage from the growing pile. "When do I get to meet this guy?"

"Tonight. That's why I made extra fries."

"What's he like?"

"He's really nice. He doesn't believe in sex before marriage like Jan does either." Willow looked sideways through her curls at Denver. "Because he's a minister's son."

"Really?" Willow's revelation surprised Denver. "You and a minister's son?"

She raised her head. "Stop using Dad's tone and go get those fries before they burn."

On the way to the sliding glass doors, Denver looked over his shoulder. "You realize you're starting to sound a lot like Mom with your bossy self."

Inside again, Denver poured the steaming fries into a plate lined with paper towels. "Shouldn't this Mark guy be here by now?"

The doorbell rang, and Willow nodded toward the hall. "Let him in while I plate everything."

"You sure got demanding while I was gone." Denver opened the door, revealing a young man with dark hair, a scruffy hint of beard lining his chin, and a big smile.

"Hey, you must be Denver. I'm running late, is Willow mad?"

"She said something about boiling you in hot french fry oil."

Willow's flats slapped down the hall toward the door. "Don't believe a thing my big brother says and don't worry about being late. Just make sure you're hungry."

"No problem, Aubie"

In the kitchen, Denver took his plate to the table and came back to help with silverware. "Aubie?"

"Because of her auburn hair," Mark said.

When plates of browned fish fillets, hot fries, and creamy slaw were ready, everyone sat at the table, where Mark said a short blessing and then raised his head. "I'm sorry about your mom and dad, Denver."

"Thanks. How did you and Willow meet?"

"At the grocery," Willow said. "He said my hair caught his eye and he got behind me at the checkout."

"That's right," Mark said, grinning at Willow. He faced Denver. "Aubie said you have a major in solar engineering and you got a side job at the sign language school designing a system for the guy who built it."

Chewing a hot fry, Denver held up a finger until he swallowed. "Jon—he's the artist who organized the school— asked me to do some preliminary research when I have time."

"What kind of research?"

"Where the sun rises. The best places for the panels. If they need to track the sun or not. I need to spend some time at my laptop and work up a proper proposal and email it to him."

Willow drank sweet tea with lemon. "We're learning sign language together."

"I took some online classes," Mark said. "My dad thinks I should learn it to use as a minister."

Willow took a bite of fish, chewed and swallowed. "How'd you like working with the students, Den?"

"I only had one full time student. Sometimes I'd help Akina with the younger ones. After about a month, Eliza helped when I wasn't working one-on-one with her."

"The classes were split?" Mark said.

"Jon thinks a woman does better with the younger kids."

"How old is Eliza?" Willow said.

"Absalom—he's Eliza's dad—said she's almost nineteen. Most of the parents are learning with their kids. It wouldn't make sense for a kid to know sign language and have no one to talk to."

Willow swallowed tea. "You're saying Eliza learned sign language fast enough to help the younger kids?"

"From what her dad told me, she has a photographic memory. She uses it with her painting, too."

"As in pictures?" Mark said. "Where does she get the paints to—"

"Uh-huh." Willow tipped the glass toward Denver. "First Akina and now Eliza. How many women did you meet in Ohio? Can one of them take you away from Jan?"

"C'mon, Aubie," Mark said. "Give Denver a break." Mark

faced Denver. "She doesn't like Jan very much."

About to sip tea, Denver lowered the glass. *"That's* an understatement."

The rest of supper included small talk concerning Denver's trip, the Lakefest in July he'd miss for the first time, and Willow's choice of tomato and cucumber seeds she wanted to try in the containers she'd learned how to make online. Table cleared and dishwasher humming, Denver stood by the bar and rubbed his tight stomach. "That was great. How about steak next time?"

Willow poked his stomach. "Keep eating like that, you'll get so fat that all your ladies will kick you to the curb."

"I'll work it off by paddling the canoe. I need to check my emails. I bet my inbox is crammed full."

"Mark and I are walking to the dock. Have fun."

On his bed, Denver powered up the laptop and signed in to his email account, which immediately populated with endless emails, topped by one from Jon. He hoped Denver had arrived home without any air sickness, adding to take his time with the solar plans. Denver widened his eyes at the last part, where Jon said the new teacher, a young man from Pennsylvania, had arrived.

The new teacher was a man? Denver didn't like the sound of that. Had Akina intentionally misled him, or had she simply made a mistake? Not caring for the jealousy twisting his lips to one side, he closed the laptop harder than normal. The new guy better not try to take over. Jon wouldn't allow anyone to replace a committed teacher unless extraordinary circumstances called for it.

Eliza's picture, still leaning against the dresser mirror, had dropped more crumbles of mud. Denver lifted it gently and took it to the basement, where Dad kept various cans of stuff and Mom kept picture frames for family photos.

Looking through the cans, Denver took one of clear polyurethane, found a frame that fit Eliza's picture, and took it outside to spray several thin coats on it while it sat on the bottom of his canoe, waiting before each one dried.

Gravel crunched in the path from the dock, and Willow said, "What are you up to?"

Mark leaned over the picture. "Wow, that's great work. Did Eliza do that?"

Denver snapped the top on the urethane can. "She sure did."

"Doggone, Den," Willow said. "If that's a self-portrait, she's as gorgeous as Jan." She touched the white kapp. "Did she take her kapp off while you were there?"

"Her dad let her wear regular clothes. She has black hair down to her waist."

Willow looked up at Denver. "Why didn't you take her picture with your phone?"

"I don't think the Amish allow anyone to take their pictures."

"You should show her painting to Jan. She might sell it at the gallery."

"She saw it when I stopped by her place this morning. She liked it, too, but I'm not selling it."

"All that tea," Mark said, walking toward the steps leading to the deck and the sliding glass doors. "Be right back."

Denver held up the picture. "I wonder what Eliza could do with real paints and brushes?"

"Den, I was joking about someone taking you away from Jan, but I see that look in your eyes."

"Okay, Willybeans, what look is that?"

"With big, sad puppy dog eyes. Did you seriously go and form an attachment with this Eliza person? Dang, leave it to you to—"

"She's Amish and lives in Ohio. Why would I do that?"

"That's true. Along with how she'd be shunned be her family if y'all started something, you're too smart to do that." Willow patted Denver's arm. "I won't tease you about anyone taking you from Jan anymore."

In his room, Denver touched the picture to check the polyurethane, decided he could frame it, and set it on his dresser. After a minute of taking in the colors, he touched Eliza's slender form. He'd only said goodbye to her this morning, and it already seemed like three months.

Chapter 20

Sunlight fell across Denver's bed to warm his feet. He rubbed his eyes, gritty from waking up off and on all night with thoughts of Eliza. Jon's solar plans could wait until after a few days of being at home and some more rest.

He shuffled to the window. A fine morning had dawned, one of those things he missed about home. The sun rose over the wooded shore about a mile away. The lake, like liquid silver, smooth and silky, reflected the sun, which trailed a shimmering path of gold upon its barely rippled surface.

Dressed in shorts, sandals, and a light jacket to ward off the cool March morning, he grabbed an apple, a bottle of water, and hurried down the stairs to the basement. Willow must still be asleep. He'd have breakfast with her later.

Beneath the deck, his old canoe had seen better days. Scars and dings marred its aluminum bow where he'd dragged it ashore on Goat Island and other areas on the huge lake, to hike along the shore or simply stretch out on a convenient sandy beach in the sun. Occoneechee State Park, straight across from the dock, provided the best hiking—he could walk for miles and not see another living soul, except for whitetail deer, cottontail rabbits, wild turkeys, and the ever-present gray squirrel. On rare occasions at dusk, the call of *whip-poor-will, whip-poor-will, whip-poor-will,* accompanied him as he left the woods. Unfortunately, whippoorwills and another bird he loved to hear—the bobwhite quail—seemed to be fading from the area.

Water and apple in his pockets, canoe dragged to the water, Denver sat on the chilly aluminum seat. No matter, he'd warm up soon. He dipped a paddle into the mirror surface of the lake and the water parted before him, sending a feathering wake off to the sides of the bow. The paddle strokes whispered liquid solitude on the serene surface. From a nearby rocky point, a great blue heron squawked its discontent and flapped into the air on wings that could easily span six feet. Instead of gaining altitude to find a more private point to wade with stilt-like legs for its breakfast of fish, it glided low, wingtips within inches of the water reflecting its image.

Further out in the lake's main body, the breeze stiffened, and the smooth surface gave way to small waves lapping against the aluminum hull's sides, almost as if the waves had fingers that tapped impatiently at his progress. The paddle dug deeper; the strokes stretched longer. Despite the cool air, beads of sweat popped out on Denver's forehead. Time fell away—time and angst and worry—replaced by the vision of Eliza grinning back at him, corded arms paddling, long black hair down her back, stray strands blown about her confident features.

The canoe lurched against something. He'd closed his eyes without even realizing it, to run aground on his intended landing point. The sandy shore, bordered by huge walls of crumbling rock, was the perfect place for watching the sun set in December, on the shortest day of the year. If the conditions were right—the humidity low, the air nipping at his cheeks and nose, his breath bursting in a haze as it exited his nostrils—the sun lowered in a magnificent display of bright yellow, burnt orange, and finally, as it dropped below the naked trees on the other side of the lake, molten red that faded to black.

That was his clarity. Now, at this very moment, nothing was clear.

What was love anyway? Eliza said a person's colors were at

their best when they were filled with hope. Most people hoped to find a love that made them consider no one else. Could that happen with Eliza? With every turn, with every silent moment, with sleep failing him to the point of exhaustion, she always appeared.

Denver scraped the canoe ashore and dropped cross-legged to the sand. A wave thumped the canoe against a rock hidden beneath the water with a hollow, metallic thud.

His heartbeat would sound like that when he told Eliza goodbye for the last time. Did that have to happen? Yes, it did, because asking her to leave her family—only to be shunned by them—would be beyond selfish. Not only that, if he told Absalom how he felt about Eliza, he'd demand he become Amish.

Stay home or go back to Ohio?

And to Eliza?

The canoe thumped once more. Even more hollow … even more empty … like the answer he refused to acknowledge.

Chapter 21

By the creek behind the schoolhouse, Eliza waited for the sun to rise. Denver was coming back tomorrow. The fear that had gripped her when he left—the fear that she would never see him again despite his plans to return—would only leave when she saw him.

The new teacher had taught her many new words, ideas, and expressions to match emotions, including more grammar like Akina had taught her, which helped her sign as well as either of them, but his face never held her attention.

Denver never left her. His smile, his warm glance, his blue eyes that always crinkled on the edge of laughter when they signed to each other, never left her. He stayed with her—in her mind, in her heart, and in her hopes.

Occasionally, although the memory made her cry, she allowed herself to think about their conversation concerning the impossibility of them being together, when he said she could never see her family again if she left them.

The sunlight beneath the horizon changed from dingy red to orange to yellow, until it broke through the haze hanging over the distant trees, bathing her with warmth. The sun rose higher, the light grew warmer, and a combination of tears—from the inspiring scene she'd never painted, from the happiness that she'd see Denver soon, from the sadness that would grip her heart when he left again—streamed down her cheeks.

If he asked, could she leave her family? And more importantly, Papa?

Like the blinding sun rising over the woods, the answer to their problem—at least for Denver—became clear. To avoid the pain of leaving her forever, and the pain of hurting her, he might not come back.

Eliza took a flat stone from the creek bank, its edges knife-sharp. Options to pain existed. Options to the fading of her colors—love and hope—without him.

She loved him that much. The rock fell from her limp fingers.

One way or another, *some* way or another, no matter of any Amish rules, the Creator would create a miracle for her and Denver.

She whirled and left the creek.

And she would do her part to make sure that happened by telling him she loved him as soon as he came back.

Chapter 22

In a hard airport seat at RDU, Denver squirmed. Just freakin' great. The plane was grounded due to mechanical issues and another one hadn't been assigned to take its place.

Well, at least he hadn't gotten upset about Eliza anymore, like that day on the lake. More sleep helped. Willow's great cooking helped, too. Heck, even her constant teasing helped him look forward to flying to Ohio again.

Jan had helped, too. Except for when she was busy with weekend art shows and outings with girlfriends, she visited every other Saturday or so, which included dinner in Clarksville, small talk, and TV. She never mentioned marriage again, thank goodness, including the subject of how she'd tried to seduce him when he flew in from Ohio.

Although Denver had managed to keep his mind off of Eliza, her gray eyes still peeked from the forest of his memories on occasion. When that happened, he kept telling himself—like he'd done a million times before—how he cared for her as a friend, which meant he could never hurt her.

Yep, no doubt about it—her life was with her family in Ohio and his life was in Virginia with Willow. Since they loved the area so much, they might work here and stay close, even sharing the house.

Along with that, since things were okay with Jan, why not give their relationship a chance? He shook his head. Funny how he had to keep telling himself that.

His watch read thirty-five minutes past his original flight

time. He might get to Ohio faster if he walked. What the heck was taking so—

On the phone in his belt holder, Jan's violin ring tone played. Denver swiped the screen. "Just in time. You can keep me calm while—"

"Denver! Are you still at the airport?"

"That's what I was gonna tell you. What—"

"Be quiet and listen! Do you think you could get Eliza's dad to let you bring her back here with you?"

"Why the heck should I do that?"

"I just showed her painting to a collector at the Amish section of the Folk-Art Gallery. You'll never believe it—he's offered 25,000 dollars for it! That's why I need—"

"How could you show him the painting when it's hanging on the wall in my bedroom?"

"Remember when you stopped by and I saw the painting?"

"Yeah, but—"

"Stop interrupting! I took a picture of it with my phone while you were asleep. I was showing it to this collector and he pulled out his darned checkbook and started writing before I could even tell him I didn't have the painting. You've got to get her back so she can do shows like Jon. Think of all she could do for herself and her family with the money."

"C'mon, Jan, 25,000 dollars? You're pulling my leg."

"I am not!"

The announcement came for the flight number that replaced the grounded plane, followed by another announcement that it was boarding now.

"Nice try, Jan." Denver stood. "My flight's ready to—"

"Forget the flight, Denver Andrews, I'm telling you the truth! This collector loves Amish folk art that much, and he absolutely fell in love with Eliza's painting."

Denver dropped to the seat. "You really are telling the

truth?"

"I couldn't be more serious. Try to get her back here, okay?"

"I doubt her dad will let her."

"Do the best you can and let me know."

Jan ended the call. A second boarding announcement came for the flight. Denver jumped from the chair and ran to the gate.

Backpack stowed in the plane's overhead compartment, he tried to wrap his mind around his problems. How would he ask Absalom to allow Eliza to travel so far away from her home? Trusting him while Eliza stayed in the schoolhouse was one thing, while trusting him to take her all the way to Virginia was something else. Then there was the question of where she'd stay, which he had no answer for either.

The plane's engines rose in pitch. He lurched in his seat as the airliner taxied toward the runway.

Jan! She planned shows for artists and might have an idea. He jerked his phone from his belt and called her number.

"Why aren't you in Ohio yet?"

"Give me a break, the plane's taxiing now. Do you have any idea where Eliza might stay while she's here? I can't think of a—"

"I just got off the phone with Willow. If you can get Eliza here, I suggested she stay at your house."

"What gave you that idea?" Denver clamped his eyes shut. If Eliza stayed with him, how could they handle being together without their feelings growing even stronger?

"She knows you, with your sweet self," Jan said. "Meaning she'll be comfortable around you. Willow thinks it's a great idea and is looking forward to meeting her. Don't you think it's a great idea?"

"That depends on what her dad says."

"You'll sweet talk him into it, I'm sure. Let me know how it goes, bye."

The plane leveled out. Denver unbuckled his seatbelt. Flight attendants pushed drink carts along the aisle. One stopped beside him. "Something to drink?"

"Two beers if I can have them, please. I need to relax, and I mean *really* relax."

At the Columbus airport, Denver climbed into Jon's pickup and tried calling him to tell him about Jan's idea, but the screen went blank when he swiped it because he forgot to charge the phone at home. Gritting his teeth at the exit, he hit the accelerator, causing the tires to squeal.

At the schoolhouse, he hopped out, backpack in hand, and met a muscular guy wearing shorts coming out of the door, carry-on in his hand. "You must be Denver. Nice to meet you but I've gotta go."

Denver grabbed his arm. "Look, I know you probably miss home, but what's the chance you could teach three more months?"

Eyeing Denver's hand, the guy pulled his arm free. "No way, I need to see my girlfriend." The guy winked. "If you know what I mean."

The pickup disappeared in a cloud of dust. The schoolhouse door opened. "Hey, stranger. Feel like getting lucky?"

Denver whirled to face Akina. "Boy, did I need that."

"Anything else you need? Come on in where it's private, I'll see what I can do."

Inside, Denver dropped his backpack by the door. "Where's Eliza, I thought—"

"Sure you did." Akina pulled his head down and kissed him—thoroughly, deliciously, and in a manner that said she was ready for more than kisses.

Denver pulled away. "C'mon now, didn't you jump the bones of that hunk while I was gone? He even said he had a girlfriend, something we have in common."

Akina punched Denver's shoulder. "Better be glad I know you're kidding, or that would've been a lot harder." She started to pull his head down again but stopped, lips in a sultry pout. "That's right, you asked about your Amish goddess."

"How'd things go while I was away? Did she do well with the other guy?"

"She learned everything he taught her."

"I knew she was special."

Akina poked Denver's ribs. "Tell me something I don't know." She went to the door. "Should I lock this so you can show me how much you missed me?"

He went to the desk and sat. "We need to talk."

Folding clothes at her bedroom window, Eliza dropped her blue jeans when Denver pulled up in the pickup and climbed out. Finally, she could tell him she loved him. She took a step and stopped. Not yet. Give him time with Akina. Then she'd talk to him alone.

She added the jeans to the others on the bed and sat. Breath after breath she waited. She clasped her fingers together, pulled them apart. He had to admit he loved her. *Had* to. Then they could tell Papa and see what he said.

Eliza went to the window. The pickup was gone, so the other teacher had left. Time to see Denver.

She passed Jon, Becca, and Ellie at the kitchen table. Becca was forming Jon's fingers into a sign while Ellie watched. Samuel sat in a carrier on the table, pacifier working in and out between his lips.

At the schoolhouse, Eliza knocked on the door and went in. Sitting in a chair on one side of Denver's Desk, Akina stood. "I told you he'd come back. I'll let you two catch up."

She left, and Eliza went to Denver. "Deevrr, I'm happy to see you."

"I'm happy to see you, too. Where's your papa? I need to talk to him."

"Can't we talk first?" she signed.

"I really need to talk to your Papa. If he agrees to what I ask, we'll have plenty of time to talk."

Eliza couldn't argue with that. "He's in Jon's workshop."

Denver followed Eliza to the barn. If Absalom allowed her to go home with him, they had to be friends and nothing else. Like he'd already decided, he had his life and Eliza had hers, *especially* if she came to Clarksville.

Footsteps swished in the grass behind him. Akina tapped his shoulder. "Are you going to tell Absalom about that collector?"

"Yeah, wish me luck."

"I'd like to be in on this conversation. It'd be great if Eliza's art hit the big time."

"I appreciate you understanding why we can't fool around anymore."

"It's no problem, but I'll still miss you."

"Can you teach the next few months alone?"

"I can handle it."

"Is that hunk teacher coming back next time? Maybe he's an ex-Marine and you could steal him away from his girl."

"Shut up. If I were into stealing men from women, I would've taken you from Jan the first week you were here."

In the workshop, which smelled of fresh-cut wood and

sawdust, Absalom turned a band saw off and removed safety glasses. "I'm glad you're back, Denver. Eliza hasn't been the same without you."

Denver leaned against a table. How to tell Absalom, an Amish man who loved his daughter so much, who was so protective of her, that he wanted to take Eliza back to Virginia? Regardless of all the scenarios he'd imagined on the plane, none seemed to fit.

Absalom tilted his head to one side. "Why the frown? Aren't you glad to be back?"

Denver signed to Eliza, "I have a lot to tell your papa. Do you mind waiting outside with Akina? It's complicated. If everything works out, you'll know soon."

Eliza and Akina left.

"Now you're worrying *me*," Absalom said. "I couldn't read your signs but I didn't need to. Why did you send Eliza away?"

"It concerns her art. Do you know about Jon being an artist, and how much money he makes with his paintings?"

"I know all about it. He does well financially."

"What would you say if I told you Eliza could do as well?"

"I'd say you need to explain it a lot better than what you're doing."

Denver couldn't argue that. "Jon comes to North Carolina for his art shows, at a gallery where a friend of mine works. I stopped by to see her on my way home, and she took a picture of the painting Eliza gave me."

"Pride is something the Amish try to avoid," Absalom said, brushing sawdust from his hands. "Still, I admit to pride in Eliza's talent. I'm not surprised others enjoy her talent like I do."

"This is a lot more than simple enjoyment. My friend showed the picture to a collector. He assumed she had the painting at the gallery and offered 25,000 dollars for it."

Absalom shrugged. "I love the Amish life. As long as I have enough money to meet my families' needs, I'm satisfied."

Denver hesitated. He hated to bring up Absalom using Jon's workshop and its electric woodworking machines, which, on the surface, could be called hypocritical, but this was important enough to use whatever he could as a tool to make Absalom understand. "How long has Eliza been painting?"

Absalom pulled a stool from under a work table and sat. "She started the year she turned five. She threw them away until she showed me one and I smiled and nodded. She still threw them away until she was satisfied. I guess she has about fifty, give or take."

"I hope you understand how much that many paintings could be worth." Denver waved a hand toward Jon's woodworking machines. "You could have a workshop like this. Your children could go to college. You could even have a solar electric system put in like Jon is doing. I understand the Amish help their neighbors financially when they can, and you could do that. You could get a pickup and—"

"You talk nonsense. We'd be shunned from our order and I'd lose my friends. What good is all that then?"

"I'm sorry for saying so, but what good is a religion that has so little forgiveness at its foundation?"

"Being Amish is about the discipline necessary to follow God's word." Absalom's deeply tanned crow's feet tightened into a series of intense chevrons. "What do you English know about discipline? Flaunting your half-naked bodies in town. Cursing like it's a second language. Having sex out of wedlock and killing your unwanted children because they're nothing more than a nuisance."

"Judging all of us for the actions of some isn't something God would like, Absalom."

"You just judged all Amish by saying we don't forgive."

"You're right, I'm sorry." Denver worked his jaw. Regardless of his mistake, he needed to get to the point.

"You *should* be sorry," Absalom said. "I'm Eliza's father and it's my job to take care of her." The chevrons calmed to their former intensity. "I suppose I could help my order with the money. Of course, I'd have to get permission from my bishop. We can ask Eliza. I suppose she wouldn't mind you taking her paintings to sell."

"I'm glad you understand. Now we need to—" Denver closed his eyes for a second. Absalom didn't understand the part about Eliza holding art shows so she could be as successful as Jon. He'd agreed to the idea in part; maybe the rest would be easy.

"Why so quiet?" Absalom said. "I thought you'd be happy I agreed."

"Eliza needs to get proper exposure for the best prices for her work. That means attending art shows in a gallery like where Jon went and where my friend works. The gallery has a Folk-Art section with an Amish section, and—"

"No, Denver. Jet planes and cities would scare her."

Denver took his phone from his belt holder. "She can stay with my sister and me. We have a nice home beside a huge lake. It's near the woods like here. It's peaceful and beautiful like here, too. I think she'd love—"

"How do you know what she'd love?" Absalom's tanned chevrons again deepened to dark chasms.

"I have pictures of our home and my family on my phone."

"Akina told me what happened to your mother and father. I'm sorry, but—"

"Thank you, I appreciate it. My sister's just a little older than Eliza. She's learning sign language. They'd be friends in no time."

"Show me your pictures. That doesn't mean I'll agree."

Denver started to press the power button but stopped. "I forgot to charge my phone before I left home. Akina has a charger. I can—"

"Don't bother." Absalom stood. "You can sell Eliza's paintings if she doesn't mind, that's all."

The door to the workshop opened. Eliza ran to Absalom. "Papa, I go." Her words were slurred, but the meaning was clear in her widened eyes and the sincerity in her voice.

Absalom faced Akina. His cheeks above his beard burned like the embers of a fire within a tangle of brush, thick and brown. "So, the English listen to private conversations, too."

Denver translated. Eliza shook her head once, twice, and a third time. "No, Papa, I go."

"You'd be afraid away from home, Eliza."

"She's not afraid," Akina signed and said. "Or haven't you noticed that about your own daughter?"

"She's my daughter. I know all I need to know about her."

"Really?" Akina's voice took on a low, ominous tone that Denver had never heard, probably her Marine voice when giving orders. "Have you been deaf most of your life?" she continued. "Have you had to deal with children teasing you? Making faces at you? Making you feel less than human because you were deaf?"

"No, but—"

Akina cut the air with signs. "No, you haven't, but I'm sure Eliza has. Haven't you seen how strong she is? If not, she might be dead by now."

"Akina's right," Denver signed and said. "What got me interested in teaching deaf children was a documentary filmed in Africa. Children who never have the chance to learn sign language can suffer to the point of suicide. They can even suffer in their own family because they're made to work while the other children go to school."

Eliza took Absalom's hand. "Papa, please …"

Denver watched a tear roll down Absalom's cheek. What guilt did he carry within that single drop of grief? Absalom's sawdust-stained fingertip wiped the tear away.

"I never could say no to you, Eliza." Eliza patted her ears and shook her head. Absalom smiled and nodded, and they hugged.

Denver slipped his arm around Akina's shoulders. "Great job, fellow teacher, translating to Eliza like that."

"Pretty smart, huh?" Akina said, smiling up at him. "Absalom, Denver and I are going to the schoolhouse to discuss my teaching alone until Jon can get someone else. See you in a little while."

Chapter 23

In the schoolhouse, Denver sat at the desk. Akina went to her desk for a notepad, pulled a chair over, and sat across from him. "You know if Jan sees you and Eliza looking at each other like *I've* seen you looking at each other, the fireworks she makes will be nothing compared to the ones your town has in July."

A vehicle horn beeped. "Wonder who that is?" Denver said.

Akina went to a window. "It's Dan pulling up to Jon's house."

"Maybe he forgot something."

"Not him, that's one seriously in love guy. Hey, Jon came out and waved him inside." Akina waited a few seconds. "Jon's coming this way." She opened the door.

Denver leaned over to look outside. Jon's hands were clenched into fists and his face was red. He stomped up the steps and slammed the door behind him. At Denver's desk, he looked down like a father about to punish his son. "We need to talk, Mr. Andrews."

"Jon, what's—"

Jon held up his hand, then faced Akina. "You don't need to hear this. Unlike Denver, you've been a great teacher. Do you want to wait outside?"

"I don't know what's going on, Jon, but Denver's just trying to—"

"I'll take that as a no. Denver, Dan stopped in town and called to tell me how you tried to get him to take your place for the next three months. Not only did you make a commitment to the children, you made a commitment to me. I consider you backing out on them—and me—an insult."

"Jon, you don't understa—"

"I'd have you leave and never come back if it weren't for the children. What do you have to say for yourself?"

The door opened and Dan came in. "Jon, Absalom told me what's going on. I'll stay and teach three more months."

"What's this got to do with Absalom?"

"That's right, you don't know. Denver, you want to fill Jon in?"

"I thought you wanted to get home to your girlfriend?"

"Like I told Jon a minute ago, I came back because I thought she wouldn't mind, but I thought she did when I called her. I just called again and she understands." Dan went to the door. "I'll let her know I'm staying."

Jon faced Denver. "Well?"

Denver told Jon everything. He went to the desk and leaned against it. "I'm sorry about jumping you. I guess I was overreacting out of concern for the children."

"No problem, Jon, I get it."

"Good. As far as Eliza and her art, I bet I know who the collector is because he loves Amish folk art. If it's him, he's wealthy and kind of eccentric, which is probably why he offered so much for her painting. Still, he influences other collectors. When Eliza has her show, she'll become extremely important in the art world. Too bad I didn't see that painting she made. I never thought about using all that stuff from the woods."

"That is so cool," Akina said, elbowing Denver. "This guy here knew she was special all along."

"We've got a lot to do." Denver silently thanked his parents for their generosity to him and Willow. He could easily afford to fly Eliza home and pay for whatever she needed.

Jon rubbed his chin. "We *do* have a lot to do. I'm sure Jan wants that painting as soon as possible."

"I think Denver might want to hold on to that one," Akina said.

"Why?" Jon asked Denver.

"She took me out to gather everything she uses to make what she calls her colors. We came back here and she painted it for me as a gift."

"Then we need to ask her if she has another one like it. We can pick it up at Absalom's house and you can take it to Jan."

"She has a lot more," Denver said. "Maybe we can ship them. She won't be able to schedule a show soon anyway."

"Let's see what they say," Akina said. "They probably have plenty of questions about—"

Absalom stuck his head inside the door. "Can Eliza and I come in? She's excited and wants to know everything she has to do before she and Denver can go to Virginia."

"We were thinking the same thing," Jon said. "First we need to ask her if she has another painting like the one she gave Denver."

"I don't blame him," Absalom said. "She gave him that one as a gift."

Denver hated how all the excitement had made him forget to translate everything to Eliza. He'd have to do better at home. He faced her and signed, asking if she had another painting like the one she gave him. She signed that she did, and Denver passed that on to everyone. "Sounds like we need to take a drive to Absalom's house."

"What do you think, Absalom?" Jon said. "It won't take long."

"I've never ridden in a pickup. My bishop sometimes gets rides to visit other bishops in the area, so it should be all right."

Denver signed everything to Eliza, and her eyes crinkled with humor. "Tell Papa I'll buy him a pickup when he learns how to drive."

"Okay, funny girl, one thing at a time. We need to get your picture so we can get to Virginia."

Denver translated to Jon, who said, "Take the pickup you drove from the airport. I'll tell Dan what's going on so he can unpack."

"Good idea," Akina said. "There's enough room for me to go, too."

Everyone piled in the pickup. During the drive, Denver glanced at Absalom, whose head turned with the miles like a child marveling at a new wonder. A little less than fifteen minutes later, they parked in his dirt driveway.

He looked at Denver. "I have to admit, this is a lot faster than a buggy."

In the back, Akina said, "And dry in the rain, too."

"Warm in the winter and cool in the summer," Denver said. Not that it would ever happen, but wouldn't it be something if Eliza's art—and this short drive—led Absalom to go modern?

"Pull around back," Absalom said. "Oneita and the children are usually there."

Denver did so. Clothes hung from a line, but no one was there. From a barn—wood planks weathered gray, tin roof bleeding streaks of rust—a boy and a girl appeared in the open double doors. "That's Tess and Ethan," Absalom said, getting out of the pickup. "Eliza hasn't been home since Christmas. She might like to say hello."

During the walk to the barn, Denver pointed at the well pump at the far end of the backyard. "Boy, I'm glad I don't have to haul water from that at home."

"I had the well installed when Eliza was five, as soon as the farm started making a reasonable profit. We used to get our water from the river down that path to the left. We had to boil it to make it safe, too. That was extra work, but we made sure we boiled every single drop."

"Good idea," Akina said. "Bad water can kill a person, especially a child."

Absalom closed his eyes for at least three full seconds. What could make him react to Akina's comment like that? She looked at Denver, questioning him with raised eyebrows, and he answered with a shrug.

Eliza slowed until Absalom got ahead. Denver slowed with her in case she wanted to sign something to him. Instead, she smiled at him while entwining her fingers into his. All Denver could do was smile back. Yep, like Akina had said, he'd have to be careful about them smiling at each other like this around Jan, or fireworks would fly for sure.

Tess and Ethan came running, black clothes dark against the greening yard. Tess beat Ethan by a few steps. "Papa, did you come in that truck? Who are these people?"

"Better not let Bishop Marley see you riding in a truck," Ethan said.

Absalom placed his hand on Eliza's shoulder. "Now, Tess, don't you know your own sister?"

"That's Eliza? I'm not used to seeing her wearing clothes like that."

"Or wearing tennis shoes," Ethan said.

"Has she gotten taller?" Tess said

Denver signed everything to Eliza, and added, "You are taller." He tapped his chest. "In here. Show your sister how to say hello in sign language. I'll keep translating so you can."

Eliza knelt in front of Tess, signed "hello," and Tess repeated it perfectly. "I like talking this way. I can tell Ethan things he won't understand. Can you teach me how to say 'your feet stink, you need a bath?'"

Absalom nudged Ethan toward Eliza. "Say hello to your sister. You saw Denver show Tess, go ahead."

"Why didn't you show us on the weekends?"

"Because you left me too much work to do. Go on, tell Eliza hello."

"Come on over here, handsome young man," Akina said. "I'll teach you sign language so you can show all the pretty girls around here."

Ethan took his wide-brimmed hat off and stepped over. "None of them are as pretty as you."

Denver elbowed Akina. "Pretty *short,* you mean."

"Shut up," Akina said. "Okay, Ethan, tell Eliza hello."

Ethan made the sign. "Hi, Eliza." Eliza returned the sign, then added something else, and Ethan said, "What did that other sign mean?"

"She called you stinky feet," Akina said.

Tess giggled. "I need to remember that one." Eliza stood and opened her arms, and Tess said, "What does that sign mean?"

"I know," Absalom said. "Now that she can talk to you, it means she wants something from you she might never have had."

"A hug?" Tess said

"Try and see, Tess. You too, Ethan. Then I'll take Eliza inside to see your mama."

Eliza took Tess and Ethan into her arms, mouthed "Thank you," to Denver and Akina, and let Tess and Ethan go.

On the back porch, the screened door slammed. A woman similar to Eliza, but shorter, crossed her arms.

"All right, you two," Absalom said to Tess and Ethan, "wait for us in the barn. It's time I had a talk with your mama."

"About what?" Tess said.

"Something I should've talked to her about a long time ago. Go on now, do like I say."

Denver and Akina followed Absalom and Eliza to the porch, where Oneita uncrossed her arms. "Why did you bring these English here wearing their English clothes? And why is Eliza wearing English clothes, too? It's bad enough you stay with them all week—now you bring them here and have them talking to Tess and Ethan when we aren't supposed to interact with them."

"Tess and Ethan were getting to know their sister. I think I understand why you've never been a proper mother to Eliza, but that excuse won't do any longer. She can speak with her hands and hear with her eyes better than any hearing and talking person I know. She can listen better, too, because she listens with her heart."

"I raised her and fed her—I made sure she was dressed and clean. That's what mothers do."

"You didn't treat her like you did Ethan and Tess after she lost her hearing. Worse than that, you know it."

Absalom faced Denver and Akina. "I need you to translate to Eliza. I'm going to explain why I think her mama has treated her like she has for all these years. Let's go inside, I want to see Ivy first."

"I'll wait out here," Denver said. "Akina's better with signs."

"This is important, Denver. I'll be trusting you with my daughter in Virginia. You need to hear everything in case she wants to talk about it."

"I don't know what you want to talk about," Oneita said. "Do whatever it is you came here to do and let me get back to work."

Absalom whirled around. "Do you not have one bit of respect for me? As your husband? As the father of our children?"

"I ..." Oneita's throat muscles worked with a hard swallow. "I respect you, Absalom. I ... I'm sorry if I act like I don't." She went inside, and everyone followed.

Denver's stomach churned worse than when an airliner took off. It seemed he was about to be involved with a discussion on how a family member had mistreated another family member who was deaf—this family member being the deaf child's own mother at that.

Absalom hung his hat on a peg by the door, then peeked into Ivy's crib. "She's sound asleep." He faced Oneita. "We will not argue. We will not fight. We will not raise our voices. Do you understand?"

"I still don't know what you want me to say."

"Do I need to ask again?" Absalom's voice whiplashed throughout the room.

Oneita sank into one of two rocking chairs that flanked a table with a lamp. The nearly invisible wisp of smoke rising from its yellow flame smelled of kerosene. "No." Her hands shook in her lap.

Absalom took three chairs from the rough-hewn kitchen table and placed them in a row near the rocking chairs. "Please have a seat."

"Standing's fine." Denver nudged Akina's arm. "Right?"

"Sure, standing's great." Ivy whimpered in the crib, and Absalom peeked at her. Akina leaned near Denver's ear. "We need to keep standing so we can run, right?"

"No freakin' joke."

Eliza had left and returned with a stack of paintings. She placed them on the kitchen table and was looking through them. Absalom touched her shoulder and said to Denver, "Tell her to watch your signs. This will clear up something she asked me a while back."

Denver signed to Eliza what Absalom had said. Eliza took the middle chair. Denver and Akina took the chairs beside her. Absalom sat opposite Oneita, in the other rocking chair. "Eliza, your mama and I lived in another state when we were first married. You aren't our first child either."

Eliza raised her hands toward Denver. "Ask Papa why I don't remember."

Denver did as she asked. Absalom glanced at Oneita, then faced Eliza. "We moved here before you were born. Our first daughter looked exactly like you when you were born."

Eliza raised her hands, and Absalom signed, "Wait."

"I won't go into how, but she died when she was five years old. I don't have the words to describe what it did to me." He glanced at Oneita again. "It nearly killed your mama. She begged me to move so she could end her grieving."

"So you came here," Eliza signed, with Denver translating.

"That's not important. What's important is how she's never been a real mother to you."

Denver lowered his hands and faced Akina. "Do you mind translating so I can concentrate on listening? Like Absalom said, I need to hear all this in case Eliza needs to discuss it."

Akina raised her hands, and Oneita said, "I need to say something."

"It's about time," Absalom said. "After eighteen years."

"It's no excuse, but no matter how hard I tried to comfort Eliza when she cried, nothing worked."

"I thought that was part of it," Absalom said. "Eliza, when—"

"I'm not through, Absalom. It was the same when I told her I love her and she didn't smile. It was the same when I tried to explain something and she only looked at me with confusion. Then, when our other children came along, I thought I should concentrate on the life I wanted for them."

Oneita's body seemed to shrink in the rocking chair, like a dark ghost illuminated by the flickering yellow flame of the lamp.

"It was wrong—I knew it then and I know it now. Now it's too late for me to be a mama who loves her daughter like I should."

Eliza's eyes focused on Akina's frantic signs—hands and fingers flying up and down, side to side, back and forth, until they stopped. She went to the table and took a picture from the stack to show Denver, similar to the one she'd painted for him. She returned it to the stack and came back to sign, "She's right, it's too late. I want to leave."

"Please, Eliza ..." Oneita's voice, edged with tears, cut through the room. "I'm ... I want to make up for my mistakes."

Akina translated, paused, and signed again. "Can't you give your mother a chance? When a person sees their mistakes, it's a good idea to listen."

Eliza clenched her hands into fists, released them, clenched them again, and raised them. "A mother does not slap her daughter because she doesn't understand why she can't get water at a river."

Akina translated to Oneita. She shrunk back into rocking chair again, eyes blinking, chin trembling. "You remember that day?"

"I remember."

Oneita covered her face with her hands and wailed pitifully. Absalom went to her, took her in his arms, and Eliza signed, "How can you comfort her when she was no mama to me?" Her hands paused, slashed the air again. "Ever."

Still signing, Akina stood. Denver admired her dedication to Eliza and her family, which had almost been torn apart by a misunderstanding caused by deafness.

Absalom left Oneita to take Eliza's arms within his hands. "I comfort her because I know why she slapped you. Yes, it was wrong. I didn't know about it then or I would've had words with her. Still, the pain of why she slapped you has scarred us all, and you need to know why she did it."

"Please, Absalom," Oneita wailed, "don't say our daughter's name. Let us both—" A huge sob took her breath. "Let us both lie in peace." She crumpled to the rocking chair again, face in her hands, shoulders heaving.

Absalom faced Eliza again. "See how much she suffers from losing her first child? I know you don't think so, but that's a hint of how much she can love."

"Not how much she can love me, Papa."

"Even love sometimes comes with pain. When we lived in the other state, our drinking water came from a river. We boiled our water like we did here, but …" Absalom's face contorted as if he were about to cry.

"What, Papa?"

"I found a cup of water by the bed in her room a few days after she died. We think she got it from a bucket of water that hadn't been boiled. I had the water tested. It had something called E-coli bacteria in it."

"I don't understand."

"It's hard to explain, but it's what made her sick."

"Did you take her to the doctor?"

"We lived about a day's buggy ride from the nearest town. By the time her fever grew to where we knew it was serious, it was too late. She died on the way there."

"I'm sorry for what happened, but—"

"Eliza, your mama slapped you at the well so you wouldn't leave us like our first child left us. Can you say you wouldn't have done the same thing in her place?"

Eliza's gray eyes darted toward Oneita, then back to Absalom. "If not for you, Papa, or my colors, my life would have no happiness. A large part of that is her fault."

"I understand. Still, you need to remember—not being able to forgive is bad enough, but not being able to forgive when a person has a reason shows a lack of what you would call your colors."

"I'm not saying I won't forgive, I'm saying I need time to forgive. The pain" —Eliza placed her hand over her heart— "is too much too soon, like for you when my sister died. If you understand, tell her. Then I want to leave."

Absalom faced Denver. "I need to tell my family what's going to happen with Eliza's paintings and where she's going. Take her to the pickup and send Ethan and Tess. I'll come when I'm through."

Chapter 24

Denver took Eliza to the pickup. She put the pictures inside and slammed the door. Tess and Ethan came out of the barn, and Denver waved them over. "Your papa said to go inside." They ran up the porch steps.

Pointing toward a path that came out of the woods, Akina said and signed, "Looks like someone's been fishing."

A man and two young men, all dressed in Amish clothing and carrying fishing poles, walked toward the pickup. The man carried a stringer of fish. They all stopped, and the man said, "Are you waiting for someone?"

"Are you Mr. Miller?" Denver said. "Absalom said you and your sons were helping while he and Eliza went to sign language school." He translated to Eliza.

"That's us." Mr. Miller waved toward his sons. "This is my oldest, Hannes. His younger brother is Timothy."

Eliza whipped her hands toward Hannes. "Did you learn a lesson that day?"

"Why's she flapping her hands like that?" Hannes said.

"You should know," Timothy said. "You're the one who told Papa to tell Mr. Gray about the sign language school."

"Whatever." Hannes took the fish from Mr. Miller and stomped toward the main road.

Denver translated everything to Eliza, whose jaw muscles tightened. She didn't like that guy one bit.

"Please pardon my son," Mr. Miller said. "He was used to

having his way until he and Timothy got into a fight last year, when they went fishing."

"I never said that's what happened, Papa."

"I know, I know. Hannes said he was chasing a raccoon and ran into a tree. Forget about it. At least he's been quieter since then."

Eliza grinned at Denver's translation, and Timothy said, "Tell Eliza I'm sorry. Tell her I'm glad she's learning sign language, too."

Denver translated to Eliza, who nodded. Denver looked at Timothy, whose eyes had been focused on his hands while he signed. Why not plant a seed in this curious young man's mind? "Timothy, maybe you can think about learning the basics of sign language so you can teach some of the kids around here."

"I might like that." Timothy trotted toward the driveway.

"Any idea what his apology was about?" Denver asked Mr. Miller.

"Hannes used to tease Eliza when Absalom brought his family to our home. Timothy did too, but only if Hannes elbowed him enough. Eliza never seemed to notice, so I let it go. I better get home myself. Nice to meet you."

Denver translated to Eliza. She climbed in the pickup and closed the door.

"What a day for your Amish goddess," Akina said.

"You did a great job signing while ago," Denver said.

"Too bad Eliza's in the pickup. You could reward me with a kiss."

"You know we're done kissing."

"Like you said about Dan, I'll have to corrupt *him* now."

"Not until I leave. Eliza needs identification for the flight—that doesn't happen overnight."

"I'm just teasing. Dan's out of luck."

Denver parked the pickup in front of the schoolhouse. He'd gotten Akina to call Jon and remind him how Eliza needed ID for the flight. Eliza signed how she needed clothes for the trip, including jeans that wouldn't show her ankles and a dress for the flight. When she finished signing, she crossed her arms, which could only mean she was still upset about the scene with her mother.

When everyone got out of the pickup, she ran inside the school and slammed the door. "She's had a hard day," Denver said. "Y'all mind if I talk to her about it?"

"I'll show Jon the paintings." Absalom said.

"I'll visit that stinky outhouse," Akina said to Denver. "That'll give you and Eliza a little time to talk."

Inside the school, Eliza was sitting in her usual desk, head hanging down, black hair hiding her face.

Denver took the desk beside her. A tear ran down her cheek and fell to the desk. She raised her head and signed, "Why does it hurt so bad?"

"Having a mother who treats a child with less love than her other children would make anyone hurt. I'm glad your papa was there for you, and your colors."

Denver placed his hand on Eliza's. Making her mad wouldn't help, but it was better to forgive and move on, although that might take a while. "Like your papa said, it's a good idea to forgive you mama."

Eliza's eyes narrowed.

"I'm not saying now, but when you're ready. Some people stay mad at someone as long as they live, and that's not good."

Eliza smiled, just a hint. "I liked signing with Tess and Ethan. It was like meeting them for the first time."

"When you get to know them better—and your mama—you

can have the family you always wanted."

"I'll be with you in Virginia soon." Her hands lowered and then rose in mid-air, like a butterfly rising and falling in a breeze. "Remember when we talked about our feelings for each other?"

"I remember."

"Now we can see what happens with them."

Denver didn't know how to answer because she'd left out how she would never see her family again if she left them for good. Like he'd already decided—more than once—he had his life and Eliza had hers. Time for a gentle reminder.

"Your papa wouldn't want you to be away very long, especially since you'll be getting to know your family."

"I—" In mid-sign, Eliza's hands faltered. "I wouldn't want to be away from him for long either." Her head fell again.

Denver cupped his hand beneath her chin and gently lifted. He'd find a way to make her happy, and reminding her of where they were going was a start. She slowly lifted her head. He took his hand from under her chin and signed, "Try not to think about that now."

"Do you know something I can think about that will make me feel better?"

"You'll stay with my sister and me. Her name's Willow, and she's learning sign language."

"Akina told me what happened to your mama and papa after you went home. It made me cry for you, and I wanted you with me." Eliza's chin trembled. The muscles in her throat worked with a firm swallow. "You must've had a wonderful family."

"I still do with Willow. We're pretty close for a brother and sister. My parents left us a house on a huge lake, and we go out fishing on our boat. I have a canoe we can go out in, too. Doesn't that sound fun?"

"Leaving you when the show is over won't be fun."

"Willow will help keep your mind off of that. She's always teasing me like Tess teases Ethan."

"Really?" Eliza tousled Denver's hair. "We can tease you together."

"Do you swim?" Denver signed.

"I never tried."

"Good, I can teach you." Denver snapped his fingers. "Oh, wow, with the extra time it'll take to get your ID, we'll be there for Lakefest. You'll love that, too."

The door opened, and Akina signed, "How's it going in here?"

"I'm better," Eliza signed. "Denver was telling me about his home."

"He told me about that. The lake sounds great, maybe I'll visit one day."

"Sounds good," Denver signed. "We can trade emails before you leave."

Eliza shook Denver's arm. "You didn't ask me if it was all right if Akina comes to see you."

"She's my friend. Isn't it okay for a friend to visit?"

"She's teasing you," Akina signed. "Look at that grin she's trying to hold in."

"You are?" Denver signed

Eliza tousled his hair again. "I'm starting now so I can catch up with your sister."

Behind Eliza's back, the huge airliner's seat vibrated. She glanced at Denver to her right. She'd soon meet his sister and actually live with them for as long as Papa allowed.

Picking up speed, the airliner rolled along a black road bordered with white stripes. Her seat shook harder, tilted, and an unseen hand pressed her into the cushion. Denver's hand on the rest beside her clenched into a fist, and she placed her hand over it. He took his hand from beneath hers and signed, "I'm okay when we're up. It's the take-offs and landings that make me nervous. It doesn't bother you?"

"I told you I was strong, remember?" She lowered her hands. Bring up Papa's last words at the airport or not? Yes, because she wanted know Denver's opinion about it.

She waited until the pressure left her back, until the vibration beneath her hands eased, and until Denver's complexion changed from ashen white to normal.

"Better?" she signed.

"Finally." He released his seatbelt.

"Deevrr," she said, raising her hands, "Can we talk about what Papa said, about me going back home soon?"

"We expected it."

"You think he won't let me stay long?"

"He wants you to get to know your family. That's a good idea, right?"

"If the people who come to my art show like my paintings, I want to stay with you and paint more instead of going back home right away. You told Papa that in town for me when we got my ID, remember?"

"I remember, but he didn't say you could."

A woman pushed a cart lined with bottles down the aisle. She stopped and spoke to other passengers, handed them something to drink, and continued to the next passengers. The woman was far away, so Eliza faced Denver and raised her hands. "Do you have a woman who's a special friend to you?"

"Willow and Akina are my friends."

"I think Akina was sad to see you leave. She hugged you a long time at the airport." Eliza lowered her hands. He didn't answer her question about having a special woman friend, and not answering meant he was hiding someone. "I understand if you have a special woman friend besides Akina."

Denver's chest rose and fell with a slow breath. He raised his hands. "I'm seeing the woman who works at the art gallery."

"Why didn't you tell me before?"

"I … well … I don't know. I'm sorry, okay?"

Denver's reddening cheeks signaled confusion and embarrassment, while his hiding Jan, even though he had admitted to having feelings for Eliza, signaled he didn't care for Jan as much as he thought he did.

He touched her hand. "Do you forgive me?"

Eliza knew the answer to her next question before she signed it. "Do you love her?"

"We're dating, that's all."

She held in a smile. Jan might think she could keep Denver, but she didn't how to fight for Denver like Eliza knew how to fight for Denver. The time to start might be now. "Maybe you should see someone else."

"Willow tells me that all the time."

"Your sister sounds like a smart woman."

"I have a lot to thank Jan for, and you do, too. She spoke to Jon about me wanting to teach sign language and set it up."

"And 'you do, too' means I have to thank her for taking the picture of my painting and showing it to that collector. If not, along with her helping you come to Ohio, we would've never met."

"Exactly." Denver paused his signs, likely to change subjects. "Does your mama like her new washing machine?"

"She's likes it fine, but not the generator. Papa told me she thinks it stinks and makes too much noise."

"Too bad they won't try anything else electric."

"Tess and Ethan want a refrigerator instead of an ice box. I think papa might like one, too. Every time he takes the buggy to get ice, he makes a face."

"Are you nervous about your show? It'll be in a city called Raleigh. Lots of people will want to meet you."

"What do you think of it?"

"I feel closed in when I drive between the tall buildings. I like the wide-open view of the lake I get from my bedroom window."

Eliza placed her hand over her mouth, but she doubted she could hide her crinkling eyes.

"What's so funny?" Denver signed. "I see your eyes laughing."

Finger in the air asking for a pause, Eliza waited until her urge to laugh ended. "Your bedroom has a view I'd like. Can I sleep with you?"

Denver's clean-shaven cheeks transformed into a reddening sunset. Maybe he wanted her to sleep with him? To lie warm in each other's arms? To touch, to kiss, and to finally admit how much he loved her. Then they could marry and do more than sleep.

The ember Eliza had kept warm within her while waiting for the chance to pursue their relationship flared—a focused point of heat in her womanhood, flaming with need like when she showered and thought of him.

Whatever she had to do to make him see they belonged together she'd do, both for her and his sake. Their colors were destined to be together, and she'd make sure Jan understood that, no matter what it took.

Chapter 25

The busy airport, where people streamed back and forth like currents in a river, struck Eliza as resembling a hive of hornets. Instead of a gray nest hanging from a tree, this human nest was inside a building with numerous glass doors, where numerous people darted and glanced and were searched by other people in uniforms, until they eventually left those doors, like hornets leaving their nest in search of another home.

By the time she and Denver climbed into his pickup, she couldn't stop yawning.

They left the airport and turned onto a wide, black road, nothing like the narrow road between her home and the small town nearby. On vehicles to the sides and in front of them, red lights dimmed and brightened, dimmed and brightened. Some flashed yellow lights, then swerved left or right. The lights and colors resembled angry eyes in the dark, eyes only intent on their destination, eyes only concerned with their metallic owners. Denver's fingers opened and closed on the steering wheel while his jaw worked. He didn't like this herd of glaring, darting, beasts any better than she did.

Tall buildings loomed ahead, with windows illuminated from the inside. This was nothing like the woods, where the trees welcomed her with their living presence. These immense stone-sided buildings soaring into the night created the illusion of crashing down on her. Eliza shuddered at the feeling of being overwhelmed.

The buildings and vehicles dwindled to a few here and there. Denver drove over a bridge that spanned a large body of water and continued on the wide road. To their left, cars traveled the opposite way, including several multiple-wheeled, house-sized vehicles, almost like lumbering bulls with flanks of silver gleaming in the night. Thank goodness one of those things had never passed the buggy on the way to town, or it might've scared the horse into running away.

Denver turned onto a different road, and they entered a small town. Between glances at her and yawns, he'd signed nothing the entire time, likely trying to stay awake by watching the road.

Leaving the town, he steered onto a narrower road, where two yellow lines marked its edges. Every so often, either two white lines or one broken line marked its middle, similar to the road leading from Papa's farm to the nearby town. Comforted by a familiar sight, Eliza yawned, settled into the seat, and closed her eyes.

Driving north along highway 15, Denver lowered the pickup window enough to allow the rush of night air and the ozone aroma of a recent shower to keep him awake. The red dashboard LED clock changed from 2:29 to 2:30. Not a single vehicle traveled the road. In spite of the air whipping in his ear, his eyes grew heavy on the long straightaways.

He glanced at Eliza.

The dim glow of the dashboard lights illuminated her profile, head jostling with the pickup's movement. Denver allowed himself a slight smile at the prospect of carrying her to the guest room and tucking her in. He'd be tempted to kiss her goodnight if she stayed asleep.

He squeezed the steering wheel. How could he be so stupid to have those thoughts when there was no way they could be together?

He eased his grip on the steering wheel.

She'd surprised him by asking if a "special" woman cared for him, and she'd surprised him even more by taking the news of Jan so well. Her joking about how he should see someone else pleased him to no end, because he absolutely loved Eliza's slight but significant way of poking fun at him. He and Jan sometimes shared a laugh, but they were few and far between when compared to his and Eliza's teasing.

Yes, she'd have to leave one day. Until then, whenever that might be, he wouldn't think about it. Instead, he'd try his best to make their time together as special as possible, preferably without romantic involvement.

He pulled into the driveway, which activated the motion detecting front porch lights. Wake Eliza or not? Idiot, she'd wake as soon as he tried to pick her up to carry her inside. He opened the pickup door enough so the interior would light and nudged Eliza's shoulder. Her eye's blinked open, and he signed, "We're home."

She yawned, shook her head, and signed, "You could have carried me, I'm not heavy."

Denver touched her bicep. "Maybe you should carry me?"

"No." Eliza poked his stomach. "That would break my back."

"Okay, enough teasing. I'm tired like you are."

Backpack in hand, as well as Eliza's suitcase, Denver met her at the front of the pickup. Instead of coming to the porch, she went to the side of the house, faced him, and signed, "I want to see the lake and the dock and the boat."

Denver set the luggage on the front porch, and they crunched along the gravel walkway, lit by solar lights.

Similar to the wet clunking sounds of driftwood washing against a rocky shore, the dock jostled side to side with their steps. At the end, Eliza signed, "This is more beautiful than my river."

"Mom and Dad really loved the lake. I—" A surge of sadness hit Denver. He didn't want it to show in his faltering signs, so he quickly continued. "I guess that's where I get it from."

Eliza looked away and then back, her expression unreadable. She came to Denver. "I can tell you miss them. I wish …" She came even closer, to slip her arms around his waist and lay her head on his shoulder.

Trying to hold in tears, Denver clung to her like a drowning man. Still, painful sobs burst from his throat for dual reasons—mom and dad were gone, and the woman he now held, who he could dream of spending the rest of his life with, would leave one day and never come back.

He forced his sobs away, but when he took his arms from around Eliza's back, she held on tighter, faced him, and gently, tenderly—even timidly—kissed him.

Resistance to their impossible situation fell away, including the sadness about his parents. The kiss took on a life of its own … soft and sensual … warm and inviting … amazing in every way.

Eliza ended the kiss and slowly raised her hands. "I don't like it when you're sad. I'd do anything to make you happy."

The statement almost brought Denver to tears again. The only thing that would make him happy was if nothing and no one kept them apart. He raised his hands. "I'm happy you're here. Do you believe me?"

A slow nod and downturned eyes, as if she were thinking the same thoughts about no one keeping them apart.

He took her by the hand and left for the house. Time for a good night's sleep and to see what things looked like between them in the morning.

Chapter 26

Sunlight streamed into Denver's room. He glared at the clock on the nightstand that read a little after 12 p.m., then swung his legs around.

And almost stepped on Eliza.

Sleeping peacefully on the floor, a blanket tucked beneath her chin, she could've been a child napping.

He ran his fingers through his hair. How could he keep from falling completely in love with her before she left? Then again, it might be too late already. That realization churned in his gut as if he'd swallowed a live twenty-pound striped bass whole.

He left the bed on the other side, circled to kneel and shake her shoulder. Her eyes fluttered open, and he signed, "Didn't like your bed?"

"I'm not used to being alone in a strange place."

"What about the first night you slept at Jon's house?"

"Don't ask me questions like that." She shoved Denver, and he thumped to the floor on his behind.

He stood. "Okay, okay, no need to get rough."

Eliza yawned. "I looked around before I went to sleep. You and Willow have a very nice home."

"Are you hungry? I smell bacon. Willow's probably making us breakfast."

Still in her dress, Eliza rose from the blankets that Denver recognized from the guest room and tucked them under her arm. "Can we go shopping today? Becca and I didn't think about something to sleep in."

Denver took the blankets from her and dropped them to his bed, then wrapped a summer-weight robe around his pajamas. He'd thought she might slip into his room and wore them in case. "I'll introduce you to Willow and we'll have breakfast. She'll take you shopping if you mention clothes. I've got a few things to do after we eat."

"Do you think she'll like me?"

"When I called her from the Columbus airport and told her we were on the way, she was on the internet learning more signs." He pointed at a nail in the wall over his dresser. "See that empty hanger? That's where I put your painting after I framed it. When I talked to Willow before we caught our flight, she said she liked it so much, she hung it in the living room."

"I'm happy people like my colors. When you told me about the man who paid so much for the one I had at home, I couldn't believe it."

Knock-knock.

"You up, Den?" Willow said. "Eliza's door is closed. I think she's still asleep."

Denver signed, "Willow knocked on the door and asked if I was awake. She thinks you're still in the guest room. I better answer. I'm up. Be out in a minute."

"Will she mind me sleeping with you?"

"She'll understand how you were uncomfortable in a strange place."

Eliza looked in the dresser mirror. "My hair's a mess." She took the brush from his dresser and stroked her hair until smooth and shiny, including the ends hanging to her waist.

Turning to face Denver, she signed, "I'm sorry about kissing you last night. We can't be together, so—" The familiar butterfly of her hands faltered, wings hanging in mid-air, losing their will to fly. "So I shouldn't do that."

Denver couldn't stand to see her this way, especially when the intimacy of her brushing her hair in his own bedroom had left him breathless. He grinned as if he were a clown. "Do I look like it bothered me? You made me feel better. Besides, I love being with you."

"I love teasing you."

"Does teasing me make you feel like a big kid? That's what it does to me."

"I don't think 'big kids' kiss like we did. It made me have feelings I shouldn't have."

Denver agreed, but he didn't dare sign it. "It's okay. Those feelings are natural when people kiss."

"Not when the two people have to leave each other one day."

"Let's not think about that and eat." Denver didn't care to think about her leaving either. Time to get it off his mind with breakfast, if that were possible.

In the kitchen, evidenced by the aroma, Willow sipped coffee. She set the cup down, offered her hand to Eliza, and Denver raised his hands to translate. Instead of speaking, Willow shoved Denver's hands away and signed. "Hi, Eliza." She was a little slow on the letters for Eliza's name, but she signed them perfectly. "I'm glad Denver brought you back."

"He told me all about you," Eliza signed. "I'm sorry about your parents."

"Thank you. We'll be okay."

Denver raised his hands to sign for Eliza and to see how many signs Willow had learned. "It looks like you and Mark have been practicing a lot."

"What's that sign?" Eliza signed.

"You mean this one?" Willow signed. Pointing her fingers on one hand down, she touched her thumb and pinky together. "My three upside-down fingers kind of make an M. I made that up for my boyfriend's name—Mark."

Eliza raised her hands toward Denver. "You didn't tell me I could make a sign for my name instead of signing all the letters."

"Do you want a sign for your name?"

Eliza's expression took on a faraway look, like a person concentrating. She made the sign for A, then signed, "I'll use A for artist, except it means my name when we're signing about names. What about you and Willow?"

Willow made Mark's sign, pointed it up, and signed, "That looks like a W. It's what I use." She poked Denver's chest. "D for dummy for you."

Eliza laughed. "Denver said you like to tease him."

"I'll use C because I like paddling my canoe," Denver signed. "You want to wash up before breakfast?"

Eliza nodded and left, and Denver told Willow why Eliza had slept in his room. She looked at him sideways. "Yeah, right, tell that to someone who thinks she's ugly. Jan will get jealous when she sees her."

Denver didn't doubt that one bit. "Never mind. Can you take Eliza clothes shopping after breakfast? I want to put up those art supplies I ordered online while we were in Ohio."

"I already took care of it, big brother. That's one of the nicest things you've ever done. What's the chance Eliza will be the woman who takes you away from Jan?"

"Don't even go there," Denver said, shaking his head. "Be right back after I wash up, too."

Beside Denver at the bar, Eliza enjoyed the rich coffee Willow had flavored with what she called french vanilla creamer. She'd also made her and Denver something called an omelet, flavored with bacon, tomatoes, mushrooms, and cheese. Between bites and sips, she glanced around the huge house. Behind her, the kitchen opened into a huge living room with tall ceilings trimmed in wooden beams that peaked into an upside-down V. The outer wall, filled with huge windows, faced the lake and the dock, where she and Denver had kissed last night.

During her and Papa's conversation at the airport, before her family had waved goodbye, his request that she return home as soon as possible had touched her. Denver signed for him that he no longer wanted her to feel separate from anyone, that he wanted her to return so she could rebuild the ties that he should've made sure she had all her life. It was obvious Papa felt guilty, by how he looked at the ground every few words.

His request couldn't be ignored, but she couldn't ignore how she felt when Denver's blue eyes met hers, when he smiled as they teased, and finally, the warmth and taste of his lips during their kiss on the dock last night.

Along with how she was attracted to him, she liked the way he looked at her, with caring in his kind eyes. Not only that, his tears when he'd said goodbye at the school three months ago proved how much she meant to him, regardless of refusing to admit it. If it was the last thing she did in this life, she would make him admit it, despite how he said they could only be friends.

Plates empty, Denver signed, "I'm gonna get dressed."

At the sink washing a pan, Willow said something Eliza didn't catch. She shot a questioning glance at Denver, who signed, "Willow's going to take you clothes shopping while I do a few things."

Eliza took their plates to the sink, tapped Willow on the shoulder, and signed, "You're still in your pajamas. I'll wash these so we can go shopping. I've got something Denver calls a credit card."

Willow faced Denver and signed, "I couldn't quite read all that."

Denver signed and spoke what Eliza had signed. Willow gave Eliza an OK sign and left. Dressed in jeans and a pink blouse, she came back and signed, "When is your first show?"

"Saturday. Are you coming?"

Willow signed to Denver, "Sign what I say. It's too much." Denver held up his hands, and Willow continued. "I'm going camping with my boyfriend and his parents after Lakefest and the fireworks."

"What's 'Lakefest' and 'fireworks?'" Eliza signed. "You mentioned it at the school."

"A big deal for our town," Denver signed. "Saturday morning, it closes main street so vendors can sell crafts and all kinds of food. That night, people take their boats out on the lake to watch a huge firework show. They're fired from the old bridge."

"But what's fireworks?"

"They're colors exploding all over the night sky. Knowing how you like colors, you'd love them."

Willow signed to Denver, "You two should go out on the boat."

"Good idea," Denver signed. "We'll have to rush to get back in time, but I'll pack us something to eat and a few bottles of water before we go to Raleigh. After we get out of whatever nice clothes Jan makes us wear, we can jump in the boat and take off."

"That reminds me," Willow signed to Eliza. "Time to shop."

On the way to get her purse, Eliza smiled until her cheeks ached. Time to use her credit card for a pretty dress for the show.

Chapter 27

Eliza carried several racks of clothes to her room, Willow beside her with the rest. Most were flowing dresses purchased at a place she called a "thrift shop." They also stopped by a store specializing in women's clothing, where Willow insisted Eliza buy more bras and panties. The reds, greens, and blues intrigued her. She bought several pair, but one pair specifically caught her eye—nothing more than two white see-through lace triangles connected by a thin waistband that rode high on the hips of the woman pictured on the label. She added the package to the rest at the last minute. Eliza felt a twinge of guilt about it—well, she felt more devious than anything. If she ever got the chance to show them to Denver, he wouldn't dare think about Jan then!

She lay the clothes across the guest room bed, and Willow took her to the basement, where Denver seemed to be waiting for them. Overhead lights illuminated half the room. The other half was dim due to sheer curtains pulled over two sliding-glass doors. A few feet back from the doors sat a cloth covered frame of some kind. A case resembling a suitcase sat on a table beside the frame.

Denver waved Eliza to the sliding doors, placed a cord in her fingers, and signed, "Pull the cord."

Eliza pulled the cord. The curtains opened, light flooded this side of the room, and Denver signed, "Now take the cloth off that tall thing beside the table."

The tall frame consisted of three wooden legs with a shelf that held another large frame of what looked like white cloth. Attached to the back of the cloth, four thin pieces of wood formed a large square. "What is it?" she signed.

"It's called a canvas." Denver opened the case and took out a tube with a red square on the label, then put it back. "This is oil paint. You use these" —he pointed to a shelf on the wall beside the sliding doors— "and the brushes in those jars to paint on the canvas."

Eliza ran her fingers over the tubes. So many colors, and she wouldn't have to gather and mix them to get the right shades for whatever she painted. "You—" She dropped her hands and raised them again. "You bought these for me?"

"Sure. Willow set everything up before we got here. I stayed to check it out while you went shopping."

For as long as Eliza could remember, she wanted to be treated like this by all her family, not just Papa. He did the best he could, but now that she could use sign language, she could have this with the rest of her family, too.

Willow came over. "My big brother's a sweet guy, don't you think?"

Eliza threw herself into Denver's arms. Closing her eyes tight, she swallowed again and again, but the tears came regardless. This was how a family cared for each other—how her family might care for her when she went home. As much as she wanted to stay with Denver—to see if he loved her like she loved him—the choice would tear her apart.

Denver rubbed slow circles on her back. She stopped crying, pulled away to wipe her eyes, and faced Willow. "I don't think he's sweet, I know he's sweet. How can you be so nice to me? You don't even know me."

Denver translated to Willow, who said something, which Denver translated to Eliza. "Willow says since I'm a great brother, she knew you'd be a great young woman when I said I was glad you were staying with us."

Eliza raised her hands. "I don't know what to say. This makes me feel happiness I never felt before."

Denver translated this to Willow. She then spoke to Denver, who translated to Eliza again. "I'm glad you like it, Eliza. I hardly know you, but I feel like we're sisters all ready."

Eliza half-laughed, half-smiled. "Do sisters shop like we did? That was fun."

Grinning after Denver's translation, Willow signed, "Oh, yeah, no doubt about it." She faced Denver, spoke for a bit, and he raised his hands toward Eliza again.

"Willow wants to have a cookout Wednesday and invite Mark and Jan. You should meet her before the show."

Eliza nodded in agreement. She should meet the woman who made all this possible—especially meeting Denver—but she tightened her lips at the idea of meeting the person who considered herself a match for him.

Willow went upstairs. Eliza went to the paints, and Denver joined her. "Let me show you all the brushes and how to clean them, and this thing." From the table he took a thin, oval piece of wood with a hole and a slot in it, slipped his thumb into the hole so the oval rested on his forearm, and returned it to the table. "I know what this is, but I don't know the sign. You squeeze the paint on it and mix it until you get the shade you want."

"Why is it so shiny?" Eliza took the piece of wood from the table and slipped it over her thumb.

"Willow did that." Denver pointed to a can. "It had to be treated with that oil. I don't know the sign for it either. I could spell it, but …"

"Maybe later." Eliza returned the oval to the table. "You and Willow are wonderful."

"We're pretty cool."

"Do you need a jacket?"

Denver's shoulders bounced with a laugh. "When I use 'cool' like that, it means we're wonderful. Let me show you how to clean the brushes and this wooden thing."

Instructions clear on cleaning the wooden thing, including all the brushes and cleaning solutions lining the shelves on the wall by the sliding glass doors, and the rags and rolls of paper towels to clean the brushes with, they returned to the canvas, and he signed, "Any ideas for your first oil painting?"

"It's a secret." Eliza poked his ribs. "No peeking until the show."

"You can finish by then? That's right, back at the schoolhouse, you painted that picture in about an hour."

She shooed him away as if he were a worrisome fly zipping around a horse's ears. "Go do something. I need to learn how to use these colors."

Denver climbed the stairs. She looked through the tubes of paint and practiced holding the piece of wood. He returned with a shirt, deep blue with long sleeves. "You'll need this to keep clean while you work."

Eliza raised the collar to her nose and recognized the aroma of his hair. "Is this yours?"

"I'd like you to have it."

"To keep?"

"Yes, to keep. I'll leave so you can work."

Eliza slipped his shirt on and sniffed the sleeves, taking in the familiar scent of the soap he used. Wrapping her arms around herself in a tight hug, she attempted to recreate how Denver had held her on the dock last night. If nothing else, if she left and never saw him again, at least his shirt would comfort her in Ohio.

Chapter 28

Sitting at the bar, Eliza watched Denver dip a slice of bread into an egg and milk mixture to make french toast. She'd eaten two with syrup, sweet and sticky, and a spice Denver signed as cinnamon, which, by the familiar taste, Mama used in apple pies.

Eliza licked syrup from her fork.

Willow and Mark had gone out for breakfast and planned to practice some new signs at his house, followed by shopping for the cookout later. What better way to start the day than to have Denver to herself?

He dropped the bread in a pan on the stove and rinsed his hands. "You excited about the cookout tonight?"

"I'm more excited about you teaching me to swim." Eliza sipped milk. "Finish eating. I'll brush my teeth and get a surprise ready." She ignored Denver's questioning signs and left for the bathroom.

In the guest room, she changed into a one-piece swimsuit—a secret gift from Willow—and returned to the kitchen to tap Denver's shoulder while he ate. He whirled around, eyes widening. "Willow gave you that I bet. It's a little skimpy because you're taller than her."

"Willow showed me how to shave my underarms and legs. I like how smooth they are, want to feel?" Eliza pulled his hand toward her thigh, but he jerked it away.

"I—" His throat worked with a hard swallow. "That's okay,

I can see without touching."

Eliza held in a grin at his bashfulness. "What does your bathing suit look like? Do you need help putting it on?"

"Not a good idea with your teasing self. Let me get ready."

Denver left for his room, and Eliza sat at the bar to wait. Willow was wonderful, but he held his teasing in around her. If they were to see where their feelings might take them, she'd rather he tease her as much as he'd like.

A tap on her shoulder startled her. She faced Denver, who turned around. "Like it?"

"It's colorful. The flowers look like they came from Mama's garden."

At the dock, Denver took something called a "lifejacket" from a compartment on the boat and showed Eliza how to connect the straps around her. On the bank, they waded into the cool water, until the lifejacket lifted from her body. "What do I do?"

"Try swimming on your back." Denver pushed off into the water and turned onto his back. Kicking his feet, he paddled with his hands, creating small swirls of water beside him. "It's not hard." He returned to the bank. "Your turn."

Eliza repeated his motion. The water slipped past her as if she were a huge bird flying backward through the air while facing the sky. She stopped to touch bottom but couldn't and swam to Denver, who signed, "Is there anything you can't do? I bet you could swim without the lifejacket already."

"I was trying to fly like a bird through the water instead of the air. Remember when you taught me what 'imagine' means?"

"I remember."

"I do things by imagining them. I do it with my colors, too."

"You just imagine it?" Denver's eyebrows arched like a rainbow. "Most people have to work hard to learn new things.

You learned sign faster than I ever thought possible."

"When you show me a sign one time, I always see it in my head."

"That's because you have a photographic memory."

"What's 'photographic?'"

"It's another word for a picture. Having a photographic memory means you see something one time and it stays in your head like a picture."

"I see words in books but don't know how to say them."

"Words are a lot different than seeing something, but we went over some letter sounds with the words you remember. Have you learned any words with the letter sounds we went over?"

Eliza paused. She'd learned "I love you" so she could tell Denver that before he left after his first three months at the school. Now, since she had to leave instead of him, and she had no idea when, she shouldn't tell him unless he told her he loved her first. "I haven't tried any new words. Signs are good enough."

"I like signs, too. I've learned a lot more since I met you." Denver swam to a ladder hanging from the dock and climbed up. Eliza followed. At the end of the dock, he dove in. She admired his firm body, the way his muscles rippled in his legs and back as he sliced into the water. He surfaced for a moment and disappeared again. A bubbling swirl marked where his feet kicked.

Eliza unsnapped the lifejacket, dropped it to the dock, and repeated Denver's dive. The darkness beneath the water blurred her vision. A twinge of panic almost caused her to not imagine a bird flying across the sky in easy, steady strokes. She kicked toward the light at the surface and rolled onto her back to swim like Denver.

Denver joined her, swimming on his back also. "You scared

me. I was coming up when you dove in." Kicking, he raised his hands again. "Look at you, swimming just like me."

A huge bird, with a white underbody darkening at its wingtips, soared overhead. Denver turned his head to follow it, and Eliza slipped beneath the water's surface to pull him under by his feet. She surfaced and so did he. He whipped his head around, slinging water from his hair. They returned to their backs. Grinning, he signed, "You and your teasing."

"I'll stop for a kiss." Eliza lowered her hands into the water and raised them again. "I shouldn't sign things like that."

Denver swam closer. "We're just teasing. You know, like big kids. Don't worry about it, okay?"

Eliza flicked her hand in the water to splash him. "I'll try, if you forget about Jan while I'm here."

"Jealous?"

"Not if I kiss better than she does."

"I'll put it this way." Denver returned the splash. "You don't have anything to worry about."

"Does she swim?"

"She dog paddles mostly. She usually puts her hair up and wears a ski belt. She doesn't like to mess up her hair."

"Does 'dog paddle' mean swimming like a dog?"

"Pretty much."

"What's a ski belt?"

"It's a belt that helps you float, kind of like a life jacket. I'll give her a call and tell her to bring her suit in case we swim later. She wouldn't want you to make her look bad when she sees how you learned in one lesson."

"How would I make her look bad?"

"Some people think it makes them look bad when someone else does something better than them. In the south we call them 'high headed.'"

'High headed' described the boy Eliza had punched in the

nose. He thought he was better than her because he could hear.

Denver returned to the dock and waited. Eliza climbed the ladder. He took towels from a box built into the boat and gave her one. "I'll take these in to wash and put more back. We keep some on the boat in case someone wants to swim while we're out on the lake."

"Do you wash the lifejackets and ski belt?"

"We leave those on the boat in the compartment." "Ready to go in?"

"I want to lie in the sun."

The doorbell rang. Denver checked his watch—a little after five—and hurried down the hall. Jan must've left work early. She usually stayed until four, and it took over an hour and a half to drive from Raleigh.

The bell rang again. He opened the door and she glared at him. "It's about time. I leave work early for my swim suit and get caught in traffic anyway. Then you won't even let me in when I get here." She shoved by Denver and strode down the hall, high heels clicking on the hardwood floor.

"Hi, Jan," Denver said, not following. "Nice to see you, too."

She whirled around, compressed lips and narrowed eyes relaxing. "I'm sorry. Trying to get ready for the show Saturday has been a nightmare."

"How are the conservators doing with sealing and framing Eliza's paintings?"

"It's coming along. From old to new they show the progression of her work as it matured." Jan touched Denver's arm. "Would you believe the collector who bought the painting asked me to not advertise the show so he could choose first?"

"He was joking, right?" Denver hoped that was the case. It

wasn't fair to the other collectors, or Eliza, to not advertise.

"I wasn't sure," Jan said. "Needless to say, it's being widely advertised."

"Sounds great," Denver said. "Eliza's in the basement. She's working on a large oil painting with the supplies I bought. She says it'll be ready for the show."

"Really? As much as I love her work, I can't wait to see what she can do with proper paints."

"You won't be seeing this one until the show. She turns it around so Willow and I can't see it."

"She's secretive, I like that." Jan took a step toward Denver. "Do you forgive me for coming in here like a madwoman? I'm going in late tomorrow. That means we can snuggle on the couch after Willow and Eliza go to bed."

"You're under a lot of stress. I'll let you slide this time."

Jan kissed him. The familiar touch, which had excited him in the past, could've been the lips of a cold, dead fish.

She ended the kiss. "I think I smell steaks on the grill." She turned around. "What do you think of Willow's new guy?"

"I like him okay. I'm glad she had someone to hang out with while I was in Ohio."

Willow appeared at the other end of the hall. "Y'all gonna yack all day or help with supper?" She pointed a large knife their way, "Like now," and disappeared around the corner.

"I see your sister's her usual grouchy self," Jan said.

Denver headed down the hall. "She just wants this night to go well for Eliza. She thinks a lot of her."

Jan went to the counter, where Willow was filling bowls with chopped lettuce. "What can I do, Willow?"

Willow looked up and fingered a stray auburn curl behind her ear. "Hi, Jan. It sure is nice of you to go to all this trouble."

The muscles in the back of Jan's neck tightened, revealed by her hair up in a ponytail instead of how she usually wore it down for work. "Hi to you, too, Willow. Did anyone ever tell you your sarcasm is your best feature?"

"Did anyone ever tell you that shade of blonde looks better on a cat?" Willow snatched the knife off the counter and pointed it at Jan. "Maybe you'd like a pixie cut instead of a ponytail cut?"

Jan, her cheeks sunset red, faced Denver. "I don't have to take this kind of abuse after working so hard on Eliza's paintings, Denver Andrews."

Denver went to Willow and took the knife. "You two need to bury the hatchet for Eliza's sake. This night is so she can meet Jan."

"Is there a hatchet in the basement?" Jan said. "If you get it, I know *exactly* where to bury it."

"You can try," Willow hissed, "but that knife is sharp enough to skin your skinny behind."

"Whoa, whoa, stop all that," Denver said, waving his hands. "Mom and Dad would be ashamed of you both. It's like you're in high school again."

"I'm sorry, Den, but she—"

"*Me* nothing," Jan countered. "Like my sweetie said, we need to act like adults for Eliza's sake."

The sliding glass door opened. Mark, with a platter of sizzling steaks, came to the kitchen, got a roll of foil from a drawer, and wrapped the steaks. "What's all that handwaving about, Denver? It's like you were trying to put out a fire."

"Hey, Mark." Denver nodded toward Jan. "This is Jan. I'm sure Willow's told you about her."

Mark gave Jan a quick wave. "Hey, Jan, how's it goin'?"

"Your steaks smell great." Jan faced Denver. "I'd like to meet Eliza before we eat."

"Go ahead," Mark said. "I'll help Willow get everything ready."

At the bottom of the steps, Denver turned the lights on and off, the agreed upon signal so Eliza would know to turn the stand holding the painting. Barefoot, wearing jeans and the shirt he'd given her over one of his old T-shirts, she turned the stand and set the palette and a brush on a table. Her unbraided hair fell in loose waves down her back.

He started toward Eliza, but Jan placed her hand on his arm to stop him. "I couldn't tell how gorgeous she is from that painting. Should I be jealous?"

"C'mon, Jan, you could be a supermodel and you know it."

"Sure, but with all that black hair down to her bottom and that strong nose, she could pass for an Italian model. Doesn't matter. It'll make her that much more noticeable during the show."

They joined Eliza, and Denver signed, "This is Jan."

Jan offered her hand to Eliza while Denver translated. "It's nice to finally meet you. I'm looking forward to the show Saturday."

"Thank you," Eliza signed. "Thank you for all your help and for getting Jon in touch with Denver. None of this would have happened without you."

"I understand your mother is enjoying a new washer."

"She is."

"I don't know how she does without a dryer and a stove and a refrigerator." Jan's perfectly plucked blonde brows arched upward. "Oh, my, and a bathroom, too. I couldn't make it without a bathroom."

Signing and speaking at the same time, Denver said, "Absalom's still taking sign language classes. Jon's going to help him video chat while Eliza's here."

"That's nice." Jan said. "Let's eat."

"I'll help Eliza clean up. Be there in a few."

At the steps, Jan turned and tapped a long red fingernail to her lips. "Denver, come here a minute." Denver signed to Eliza that he'd be right back and went to Jan, who said, "Didn't I unbutton that shirt one night a few months ago when we were snuggling on the couch?"

"Eliza needed something to keep her clean. Go ahead, we'll be there in a minute."

Denver gathered the brushes and placed them in a jar half-filled with paint thinner. Even though he worked on the side of the painting that held the colors, he didn't look to avoid ruining Eliza's surprise.

She used a putty knife to scrape the paint from the palette into a trash can. He'd helped her before—once she trusted him to ignore the painting—and he enjoyed the quiet moments beside her, when she glanced between whatever work she was doing and him, sometimes sharing a lingering smile. How often did that happen with Jan? If ever?

She wiped the palette clean with a rag soaked in paint thinner, set it down and signed, "Jan's hair is very bright. Do you like yellow hair that's almost white?"

"Not necessarily."

"Did she kiss you when she came in?"

"A little one."

Eliza threw the rag in the trash. "Did you like it?"

"Not like I—"

She faced him, gray eyes stealing his words. Her hands found his, fingers entwining. Barely able to control the urge to kiss her, Denver eased his hands from hers. "Like I said, you don't have anything to worry about."

Eliza's lips curved into a sly grin. "I didn't think so." She washed her hands in a sink by the washing machine and dried them with paper towels. Denver did likewise.

On their way up the stairs, he realized a new Eliza was emerging—one confident, controlled, and not the least bit jealous of Jan like Jan was jealous of her. The thought pleased and saddened him at the same time. In his early teens, when puberty hit and high school girls caught his shy eye, he'd wondered what combination of woman he'd want to eventually marry, and Eliza, although she'd leave when they both least expected, fit that ideal.

In the kitchen, Jan was filling a plate at the counter. "What happened to being done in a few minutes?"

"It takes a while to clean up," Denver said, coming to the counter. He gave a plate with a steak and baked potato and a bowl with tossed salad to Eliza.

"Tea's on the table," Mark said. "I hope y'all like the steaks."

"And the potatoes," Willow said, signing. Denver translated to Eliza because she hadn't seen Willow's signs. She smiled and nodded in reply.

"I love the way you and Eliza talk." Jan took her plate to the table. "But I feel left out. You could say whatever you like and I'd be clueless."

"She mentioned your hair while we were cleaning up." Denver translated to Eliza and faced Jan again. "As you know, she has an eye for color. I think she found your shade of blonde interesting." He and Eliza sat opposite each other at one end of the table.

Willow snorted laughter. "It's interesting all right. I've seen that shade on a hair color box at the store."

Mark picked up a knife, shot Willow a disapproving look, and started cutting his steak. "Maybe you should apologize so Eliza doesn't think it's okay to make fun of people."

Mark's remark impressed Denver. Willow definitely needed to tone down her attitude concerning Jan.

"It's okay," Jan said. "I was young and mouthy once."

"When did you ever stop?" Willow said.

Denver had been translating everything to Eliza, whose eyes

darted between his hands and the faces of Jan, Mark, and Willow. The corners of her mouth were fighting with her cheeks to hold in a grin, and it was all Denver could do to not burst out laughing himself.

Mark looked up from his steak. "I think we all need a blessing. It's great how Eliza's life is changing, and I'd say we have a lot to be thankful for."

The blessing done, Denver signed it to Eliza, who signed, "Please tell Mark thank you."

He faced Mark. Eliza said to tell you—"

"What are you two going on about?" Jan blurted. "Don't you think it's impolite to talk when no one knows what you're saying?"

"Eliza asked me what Mark said during the blessing, and I signed how he hoped her show went well. She said to thank him."

"Steak's great," Willow said. "How's your crow, Jan?"

"Willow," Mark said, his tone low.

"All right, all right." Willow faced Jan. "Sorry about that. You know how we are, like oil and water."

"More like gas and a lit match," Jan said. "But I accept your apology anyway."

Denver continued the translation, and Eliza's mouth battled with her cheeks again. This time her crinkling eyes made Denver's fight to not laugh even harder. What a sense of humor she had, although a bit irreverent exactly like his. Denver held in a laugh again.

Stomach tight from the juicy beef, buttery potato, and delicious salad, Eliza went to the deck and leaned against the rail. Mark was wrapping leftovers, Willow was rinsing dishes, and Jan was drinking more tea at the counter.

Denver joined Eliza. A slight grin played at the corners of his mouth, and she signed, "What's so funny?"

"You make me smile, that's all."

"That's a different smile for you. I shouldn't tell you I like it but I do."

"I like smiling at you."

Eliza glanced inside; Jan was watching them. "Who do you like smiling at more, me or Jan?"

"Like I keep telling you, you have nothing to worry about."

"Then why is she your girlfriend? Don't you want a girlfriend who makes you smile like I do?"

Denver turned away. Time passed in one, two, three slow expansions of his chest. He faced her again. "I hate to bring it up, but you'll leave one day."

Eliza glanced inside again. Jan was gone. "I'm not sure I can do that."

"Your life is changing. Your family is learning sign language. Even your mama wants to make up for how she treated you."

Bees and yellow jackets, hornets and wasps—none could sting as much as the tears stinging Eliza's eyes. She turned away to calm herself. Stinging sensation gone, she faced Denver again. "I want to pretend none of that matters."

Jan opened the sliding glass doors. She wore a swimsuit that covered less than the bras and panties Eliza had bought, even less than the lace pair of panties she still hoped to surprise Denver with. The thick hair, pinned up in creamy, nearly white swirls, was ready for dog paddling. She kissed Denver's cheek, said something to him, smiled at Eliza, and went back inside.

Denver signed, "Jan said Willow's getting ready to swim. Mark can't, so he's drying dishes. Let's see how the water feels."

◈

Wearing swim trunks, Denver crunched along the gravel walkway to the dock, Eliza beside him. Willow sat near the ladder with her feet in the water. Jan, arms crossed, waited on the end. "It's about time. It's getting late and the water's cold."

Eliza took the ski belt from the boat compartment and gave it to Jan. Jan said something to Denver, who translated. "Jan wants to know how you knew she used a ski belt. I told her about me telling you this morning."

Beside Jan, Eliza dove in and surfaced to swim on her back. Willow followed her, while Denver waited until Jan buckled the ski belt. At the end of the dock, she dropped into the water and went under, leaving the ski belt on the surface. Coughing and sputtering, wet hair hanging in her face, she dog paddled to the ladder. "You and that dry rotted ski belt! I told you it could break if you didn't get a new one." She climbed the ladder and fingered hair from her eyes. "Just look at me. Now I've got to go home and fix my hair."

Denver said nothing, because nothing but laughter would come out if he did. Jan stomped toward the house. "O-o-o-oh!"

A girlish giggle floated across the now calm water. Eliza held a hand over her mouth, eyes crinkling. Willow splashed Denver. "I see you straining. Better laugh before you pee in the lake."

"Will you be quiet until Jan gets inside?" He swam toward the ladder. "Nothing's wrong with that ski belt. Dad replaced it last year." He took the ski belt from the water and checked the strap. "It looks like a mouse chewed the stitching on the inside of the buckle. How'd a mouse get in the boat?"

Willow climbed the ladder. "I don't know, but I need to leave him a treat."

Eliza followed Willow up the ladder, fingered hair from her eyes, then raised her hands. "Even a person who can't hear knew that was funny. She reminded me of a possum that fell from a tree into the river. When it finally made it to the bank, it was mad, too."

Denver signed and said, "I better check on her before she leaves. I want the show to go well Saturday."

Eliza waited until the sliding glass door closed behind Denver. Unable to hold her laughter in any longer, she dropped to the dock, rolled onto her back, and laughed until her sides ached.

"I agree," Willow signed. "That was funny."

Instead of signing, Eliza hugged her sides. The threat of laughter gone, she signed, "Since you frown when Jan is around, I can tell you."

"Slower, okay?"

"You frown at Jan, so I can tell you something."

"No! What did you do?"

Grinning and nodding, Eliza patted her chest and then signed, "I'm the mouse."

"You chewed the belt?"

"I chew sticks for paint brushes. Chewing thread is easy."

"Very funny, but why?"

"Denver said Jan is high headed."

"That's for sure. She's been a pain since she got here."

"It's our secret, okay? She could swim, so she wouldn't drown."

Willow nodded. "I have a secret for you, too."

"What is it?"

"It's a surprise for Saturday night, and I can't wait."

Chapter 29

Seated at the dresser in the guest room, Eliza kept still while Willow colored her cheeks a light pink with makeup. Willow returned the brush to the case she'd brought from her room and signed, "Wow, look at you."

Eliza loved signing with Willow, as if she were her sister. Maybe she and Tess could sign like this one day.

Willow pulled two lengths of hair from Eliza's temples and held them with one hand. At the back of Eliza's head, she fastened them with an oval silver clasp. She took a mirror from her case and held it so Eliza could see in the dresser mirror.

"I love it," she signed.

"One more thing, then the dress and shoes." Willow took a tube from the case and twisted it. The light pink color of lipstick, like on the women in the magazines Eliza had seen, glistened in the light above the dresser.

She finished applying the color, and Eliza held up her hands. "It matches my fingernails and toenails."

Willow dropped the lipstick in the case and took out a pencil. "Let's see how you like this."

On the sofa, Denver shook his head at his watch. Willow needed to finish whatever the heck she was doing to Eliza before she missed her own debut.

As far as getting ready for the fireworks, a cooler with sandwiches, water, and apples waited in the pontoon boat. Get home, change clothes, take off up the lake. Still, the Lakefest fireworks started around 9:30, and it'd be a struggle to thread the pontoon boat through the multitude of fellow fireworks watchers in their boats before the show began. Since it was Eliza's first time, he wanted to make it as special as possible, which meant getting as close to the launch site on the business bridge leading into Clarksville as possible. Her art show ran from six to eight, not much time to spare for the drive home. Even if he drove like a nut, Eliza might only get a distant view of the fireworks.

He hopped from the sofa to knock on the guest room door, but Willow stuck her head out before he got there. "I heard your big feet," she said. "Close your eyes so your absolutely gorgeous sign language student can surprise you."

"We're late, I've—"

"The longer you talk, the longer it'll take. I need to change clothes before Mark picks me up. We're going out to eat and meet his parents to watch the fireworks. Close your eyes."

"Doggone it, open—"

"So impatient, close your eyes."

"You're gonna make us late. Open the—"

"Don't make me call Jan and cancel."

Denver closed his eyes. "It's almost 4:30. We've got to get there in time to—"

Soft, warm lips touched his—Eliza's lips. He opened his eyes. Willow stood to the side grinning. Eliza, wearing a multicolored rainbow of a tie-dyed dress that fell to her ankles, with strappy sandals on her feet, held out her arms and twirled around. He stepped back to take in the whole of her in one intoxicating sight. The sandals were sexy, the dress was colorful, but what drew him in were Eliza's beautiful gray eyes, highlighted with the barest hint of liner. "Wow, Willybeans, great job. Not that she needed it."

"I didn't know about the kiss, but I think you liked it."

Ignoring Willow, Denver signed to Eliza, "You look great. Ready to go?"

"One more thing," Willow said. She ran to her bedroom and came back with a small shoulder bag and a handful of silver bangles. She hung the bag on Eliza's shoulder, slid three of the bangles on her right wrist, and took her own silver watch from her wrist and slipped it over Eliza's wrist. "Now you're ready."

Eliza opened her arms for a hug.

They separated, and Willow signed, "Have a great time. Make money so we can shop some more."

In the pickup, Denver signed, "Why did you kiss me? I don't want Willow to get the wrong idea about us."

"I was thanking you for everything, that's all." Eliza glanced behind the seat. "I'm glad you remembered my painting."

During the drive along highway 15 south, Denver tried to ignore the fact that Eliza might leave soon by keeping his mind blank. Regardless, by the time he took the exit onto interstate 85, leaving Oxford, North Carolina, his imagination interrupted with visions of Eliza's plane soaring into the sky above Raleigh-Durham International.

Cars filled the museum parking lot. He took one of the last available spaces in the overflow area and faced Eliza. "All these people are here to see you and your work. Are you nervous?"

She looked out her window and then his window. "I can't believe they like my colors this much."

"I'll stay with you to translate. People will want to talk."

"Are we late? I don't know how to tell time on Willow's

watch."

"A few minutes late. You look really great, but you always look great anyway."

"Willow's wonderful."

"She had a beautiful subject to work with."

Eliza's cheeks flushed, similar to a pinkening sky at sunset over the lake.

"Okay, we better go." Denver took the painting from the pickup.

When they rounded the corner to the front door, Jan stepped out of the double glass doors onto the white marble steps. "I can't believe you're late. All I've heard is 'where's our artist? Is something wrong? Is she sick? Did her car break down?' I tried your phone and Willow answered. You forgot that, too."

Denver topped the steps. "We had a safe drive, thanks for asking. Show me where we need to go."

Jan whirled and opened the door. Her high heels struck an aggravated beat across the white tile floor. She took a right through another door and continued down a hall. "This leads to an entrance at the rear of the Folk-Art gallery. The section where the painting will be displayed is curtained off. When we're ready, I'll step through and announce Eliza and open the curtain." She stopped at a door. "Got it?"

Denver signed everything to Eliza. Jan led them through the door and to a stand like the one in the basement. "Put the painting here and leave it covered. I want the buzz to build until the collectors just can't stand it."

Denver translated again. "Go to it, Jan, wow the crowd."

She slipped through the curtain. On the other side, the crowd's murmur rose. "Ladies and gentlemen, if you'll indulge me in quieting down for a moment, I'd like to say a few words. As you know, by strolling our gallery and studying our new artist's work, rarely are we gifted with such natural talent. Since

I've worked here at the Folk-Art gallery, I've never known an artist to have such a keen eye for nature, for life, and for her colors. Please welcome Miss Eliza Gray."

The curtain opened. The crowd of people that must number over a hundred applauded, many shouting "Hear, hear," and "bravo." Denver took Eliza's hand. Her fingers squeezed his while she followed him to where Jan stood, who was clapping also. He released Eliza's hand and stepped away to clap as well, smiling so large his cheeks ached. Eliza smiled, too, as brilliant as he'd ever seen. She'd come through so much in her life, overcome obstacle after obstacle, and now, after showing the world the colors of her outstanding talent, she was showing the world the colors of her heart.

The applause ended, and the crowd returned to its murmur, milling about while studying and remarking on Eliza's paintings, now framed and hanging around the room. Jan, who'd stepped away, returned with a tall man with gray hair tied in a ponytail. He also wore a gray handlebar mustache, a dark pin-stripe suit, and his nose took a pronounced bend to one side. Denver raised his hands to translate, and Jan said, "This is the collector who just couldn't wait to buy the painting when I showed it to him on my phone. Eliza, this is Walter D. Elliott, your biggest fan."

The man nodded. "Please tell the young lady I'm known as Dave to my closest friends."

Denver translated to Eliza, who signed, "I'm happy you like my colors."

Dave's eyebrows shot to an arch. "'Like?' Not at all, not at all, I'm completely infatuated with them." Twirling one side of his mustache, he studied the covered painting. "I'm dying to know what's under this cloth." He faced Eliza again. "You haven't had a chance to look around, but almost half your work is marked as sold to me. I currently have an architect designing a wing for my home in New York. Your paintings, along with select others from other Amish artists, will be displayed there."

Eliza signed, "Do you have any of Jonathan Raber's work?"

"I certainly do. His abstracts fascinate me, although I fail to understand what two or three even are." Dave glanced around the crowd. "I need to ask him about them when he's through telling the story of how you came to meet this handsome young sign language teacher in Ohio. Remarkable story, remarkable story. I've taken up enough of your time, Eliza. I should see if anything else catches my eye."

Dave left, arm-in-arm with Jan, and Eliza signed, "He's a nice man."

"A nice man with a lot of money," Denver signed. "After this show alone, you can buy that pickup for your papa, plus a solar grid for the farm and who knows what else."

Eliza poked Denver's stomach. "You know Papa was joking."

The next hour, several more collectors introduced themselves to Eliza and chatted with her about her work. Jan joined them. "Denver, the crowd is simply buzzing as I had hoped. Everything's sold and it's time to unveil Eliza's very first oil."

Denver signed to Eliza, who replied, "I want everyone to close their eyes."

Jan frowned at the translation. "Whatever in the world for?"

"I don't know," Denver said, "but the quicker you tell them, the quicker they'll see the painting."

"I see no need to get huffy about it."

"Just tell them, okay?"

Jan faced the crowd and clapped her hands. "Ladies and gentlemen, the moment we've all been waiting for is here."

The crowd faced her. Their voices quieted.

"As we know, artists can have their quirks. That's

understandable—that's part of what makes them artists. Eliza has requested we all close our eyes while she removes the cover from her painting. If you please ..." She faced Denver and closed her eyes. "There you go."

Eliza kissed Denver's cheek. "I wanted you to see this first because you inspired it. Even though I wouldn't be here if it weren't for Jan and Jon, I wouldn't be here if it weren't for you. I don't share my colors with just anyone." She placed her hand over his heart. "These colors, I mean." She removed the cloth from the painting—an exact copy of the painting she'd given him—but two figures stood in the path through the woods instead of one.

Denver touched the figures. "I'd know you anywhere. Who's that?"

Eliza smacked his arm. "You don't recognize yourself in the shorts and T-shirt you wore when it got warm in Ohio? Maybe my talent isn't as good as all these people think it is."

"Are we signing? We're sort of facing each other with our hands up." He pointed to a huge sun, glowing red and half-set at the end of the road behind a horizon filled with sparse clouds. "Why the sunset?"

"It's a sunrise. My painting shows two new beginnings. One is when you taught me my first word, and the other is when you held me while I cried. Between your teaching me and your arms around me, my heart felt as if it were a sun rising that day."

"It's great, Eliza, *really* great. I hope you get a good price for it."

"Unless you sell it—and you better not—that won't happen. You can hang it in your room in place of the one Willow hung in the living room."

Denver touched the raised oil paint again. Instead of pieces of leaf and mud, Eliza had painted the woods with leaves of all sizes and shapes in brilliant greens and shadowed browns, including gray tree trunks and hanging vines. "I don't care what Willow says, this stays in my room."

In the waiting crowd, someone coughed, and Jan whispered, "What's going on back there?"

Eliza kissed Denver's cheek again. "Good. I like to think a part of me is always with you."

Denver tapped Jan's shoulder. "She's ready."

"It's about time," she hissed. "Okay, everyone, Eliza's ready."

The crowd opened their eyes and edged closer. "Oohs" and "Ahs" came from several people in front.

Someone tapped Denver's back. He turned to face Jon, who patted his shoulder. "How's it going, Denver?"

"Hey, Jon, it's going great."

Jon opened his arms to Eliza, who hugged him. Hug finished, he faced Denver. "I still haven't had time to learn many signs yet. Tell Eliza how proud I am of her, and how much I love her paintings. I bought the one with the raccoon sitting in the bowl of a tree with her kits. I wanted the portrait of Absalom plowing with his horse, but someone beat me to it."

"Thank you," Eliza signed. "I didn't know you were coming."

"I couldn't miss your first show. Your papa asked me to tell you he's practiced with my laptop and can chat with you online now. We're all in awe of how quickly you learned sign language."

"That's because Denver's a good teacher."

"I like your dress and bangles. I think I see a little makeup, too. Who helped with all that?"

"Willow. She's Denver's sister."

"She has wonderful taste, but you're the perfect canvas."

"She sure is," Denver said, translating for Eliza at the same time. "How's Akina doing?"

"Three more students showed up. She and Dan are doing fine."

"I'm glad his girlfriend didn't mind him staying."

"A few days after you left, she dumped him like the proverbial hot potato. Like I said, he and Akina are doing fine. She really knows how to make a person feel welcome with her funny mix of Marine discipline wrapped up in her petite self. Dan's used to it. He left the Marines recently himself."

Denver leaned near Jon. "Eliza and I have plans. Can you distract Jan so we can get out of here?"

"Be glad to." He faced Eliza. "Make sure Denver gets you in bed at a decent time."

"Don't worry," Eliza signed, "I will."

Jon took Jan's arm, pointed toward the paintings on the far wall, and steered her away. Beside Denver and Eliza, people were gathering around Eliza's oil painting, discussing the lack of a price tag. "Excuse me," Denver said, "this isn't for sale." He slipped the cover over the painting. "But thank you for enjoying Eliza's work."

In the pickup, Denver hit the accelerator. The tires squealed, but the seatbelts kept him and Eliza from sliding across their seats. Taking the exit ramp onto interstate 85, he finally looked at her. She laughed and signed, "You must really like those fireworks."

Chapter 30

Denver parked in front of the house. "I'll grab my painting later. Didn't Willow give you an old pair of shorts and a few T-shirts?"

"She did."

"Good, meet you in the living room."

Denver traded his suit and necktie for shorts, a T-shirt, and sandals. He started out the door, but Jan's violin ringtone from his phone on the nightstand stopped him. As he checked the screen, Eliza came in, wearing cut-off blue jean shorts and a white T-shirt that showed her middle. "Did Jan call? You're frowning like you did when she met us at the museum."

"Don't worry, I'm not answering." Denver left the phone on the nightstand. "Let's go."

They untied the pontoon boat and dropped to the sofa-sized seat behind the steering console. Denver flipped the switches for the running lights—white at the rear, red and green at the front. Outboard cranked, transmission in forward, throttle at a quarter speed, the boat started away from the dock. Seconds later, the engine sputtered and stalled.

"What's wrong?" Eliza signed. "We're slowing down."

Denver turned the ignition off. "I'm not sure." He flipped the rear lights on that shined down from the metal roof, and Eliza joined him at the outboard. "Here's the problem," he signed. "The gas valve is turned off." He twisted it on. "That should do it."

He and Eliza returned to the seat. She pointed up the lake and signed, "What are all the lights?"

"That's all the people waiting to see the fireworks. They look like red, white, and green lightning bugs, don't they?"

"A rainbow of lightning bugs reflecting on the water. I'd love to paint them one day."

Denver glanced at his watch. "We need to go before the fireworks start."

Ten minutes later, as they neared the bypass bridge that arched over the lake, the first rocket shot into the sky. At its apex, it exploded with a huge, concussive boom. Denver killed the engine, and Eliza signed, "Is that why we're here? I could feel it in my chest like thunder."

"The best is on the way."

Another rocket flared upward, then another and another, all climbing high into the night sky on trails of fading fire. Seconds apart, each exploded in huge balls of blue, red, green, or white streams of sparks, like umbrellas of lightning bugs in rainbow colors, each winking out in turn.

Denver started to ask Eliza what she thought but didn't. Eyes bright with the reflection of the fireworks, blinking with each new explosion, she clutched her hands to her chest.

Watch the fireworks or watch Eliza? What a dumb question. He could see the fireworks next year, but he'd never get the chance to watch Eliza's child-like expression of wonder again.

A ball of sparks filled the night sky, a gigantic chrysanthemum of brilliant blue petals, intensely burning with life, then dying all too soon. Eliza clapped, smiled at him, and continued to watch.

The mix of emotions—the enjoyment of watching her and the realization of how he would lose her soon—made him return to the fireworks. Either that or break down into a blubbering mess.

About fifteen minutes into the thirty-minute show, Eliza rested her head on his shoulder. More of the large explosions, which had boomed at the beginning, came and went every few minutes. A particularly loud one vibrated Denver's eardrums. Eliza placed her hands over her ears and lowered them. "I could feel it my ears."

About to sign "me too," Denver lowered his hands. Could Eliza feeling the explosion in her ears mean hearing aids or a cochlear implant could help her condition? His research into the Deaf in the Amish community said their denial of technology meant they didn't allow those things. Of course, using those things—if she ever had the chance—was up to her.

The rocketing missiles stopped—the pause before the grand finale—followed by at least a dozen rockets blasting upward, to explode simultaneously in reds, blues, greens, and brilliant whites, including several of the loud blasts as earlier. The bitter aroma of burnt explosives drifted on the air. Except for the multitude of white, red, and green lights on boats dotting the water, darkness returned to the lake.

"Is that all?" Eliza signed.

"That's it, see all the boats coming this way? I'll move us behind one of the bridge pilings and wait before we go home." Denver dropped anchor and returned to sit by Eliza. "Do I have to ask if you liked it or not?"

"It was more than I imagined." She yawned. "It's been a long day."

Ski craft, pontoon boats, houseboats, and fishing boats passed. Multiple wakes rocked Denver's boat up and down, and Eliza giggled. "Does this make you feel like you're flying on a plane?"

"Would you hold my hand if it did?"

"Do you want me to?"

Denver slipped his arm around her shoulders. "I'd rather do

this."

Eliza pulled his other hand to her lap, wrapped her hands around it, and rested her head on his shoulder.

The boats continued by, some roaring with large engines, some whining with smaller engines, all trailing the gassy aroma of exhaust. The waves lessened as the various craft dwindled. Disappearing up and down the lake, their lights faded into flickers of white, red, and green.

Denver closed his eyes. Eliza cuddled into him further, warm yet firm at the same time. Nothing could be better than this. Absolutely nothing.

The lake gradually calmed. Except for the occasional roll and thump of vehicles passing over the bridge joints overhead, the night quieted. Denver opened his eyes. Eliza's eyes were closed, and her chest rose and fell with the rhythm of sleep. He could get used to this, to her, to her excitement at newfound joys, to her calm when she enjoyed quiet moments, to how she teased him with their mutual idea of humor.

Did they have a chance to be together? Denver clenched his teeth hard enough to bite a fishhook in two. Why keep asking that when her family would shun her if she married him? And when, if he became Amish, their prohibition against technology meant he couldn't live the life he wanted, including driving or flying to see Willow again, made even worse with Mom and Dad gone?

Eliza stirred against him, moaning softly, and opened her eyes. "Was I asleep?" she signed.

"A few minutes. I guess we should go."

Denver steered the boat toward the middle of the lake and eased the throttle back to a slow and easy cruise, wavelets lapping, motor gurgling. The night couldn't be clearer. Out here, away from the lights of Clarksville, stars filled the sky with an endless blanket of sparkling, winking, pinpoints of light. Clusters creamy, hints of cat-eye green, suggestions of seductive pink, alluring ambers and aquamarine slipstreams gave shape and form to the Milky Way.

Eliza.

Strong profile, stronger soul. Heart of a dreamer, an artist, a lover.

The sky and stars had nothing—absolutely nothing—on Eliza. She was nature personified; she exuded self; she exuded confidence; she was a creature of the night—completely untamable.

The lights on the dock burned into view, an end to her magic.

Eliza's gray eyes found Denver's. "Can't we stay and watch the stars?"

"Sure." Denver killed the engine. "We can eat our sandwiches, too."

The pontoons settled into the lake, gliding along with the barest whisper of water on metal. Ahead of the driver's console, Denver opened the cooler and fished around in the ice to take out two waters and two bagged sandwiches. He turned to give Eliza her supper, but she was standing beside the extra-wide seat in front of the outboard, back to him, head tilted up to the stars. She faced him and signed, "I wish we could stay all night."

"I've done it before." Denver took a roll of paper towels from a compartment beneath the seat and placed their sandwiches beside him, out from beneath the metal roof where she could watch the stars between bites and sips. He took in a breath of the warm July air, tinted with the gray aroma of the lake. "The fresh air made me sleep like a baby."

Eliza sat. "Can we sleep out here? Please?"

"That might not be a good idea. You know, with our kiss and how you'll have to leave soon."

Eliza slipped off her sandals and stood. About to take a bite of the sandwich, Denver's mouth hung open as she strode to the front of the boat, black hair down to her waist, shapely legs glowing in the lights overhead. She clicked the front gate latch and swung the door open. "Food later, I want to swim."

Tugging the waistband of his shorts, Denver joined her. "Sorry, no flowery swim trunks."

She jerked his cargo shorts to his ankles. "You don't need them." She unsnapped her cut-off jeans, kicked them free when they fell, and whirled around to reveal a pair of barely-there sheer lace panties covering her bottom, with a narrow waistband riding high on her hips. "If I can swim in my panties and bra, you can swim in your underwear.

Denver couldn't look away, but he did manage to raise his hands. "This is worse than teasing. You're a bad woman—a *very* bad woman."

"Is my body bad?" Eliza pulled her T-shirt over her head. The bra's lace cups matched the panties. "Do you like my new bra?"

"Well … yeah, but—"

She reached behind her back as if she were undoing the clasp. "Would you like it better if I took it off?"

Denver closed his eyes. There was no way he could deal with this exquisite young woman's nearly naked body right in front of him. *And* within reach. "Eliza, this isn't right. Put your clothes back on, okay?"

Eliza tapped his nose. He opened one eye, and she signed, "I love the silky feel of the night air on my skin." She neared the open gate. "You don't have to look, just be here beside me."

"Not until you get dressed."

"Please? All I want is to swim."

Despite the innocence in her gray eyes, Denver didn't know whether to believe her or not. One quick swim, climb back on the boat, eat their sandwiches, and get the heck back home before something happened beyond her teasing. Watching the stars instead of her, he kicked his sandals and shorts off.

She raised her hands in front of his face. "Raise your arms. You need the night air on your chest."

"One quick swim, that's it."

"Raise your arms before I tickle your ribs."

"Okay, okay." Denver raised his arms. She pulled his shirt over his head, then raised her hands in front of his face again.

"Doesn't that feel nice? "she signed.

"It's okay. Let's—"

She stepped away from the open gate and shoved him through it into the lake. He splashed and came up sputtering. Eliza dove in and came up beside him. She wiped hair from her eyes and the water from her face and signed, "The things I have to do to get you to swim with me. I hope your underwear didn't come off."

"Did yours? They weren't much to start with."

Eliza lowered her hands, then raised them. "All there." She looked into the sky. "What happened to the stars?"

Denver pointed. "The moon is rising. It's hard to see the stars when it's full."

Eliza swam away from the boat, her dark form joining the path of moonlight shimmering on the lake. Denver swam hard to catch up. They swirled around each other, grinning, splashing, laughing.

The moonlight dimmed, and Eliza signed, "Clouds are ruining our swim."

They swam to the boat, toweled dry and dressed, and returned to their sandwiches and water.

The meal done, Denver signed if she wanted an apple. She signed "No" and leaned back on the seat to touch her forehead. "It's raining."

Denver stuck his hand out; cold drops wet his palm. "Sure

is, we better head in."

In the driver's seat again, Eliza beside him, he turned the ignition key. The boat cranked and stalled like earlier. "Can you make sure the gas valve is open all the way?" he signed. "I was in a hurry when I opened it before."

By the outboard, she signed, "I can't turn it anymore."

Denver twisted the key. The starter whined, but the outboard refused to start. "Looks like you'll get your wish to sleep out here." To save the battery, he turned all the lights off except the red, green, and white running lights. "The rain is making it chilly." He took several towels from a compartment and gave Eliza one. "We can use these as blankets when we feel like sleeping."

Eliza wrapped the towel around her shoulders. She and Denver sat in the driver's chair like before.

In the dim circle of red and green light on the front of the boat, the rain dotted the lake's surface with increasing intensity.

"I wish I could hear the rain." Eliza's hands faltered. "I'd like to have children one day. But …"

The weight of her regret silenced Denver. She wanted to be able to hear her children say "I love you, Mama." He'd never seriously considered the idea of having children, but Eliza made him love the idea. He raised his hands. "When I got interested in sign language, I researched the causes of deafness. Some can't be helped, but some can."

Eliza's hands split the air between them. "You mean I could hear? How?"

"A doctor would decide."

"Decide what?"

"What might help, like hearing aids. Sometimes a cochlear implant can help.

"An implant? Does it hurt?"

"I don't know. I've seen videos on the internet of children

and adults—even babies hearing the first time using them and hearing aids. I loved their reactions. The adults usually cried. The kids' and babies' eyes lit up like nothing I've ever seen." Denver paused. "That's not true. Your eyes lit up like that when you learned your first sign."

"You mean before I cried in your arms. I'll always remember that. It—you—changed my life."

Their hands stilled. Denver slipped his arm around Eliza again. She snuggled her warmth into him again, too.

The rain's intensity dwindled to a light patter on the metal roof—a sound Denver always enjoyed—but a cold breeze sprang up, chilling him as well as Eliza, who shivered.

He eased away from her and signed, "We better get under those towels and get some sleep."

He took all the towels from the compartment, spread two on the scratchy outdoor carpeting that lined the boat's floor, and folded two towels for pillows. On his back, Denver pulled a towel over him. Facing him, Eliza did the same, then pressed herself—from her toes to her legs to her chin on his shoulder— into the full length of his body. She shivered once, twice, and once more. Warmth grew between them. The softness of her breath in his ear fell into the rhythm of dreams.

As if sleep were a black road illuminated with undeniable facts, it escaped Denver. If he ever doubted his love for this amazing woman, who slept with herself wrapped around him, he doubted it no more. Not only did he love her, he was *in* love with her, which was a huge difference in anything he'd ever felt for Jan. Unlike with Jan, being *in* love meant never wanting to be apart, the desire to share and uplift, and the need to live dual goals of happiness, more so for the other person instead of yourself.

Time after time, Eliza had given him hints that she loved him—so many that there was no need to torture himself with remembering them.

Who knew when she might leave? When she did, his ideals of love—and her—would be gone as quickly as he'd found them.

Chapter 31

Eliza awoke. Denver had rolled away from her during the night. She stood and stretched, breathing in the crisp air that included a tinge of warmth due to the sun rising just above the trees in the distance across the lake. At the outboard, she opened the gas valve. She didn't like lying, but since she didn't know how long she and Denver had together, she wanted to be with him as much as possible. Preferably alone.

Lying beside him again, she buried her face into his neck. His hair tickled her nose. The watery aroma of the lake from their swim filled her.

She loved him more than signs could say. When she mentioned having children, she immediately imagined him at her side, holding the hand of their son or daughter. The choice she must make when Papa asked her to come home careened in her thoughts like a pair of bulls battling over a cow—curved horns battering, bodies straining for advantage, clouds of dust rising from cloven hooves.

Like the cloud enveloping the fighting pair, a cloud of sadness enveloped her. Go against Papa's wishes or not? A tear slipped down her cheek. She *had* to try, or life wasn't worth living. She shoved the tear away with the palm of her hand.

Denver blinked and yawned. Propped on elbow, she signed, "Did you know you sound like a bull mating a cow while you sleep?"

"Yeah?" Denver rubbed his eyes. "You must mean I snore,

because I have no idea what a bull sounds like when he mates a cow." He tapped her nose. "And neither do you."

"Remember how I imagine things? I've seen it so I can imagine it. Do I have to tell you how impressive it is?"

"Can your imagination tell you how hungry I am? I'll check the motor again in case I missed something." Eliza went with him to the back of the boat, where he turned the gas valve. "Didn't you sign it was open?"

"I thought the other way was open."

Denver sat at the console and turned the key. The motor started on the third try. Eliza sat beside him. "Now we can have breakfast."

At the dock, he hopped out and tied the ropes to the cleats on the graying boards. "I'll get the cooler later."

Inside the living room, Eliza signed, "I need the bathroom. "Then you can show me how to make an omelet."

"I'll check my phone first. Jan's probably left a million messages about us sneaking out on her."

Done in the bathroom, Eliza found Denver sitting on his bed, staring at the phone in his hands. She went inside. "Is anything wrong?"

"Jan surprised me when she made my trip to Ohio possible by getting me in touch with Jon. She just surprised me again by saying our leaving early was brilliant, especially since we took the painting. Even though the crowd only got a quick look, those who saw it want oil reproductions of the paintings they already bought." Denver dropped the phone on the bed and stood. "You, my very special student, are a success. You know what that means?"

"I better paint after we eat?"

"Only If you want to."

"I love my new colors."

Denver started to the door and stopped, then went back for

his phone and dropped to the bed.

"Is it Jan again?" Eliza signed.

Denver signed nothing.

"Denver, who is—"

"It's your papa."

Chapter 32

Denver waited for Eliza's reaction. A perfect night together—even more perfect because of the gas valve misunderstanding—and Absalom might want her to come home already?

Eliza sat beside him. "Papa doesn't have a cell phone."

"It's Becca's number."

"How do you know it's him?"

"He said so."

"Jon said Papa can chat on the computer. Maybe he wants to know how the show went."

Denver read the short text, then signed, "He's setting up an online chat for …" He glanced at his nightstand clock. "It's 8:40 now. He'll be ready at nine."

Eliza's head dropped. Denver's head dropped. Those twenty minutes might as well be a countdown to the end of the world.

Absalom shouldn't ask her to come home now. Eliza's success meant she needed to stay and work to build on that success. If anyone knew the importance of a responsible work ethic, her Amish dad did. "Maybe you're right," Denver signed. "He probably wants to know about the show and that's it."

Twin butterflies, wings broken, fluttered upward from Eliza's lap. "Maybe."

"He shouldn't see us on my bed." Denver took his laptop from his desk and went to the dining room table. Eliza sat beside him.

Denver opened the laptop and signed in. The time on the lower corner—less than fifteen minutes left—made him turn away.

Through the sliding glass doors, the sun glistened on the lake. What he wouldn't give to be paddling his old canoe to the sandy beach tucked between the two walls of crumbling rock, Eliza in the front, looking over her shoulder and smiling at him. Wait until dusk. Watch the sun set. Make plan after plan after—

She touched his hand. "Your eyes are far away."

"I was daydreaming."

"Am …" Her hands faltered, a question hanging between them.

"You can ask, Eliza. You can ask me anything."

"Am I part of your dream? I know we talked about how we can't be together, but you're still part of my dream." Her hands slowed, then flashed through the air. "Giving it up might kill me."

"We all dream, Eliza. Before you learned how to sign, I'm sure you dreamt of being able to communicate with your family, and now you can. Don't you want to feel like you're part of them?"

"Like you do with Willow." Eliza's hands paused. "Yes, I would like to have that with my family."

"Your mama, too? Have you forgiven her for how she treated you?"

"All those years of making me work while never acting like a real mama is hard to forgive. Sometimes, when I try to put myself in her place, I understand how losing a child she loved so much could make her act like that. Then again, it wasn't like I could use words to say I loved her like a hearing child. When Ethan and Tess were born, I see why she acted like she loved them more, even if she didn't."

Eliza's growth as a person—not that Denver doubted her—

fulfilled his faith in her. How could he let her go?

The laptop screen flared to life with Absalom sitting in a chair, Jon and Becca's coffeemaker over his shoulder. "There you are," he said. He raised his hands. "I miss you, Eliza." He moved the laptop to one side. "Denver, I don't know all the signs. Please tell Eliza what I'm saying. Look who made the buggy ride to Jon's house yesterday."

To Absalom's right, Oneita sat, Ivy in her arms. He moved the laptop again. To his left sat Ethan and Tess. Absalom shoved the laptop away, widening the view. Simultaneously, except for Oneita, everyone raised their hands to their forehead with the "hello" sign. Oneita couldn't because she was raising Ivy's chubby hand to the baby's smooth forehead with the "hello" sign, too.

Silver teardrops ran down Eliza's cheeks. She raised her hands. "Look at you all, you make—" Smiling, she wiped her eyes. "You make me so happy."

"What did she say, Denver?" Tess said. "I'm still learning."

Denver translated, and Tess said, "Good. She needs to be happy from now on."

Denver translated again. Eliza laughed and pointed at Tess. "You're right. Are you and Ethan getting along?"

Ethan leaned his head in front of Tess's. "She doesn't like how I'm learning sign language faster than her. Papa ordered books online for us."

Oneita handed Ivy to Absalom. "Hello, Eliza, I miss you, too," she signed perfectly. Her hands hung in midair. She covered her face. Her shoulders shook. Soft sobs escaped her.

Denver said nothing. Eliza's mom had obviously come to terms with how she'd treated her daughter for all those years.

Absalom gave her a napkin, and she wiped her eyes. "Denver, can you sign for me?"

"Let me tell Eliza first." Denver signed this to Eliza, who

nodded.

"I wanted to talk to you before you left, but I didn't want to upset you. Please forgive me, Eliza. You're every bit as wonderful as your sister would've been. More than anything I want to make up for all the time I wasted in not seeing that."

Absalom returned Ivy to Oneita. "I need you to sign again for me, too, Denver. I have a lot I want to say."

"I will." Denver translated to Eliza. As he finished, her chin trembled.

"Can you give us a few minutes?" Denver said. "I'd like some water."

"Go ahead."

Denver muted the chat and turned the camera off. Eliza covered her face with her hands. Denver stood to lift her by her shoulders. She rose slowly, her entire body shaking and shuddering. He wrapped his arms around her and rocked her.

She lowered her hands from her face, wrapped her arms around him, and buried her face into his neck. Warm tears soaked him from her violent sobs. Those gradually eased also, but she still clung to him. "Deevrr, I … I …"

He pulled away and took her face in his hands so she could read his lips. "Tell me."

"I can't."

"It's okay, you can tell me."

She jerked away, shaking her head so hard that her hair flew about her face. A second passed, then another. She took several steps across the room, turned and came back, stalking like a black-maned lion at the zoo in Asheboro, North Carolina. Head down, the lion huffed hard breaths. Narrowed gray eyes searched for an escape.

"Nooooooooooo!"

The shrill shriek echoed in the room, bounced from the peaked ceiling, careened down the hall and back.

Denver took her hand but she pulled away. "You don't know," she signed, hands slashing the air.

Denver stepped close, took her face in his hands again, lifted her eyes to his. "Tell me."

She shook her head within his hands, shook it again, shook it once more.

He pulled his hands away and signed, "Trust me—don't you trust me?"

Face twisted, tears streaming, she signed nothing, and Denver understood why. If she admitted to loving him—and had to leave—she was afraid of the pain they each would suffer. He had to make her understand. Had to let her know he believed in her. Had to let her know that somehow, some way, they belonged together.

Once more he placed his hands to her cheeks. He kissed her forehead, the tip of her nose. He kissed her lips, salty from her tears, just enough so his mouth upon the exquisite smoothness of hers would tell her how much she meant to him.

He ended the kiss and waited until she opened her eyes.

"I love you, too."

Chapter 33

Eliza recognized the words on Denver's lips—the words she'd waited for so long to see.

He loves me, too!

Her heart filled and emptied. Her soul sang and cried. Her colors bloomed into rainbow brilliance. Then slowly, painfully, filled with more grief and heartache than she'd ever felt in her entire life, they withered into drab and dreary grays.

"I can't … I can't …" She clenched her hands into fists, then signed, "I can't stay."

Denver took her hands, kissed them, released them to sign, "We'll work it out."

"I don't know how. We already talked about it."

"I don't know how either but I'm not giving you up when I just found you," he signed, hands cutting the air.

"Like I just found my family."

"They'll understand, Eliza, they've got to."

"I can't—we can't—" She shook her head. "Papa's waiting."

Eliza returned to the table, snatched napkins from the holder, and wiped her eyes. Denver started to turn the laptop, but she grabbed his arm and released it to sign, "Don't say anything about us. Can you do that for me?"

"I can, but—"

She grabbed his hands and released them. "If he asks me to come home, I have to go."

"Can't we at least try? They'll understand if we tell them how much we love each other."

"That doesn't matter."

"What? You can't mean—"

Again, she grabbed his hands and released them. "Turn the computer."

Denver placed his hand on the laptop, hesitated, then turned it toward them.

"We're back," Eliza signed.

Absalom's deeply tanned crow's feet splayed deep chasms at the corners of his eyes. "Denver, why are Eliza's eyes red?"

"She's … she's tired from the show. We came home late."

"I still need to talk to her."

Denver raised his hands.

"I'm happy for you, Eliza. Jon got home this morning and said most of the people at your show want copies of your paintings in oils, especially Mr. Elliot. Jon's making a list of everything you need, and I'm going to turn the basket making shop into an art studio. Tess said I should make the window bigger so you can see the woods. Ethan said I should make the path wider so you can see the river. Your mama said I could install a propane heater if Bishop Marley agrees. We miss you and want you to come home."

"When?"

"Do you need to stay and catch up on your work? It'll be a week or so before I finish your studio."

"I'll leave as soon as I can."

Denver's hands stilled in midair. He pushed his chair away from the laptop and jerked his hands up. "He said you can stay. Why can't you stay?"

"You promised not to say anything. Tell Papa what I sign."

"But—"

Eliza jerked the chair back. "Denver is catching a cold and he didn't want you to see him sneeze. I'll come home when I can."

Denver translated, she closed the laptop, and he jumped from the chair. "You've got to give us a chance, Eliza. We can make it work. Don't you … please tell me you believe me."

Cringing at the pain in the hesitation in his signs, Eliza went to the guest room, took a credit card from the purse Willow had given her, and returned to the table to drop the card beside the laptop. "Buy me a plane ticket for tomorrow morning. When you know what time I'll get to the airport in Ohio, call Jon so he can pick me up."

Denver collapsed into the chair. Eliza turned to leave, but Denver grabbed her arm. "Why are you leaving when you don't have to? I want to show you my favorite places. There's a sandy beach across the lake where I like to watch the sun set. We could hike in the park over there. We could rent a cabin there. We could— Don't you love me?"

Eliza pulled his head to her stomach. Forehead down, he refused to hold her. Curly hair, earthen brown, a dream turned nightmare. His shoulders heaved. His head shook. Hot tears fell to her sandaled feet.

All she wanted was to stay, to love him, to marry him, to have his children. Their colors would create a painting beyond imagination.

She slowly pulled away. "I *do* love you. I think I may have loved you ever since you taught me my first word and held me at the schoolhouse."

"Go home and come back. We'll see each other when we can."

"It would hurt even more every time I left. Then we would want to get married, and that would mean never seeing my family again."

Eliza forced herself to walk—not run—to the guest room. She stopped at the door. The next words she signed to Denver would kill her.

"Jan will make you happy."

She started to close the door. Instead, she faced the man she loved more than life itself, possibly for the last time.

"I can't."

Chapter 34

Denver purchased a plane ticket for 11 a.m. tomorrow, texted Jon the arrival time, and shoved the credit card beneath the guest room door.

His stomach growled. No, he would throw the first bite of food up. A spasm of pain squeezed his chest. No, a heart attack would be too easy a way out of this mess. He dropped to the sofa and glanced at his watch. He and Eliza would be alone until Willow got back from camping with Mark and his parents. Better get himself into some semblance of normal.

A shower—hot or cold—who cared. Toweled dry, he forced a comb through his hair, then dressed to wait on his bed. The green numbers on the nightstand clock changed. Changed again. Changed again. Eliza opened the door. Raising his hands, he refused to face her. "Your flight's in the morning at eleven." She closed the door.

Willow and Mark came home around four and asked Denver if he and Eliza wanted to go out to eat with them. She also asked how the show and the fireworks went. Denver said everything went well, that Eliza had a headache, and for them to go ahead.

At six he made toast and threw it in the trash. Eliza never came out of the guest room.

On his bed, he watched the nightstand clock. Willow wasn't

stupid. He waited for her to come home and the inevitable knock on his door.

The clock read 7:35, 8:00, 8:40. A single car door slammed. The front door thudded closed. Footfalls passed his door and stopped, maybe near Eliza's door, and came back to his door. "I'm back, Den. Can I come in?"

"It's not locked."

Willow opened the door. "What's going on with you and Eliza? I knocked on her door but she won't answer."

"C'mon, Willow, really?"

"What? Oh, I forgot she's deaf. Pretty dumb, huh?"

Denver said nothing.

"Sorry about that, I don't always see the obvious. Still, what's going on with you two?"

"We're fine."

"Tell that to someone besides your sister. I'd ask if you fought about something, but you get along better with Eliza than you ever do with Jan."

"She and her dad got in touch on my laptop. He wants her to come home."

"That still doesn't explain—"

"We're just tired from last night, okay?"

"Are you sure?"

"I need some sleep." Denver rolled over. "I'm driving Eliza to the airport in the morning."

"You're gonna sleep in your clothes?"

"I'll change in a minute."

"I'm sure Eliza hates to leave as much as you hate to see her leave. You two really do get along better then you and Jan. I'm going to town for groceries first thing. If you leave before I get back, tell Eliza I'd like her to stay anytime she has a show." Willow closed the door.

Denver turned the lamp off. Except for the faint green glow

of the LED clock, the room resembled the middle of the lake on a moonless, starless night. In either the living room or kitchen, Willow's footsteps padded across the floor. A door clicked opened. The sliver of light beneath his door darkened. A door thumped closed. Outside his window, crickets chirped faintly, followed by an owl's *who-whoooo, who-whoooo, who-whoooo.*

Denver blinked, blinked again, and a hot tear rolled down his cheek, followed by a huge sigh stretching his ribs.

He turned the lamp back on to set the alarm and turned the lamp back off.

Forget the freaking alarm.

You two really do get along better than you and Jan—you two really do get along better than you and Jan—you two really do get along better than you and Jan—you two really—

Each letter, each syllable, each word—another nail in his coffin.

A hint of orange illuminated the curtains. Denver rose to the side of the bed and set his feet where Eliza had slept a week ago. In fits and starts, sleep had tortured him, until he'd finally drifted off.

To wake up, he brushed his teeth, which didn't help. Bloodshot eyes, crusty with sleep—or tears—stared back from the mirror.

He sat on the bed. Doors clicked and thumped, probably Willow making breakfast and getting ready to drive to Clarksville for groceries. The aroma of coffee drifted into his room. The air conditioning fluttered the curtains. Willow's footfalls padded to the front door when she left.

Denver tried the knob on the guest room door. Sitting on the made-up bed, Eliza wore wrinkled jeans and a white T-shirt. A single braid, thick and black, fell across her shoulder. She stood and signed, "Is it time to go?"

"In fifteen minutes. Time enough for me to talk you out of leaving."

She dropped to the bed. Her bloodshot eyes were worse than Denver's. She raised her hands. "I've been thinking about us. I'm going home instead of to the schoolhouse. We don't have phones or computers, so don't come to Ohio. Don't come to my shows. Don't tell Willow about us."

Denver slumped against the door frame. She really meant it. She didn't want to see him again—ever. The room's yellow paint swirled nauseously. He swallowed, no saliva at all. This was going to kill him. *She* was going to kill him.

"I really thought you loved me," he signed. "Maybe you don't and I was too stupid to see it. God help me. God help me."

"I want the best for you—does that sound like I don't love you? Please do as I ask. If you love me like I love you, you'll do as I ask."

"Why can't—"

"Except for what I'm about to say, I won't sign another word. I need you to stay with me at the airport until I get on the plane. I won't hug or kiss you goodbye—I'll cry if I do. Will you do this one last thing for me?"

Denver took the carry-on to the front door and slammed it when Eliza reached the pickup.

Outside the airport windows, the 737's white belly ghosted into the hazy overcast. Lights on the wings and tail blinked red. Brown exhaust trailed the engines. Denver wanted to scream like the plane screamed.

He reached for the phone on his belt holder to tell Jan about

Eliza leaving. Air filled his hand because the phone sat on his nightstand. Good. Great. Finally. It was about time he explained to Jan how they weren't right for each other. In fact, he should've done that a long time ago, especially when sleeping with Akina should've been his wake-up call.

At the museum, when he entered the Folk-Art gallery, Jan strode toward him. Blonde, almost white hair fluttered at leveled shoulders. Manicured nails slashed scarlet beside the fitted black skirt. Open-toed high heels hammered the white tile. "We need to talk."

"Eliza's gone home."

"Who do you think I want to talk about?" She whirled. "My office—now."

Denver followed. She closed the door and sat at her desk. "Sit. I don't care to break my neck looking up, especially at you."

Denver sat. "What's wrong?"

"I never took myself for a fool."

"What do you mean?"

"What do I *mean?*" Jan said, her voice sharp enough to cut cold steel. "Something happened and Eliza's gone. You need a shave and your eyes look like something out of a horror movie. Your clothes are so wrinkled they could've come from a corpse."

"Whatever. Why are you a fool and why do you think something happened with Eliza?"

"I *was* a fool. Seeing you like this—as well as at another time I've not been able to consider since the show—makes me the genius of all geniuses."

"Will you tell me—"

Jan's chin quivered. She pulled a tissue from a box on the desk. "I thought you loved me. You never said it but I thought it. Even though I saw what I saw, I think I ignored it because I didn't want to believe it was true."

"What did you see?"

"No woman wants to see the man she loves looking at another woman the way you were looking at Eliza that night on the deck."

Denver couldn't deny it. He'd smiled at Eliza that night like a schoolboy with his first crush. "Jan, I—"

"Don't." Jan threw the tissue to the desk. "Regardless of how you led me on, business is business. I'll continue to welcome her in my gallery, regardless of whatever relationship you two might have. I don't even care if you come with her, I'll be civil."

"Look, I'm sorry, but all we ever did was date. We never even said we were exclusive. And let's not forget how you saw other people."

"Don't you dare try to blame this on me, Denver Andrews."

"I'm just telling you how it was between us."

"You're saying that so you won't feel guilty."

Denver worked his jaw. "Did we say if we were exclusive or not?"

A tear rolled down Jan's cheek.

"See? You won't even admit it so you can blame it all on me."

She lowered her head. "Didn't saying I wanted to marry you mean I thought we were exclusive?"

"I'm sorry, but you never said anything about marriage until I came back from Ohio the first time."

Jan's jaw muscles tightened. "I burned the kapp you gave me last night." She raised her head, nostrils flaring. "It was a pleasure, you jerk."

Denver left her office.

At home, Willow's car was gone. Maybe she was with Mark.

Denver took Eliza's painting from behind the pickup seat and carried it to the basement, where his folded shirt lay over the case of oil paints. He placed the covered painting on the stand, gave the paints and brushes a glance, shuffled along the gravel walkway to the dock, and sat with his sandals hanging in the water.

An osprey called, a sound like a rusty door hinge squeaking. Denver shaded his eyes. The magnificent bird of prey soared and wheeled, the white underbody contrasting against the sky, blue and empty.

Denver rubbed his chin. Shave again? If ever?

A week later he rubbed his chin again, sticky like blackberry briars.

A week after that he tugged bristly whiskers.

Another week passed, and Willow yelled from the deck, "Jan's on the phone! She says it's important!"

Denver started toward the house, and his shorts fell to his ankles. Belt taken in another notch, he crunched along the gravel walkway. The quicker he got rid of Jan, the better.

In the kitchen, Willow turned from the sink. "She's on your phone in your room."

He closed the door, dropped to the bed, placed the hard plastic to his ear. "What."

"It's about time, Mr. Jerk. What's going on with Eliza? Absalom called a few days ago and mumbled something about her not coming back."

"We haven't been in touch since she left."

"Having a lover's spat?"

"You call that being civil?"

"I said I'd be civil during a show." Jan didn't say the words, she spat them. "That's not happening and you need to fix it."

"Maybe Jon knows something."

"Don't you think I already called him? He's as clueless as you are. I'm only calling you now because I had no other choice.

"Out of my hands."

"You better put it in your hands before I—"

Denver ended the call, dropped the phone on the bed, and returned to the dock.

He lowered his feet into the warm water. One sandal fell, twisting, turning, brown disappearing into blackness. How easy to sink like that … just fall and sink… fall and sink.

He looked back at the house. What would Willow think if he drowned himself? A tragic accident, evidenced by an overturned canoe in the middle of the lake? The local EMS might find his body before it decomposed to the point where an open coffin was impractical. Regardless, his death would cause Willow to cry and say over and over: "Den, why didn't you tell me why you wouldn't eat or shave? We were all each other had and now I'm alone."

No, she and Mark would probably make a life together. If not, she'd meet someone in med school.

In the cool shade beneath the deck, Denver patted the aluminum hull of his old buddy. Time for one last trip.

This time to the bottom of the lake.

Chapter 35

The black dress, hot from the midday sun, rubbed Eliza's legs as she walked through the back yard. Sweat slickened her underarms, trickled into the small of her back. Smells of cow and chicken manure, of the thick air of late August, humid and heavy, hung in the air. The sour odor of her own body, along with the musty cloth of the gray apron pinned to her dress, rose from herself. Warm grass caught between her toes.

In the dimness of the barn, she climbed the ladder to the loft, sank into the hay, and watched a stick of sunlight streaming through a crack in the wall. Watched its captive flutter of dust motes. Watched a mouse scurry across a wooden beam. Watched a wasp paste chewed wood to its nest, gray and filled with holes.

She rolled over in the prickly hay to look down at Papa's tools hanging from a board. A hammer. A set of wrenches. Large and small pliers. Scissors for cutting cockleburs out of the horse's tail. A knife used last fall for helping Vernon skin a pig. A whetstone.

Eliza climbed from the loft, wooden rungs digging into her arches. A dusting of rust coated the knife. She took it and the whetstone to Papa's workbench, spit on the stone, stroked the blade against it. Back and forth, back and forth, back and forth. The grit whispered minute vibrations into her palm. Secrets she intended to keep.

She thumbed the blade, sharp enough to stick, and scraped

it against a fingernail. White slivers powdered into the air.

The bones in her hand laddered beneath her skin, the same in her feet. Papa could hang her in the garden for a skinny scarecrow.

Or place her in the ground.

Through the kitchen she walked. Heads turned. Eyes followed. Papa waved her toward the table and her plate of food. She continued upstairs.

Her window beckoned, like a bright light pulling her to the Creator. She lay in the narrow space between the bed and the wall. Dark. A grave.

Sitting on the bed, she slipped the knife under her pillow. Not now. Not yet. Give the Creator more time to create a miracle.

Chapter 36

The empty lake amazed Denver. Not a single boat in sight—not a fishing boat, not a sailboat, not a ski boat, not a pontoon boat. The miracle of solitude to end his heartache of losing Eliza.

Over the past weeks, while he sat on the dock, nothing of the lake had caught his attention.

It was completely different now.

Almost no wind blew, just enough to ripple the water against the canoe's aluminum hull, similar to the sound of Eliza's laughter, soft and low in her throat, with the hint of her personality transforming in those early days at the schoolhouse, gray eyes focused on every sign, black eyebrows rising with comprehension, photographic memory absorbing everything she saw.

The liquid smell of water, of life, rose from the lake's gray-green surface. When everyone went to Eliza's home for her paintings, the highway had crossed a river a time or two. Absalom said it was the Mohican River, the same river that flowed through the woods near their house. Not at all, it was Eliza's river.

During one of those crossings, Denver had rolled his window down. Eliza's river carried that same liquid smell, not salt like the ocean, not dank like a swamp, impossible to describe. Alive maybe? Exactly. Like her.

He tossed the paddle into the front of the canoe. A school of tiny fish—fisherman called them butterbean shad—flipped around him like ghosts tapping fingertips on the mirrored surface.

Flip-flip.

Flip-flip-flip.

Flip-flip.

Water boiled in the middle of the shad. An elongated silver body, telltale lines down its sides, a huge striped bass gorged itself.

The shad flipped no more.

Denver gripped the cool metal sides of the canoe. Exhale until his lungs were empty, suck in until they were full, and drown before the sun faded above him.

Count or just do it?

Was he sure?

One. He rocked the canoe to the left. Two. He rocked the canoe to the right.

Three.

He wasn't sure.

Because of Eliza.

Would she kill herself, too?

No, not after everything she'd overcome. Like the question Akina had demanded an answer to from Absalom, after she'd translated the conversation to Eliza about attending art shows, "Haven't you seen how strong she is?"

Denver grabbed the paddle. There was absolutely no way he would dishonor her strength by drowning himself in the lake that she loved as much he did.

He dug the paddle into the water, so hard and so fast that a kid could probably water ski behind him.

Humor. Maybe a miracle *was* due, and not the miracle of solitude to kill his stupid self with. The best miracle would be to pack a suitcase and fly to Ohio, then get Eliza to open up to her family. Regardless of any customs, how could they shun her because of love?

The aluminum hull scraped sand. He hopped out and pulled it halfway from the water. Shave, shower, change clothes, pack a bag, tell Willow he was going to Ohio, ignore her questions, buy a plane ticket, pick up a burger for the road in Oxford because he was starved, including fries and a milk shake to start putting on weight before his clothes fell off.

At the kitchen counter with her laptop, Willow looked up when he came in. "Enjoy your canoe ride?"

"You could say that."

"About time you took it out again. Oh, you got a text tone a minute ago."

Denver took the phone from his nightstand. Jon's text asked if he was home. Why did he want to know that unless he was here? Denver texted he was home, and another text popped up.

Absalom is with me. Something's happened with Eliza and he wants to see you. I'd say more but I can't believe it myself.

"Den?" Willow stood at his door. "A car just pulled up with two men in it."

Denver went to the front door, Willow on his heels. They looked out the two narrow windows bordering the door. Absalom climbed out of the car. Jon stayed behind the wheel.

"Isn't that Absalom?" Willow said. "Except for the jeans and haircut, you described him as a huge guy with red hair." She reached for the doorknob and Denver grabbed her arm. Despite Jon's cryptic text about not believing something about Eliza, which hinted toward her suicide, Denver knew that was impossible. Maybe she'd told Absalom they were in love and he came to see if it were true.

"Willow, that text was from Jon. He said Absalom wanted to see me, and I'd like to talk to him alone."

"Does this have anything to do with you not eating or

shaving or telling me why?"

"Look, you only asked that a few times because I know you respect my privacy. I'll tell you everything after Absalom tells me why he's here."

"Good. I'd like to have my big brother back."

Denver waited until Willow's bedroom door closed behind her before he opened the front door, which Absalom, with his fist up, was about to knock. His monstrous bulk, wearing blue jeans and a white, button-up shirt, blocked the view of the car.

"Absalom, what—"

"What did you do to her?" He pushed into the hall. Denver closed the door and faced him.

"I don't know what—"

Absalom lunged toward Denver, drove his forearm into Denver's throat, and shoved him against the wall. "What did you DO to her?" Blood clouded his face. His breath smelled faintly of coffee.

Adrenalin burned through Denver, seared through his neck and chest. "Can't ... can't ..." Panicking, he clawed at Absalom's forearm.

Absalom lessened the pressure. "What did you DO to her?"

Denver swallowed, trying to ease the pain in his nearly crushed throat. Did Absalom's rage mean Eliza had killed herself? "Is she okay?" His eyes filled with burning tears. "Just ... just tell me she's okay."

Absalom's face paled. He collapsed to the floor, a huge pile of legs, arms, and reddish-brown hair, umbrella haircut replaced by a modern trim, face contorted like a man about to cry.

Denver knelt beside him. "Absalom, tell me—" Denver swallowed. "Tell me Eliza isn't—"

"She's dead, Denver. Dead and buried."

Denver grabbed Absalom's collar and shook him. "She

wouldn't do that." Despite his disbelief, he could only manage a whisper. "She wouldn't do—"

"What did you do to her?"

"She wouldn't hurt herself—she's too strong for that."

"Would it matter to you if she *did* hurt herself?"

"More than you know."

"She might as well be dead." Absalom got to his feet. "Oneita found a knife under her pillow last night. Thank God she found it before Eliza used it."

Denver fell against the wall, a cold wave of relief washing over him. "What happened after that?"

"I tried to get her to tell me about the knife, but she just curled up in bed. She wasn't like that until she came back home. What did you do to her?"

"She made me promise to not say anything. We need to talk to her."

"Is your sister here?"

"Yes, why?"

"Because I want to get to the bottom of this now, and that means talking to her, too."

"But—"

Absalom turned away, opened the door, and waved toward the car. Eliza got out, and Denver's knees almost gave way. The belt she wore creased wrinkles in the jeans around her thin waist. Head down, she came inside, and Absalom closed the door. "I took my family to Jon's house last night. He'll do anything to help, even if it means sitting in the car all day. Call your sister. We need to find out what's wrong with Eliza."

Denver looked into Eliza's eyes, but she refused to acknowledge him. He faced Absalom. "You don't think I did something to her now?"

"I— Well, I have a problem with my temper sometimes. Imagining all the wrong things during the flight and the drive didn't help. Call your sister."

Denver showed Absalom and Eliza to the living room. Despite the turn of events, the fact that Eliza was alive, especially after Absalom said she wasn't, couldn't be better news. They sat on the sofa, and he knelt in front of her. Her cheeks, once smooth and filled with color, were sunken and pale. The thick braid, always shining and neat at the schoolhouse, was frazzled and dull. He signed hello, but she didn't raise her head. She was going to keep their secret of falling in love regardless of anything and everything.

"Absalom, how did you get her to come here?"

"I signed I'd beat you if she didn't come."

Willow's bedroom door opened. "I'm glad you and Eliza are here, Absalom. I was thinking about beating my brother myself for how he's been acting since Eliza left."

Denver sat in a chair across from Eliza. Willow took the matching chair at the other end of the sofa and signed, "Hey, Eliza, you're as thin as Den."

Eliza shrugged.

"That's not important now," Absalom said. "I flew all the way from Ohio to get to the bottom of this. Eliza barely eats or drinks. She doesn't paint, even after I made her the studio. She won't sign anything." Absalom slapped his thigh. "Look at these pants. Everyone's wearing blue jeans—even Oneita—to make Eliza feel better. I had to make her wear jeans for the trip." He rubbed his hair. "Ethan and I got haircuts despite our bishop saying not to. Nothing helps, absolutely nothing."

"Denver practically lives on the dock," Willow said.

Absalom closed his eyes. His mouth worked like a man solving a problem in his head. He opened his eyes. "Your name's Willow?"

"Yes."

"I was sorry to hear about your parents. When they were

alive, did you or Denver ever do or say anything that made them feel like an idiot?"

"I wouldn't say so." Willow faced Denver. "Do you remember anything like that?"

"Just silly things. Nothing serious."

"Yeah, like when I told you I knocked on Eliza's door and she didn't answer. Forgetting she's deaf made me look like an idiot for sure."

"I see," Absalom said, "so you know what I mean. Tess—she's Eliza's younger sister—is making me feel like an idiot now." He stood. "Denver, that day we talked online, I saw your kitchen behind you. Can you bring your laptop to your dining room? My family's at Jon's house, waiting to hear from me. Jon called Becca when we got here."

Denver brought the laptop from his room. Waiting at the dining room table with Eliza, Absalom turned. "This involves you, too, Willow."

Willow joined them, and Denver started the chat. Tess appeared, sitting at Jon's table. Denver glanced at Eliza. Head still down, she refused to look at the laptop. He admired her for keeping her promise to stay with her family, so he couldn't break his promise to not tell them either. Whatever was about to happen, maybe it was the miracle they needed to be together. He turned the volume up.

"Hi, Papa." Tess said. "Is what I said about Eliza—"

"Where are your mama and Ethan?"

"They're here." Tess pushed the laptop away from her, which expanded the field of view. Holding Ivy, Oneita sat to Tess's left. Ethan sat to her right.

"Well, Absalom?" Oneita said.

"I think Tess may be right."

"I think so, too," Ethan said. "I saw the same thing."

"I've thought about it more since you left," Oneita said. "You need to come home."

"I don't know what to do about it. We'll figure it out when we get back."

"I *told* you so, Papa." Tess said. "That day at our house, Denver was holding Eliza's hand and smiling at her like I would want a boy to smile at me one day."

"Hush," Oneita said, "you already told us that. Absalom, I meant for *you* to come home. Eliza needs to stay with Denver and his sister so she can eat and look beautiful in her wedding dress. *You* come home so we can make plans to move. I'm not staying in Ohio when my grandchildren live in Virginia." Oneita ended the chat.

Willow stared at Denver. "You and Eliza are in love? I knew you liked her, but when did that happen?"

Denver went to Eliza, lifted her chin, and translated everything. Her eyes widened as she read his signs. She jumped from the chair into his arms and kissed one cheek— "I love you"—kissed the other cheek— "I love you"—and kissed him fully on the lips.

"How in the world did I miss all that?" Willow said.

"I knew they were close at the sign language school," Absalom said, "but I missed it also. At least I don't feel like an idiot anymore."

"I sure do, but I don't care. My brother isn't going to marry Jan, and I'll take being an idiot over that any day."

Denver led Eliza to the sofa, where they both sat. "I think I can speak for both of us when I say we're sorry about everything." He translated this to Eliza.

Absalom sat beside her. "Please translate for me, Denver."

"Me too, Willow said. "I don't want to miss a single word."

"Denver," Absalom said, "how did you and Eliza get so close?"

"To be honest, for me it started with the way her eyes never miss anything … the way she studies nature … the way she seems to know what I'm thinking before I sign it. Then there's her strength and the unique woman she's become. There's no way I could live without her."

"I don't know how I didn't see it." Absalom's eye narrowed. "Have you two behaved?"

Denver signed this to Eliza, who signed, "Stop it, Papa. You're embarrassing me."

"Anything else?" Absalom said to Denver, who signed this to Eliza.

She placed Denver's hand over her heart and released it to sign, "Almost from the first sign Denver taught me, I knew our colors belonged together … like the clouds turn a sunset red and shimmering … like the wind makes the leaves dance during a storm … like lightning brightens the night … like the thunder touched my heart and let me know someone was out in the world who would love me like I would love him." She kissed Denver's cheek. "And now I have that someone."

Denver had never seen such beautiful signs—even more beautiful because Eliza had meant them about him. If he told her how much he loved her for every second of every minute of every hour of every day for the rest of his life, it would never be enough.

He translated everything Eliza had signed. Absalom slowly nodded and smiled, and Willow said, "Wow, you two need to write a romance novel about all this one day."

"What I want to know," Absalom said, "is why you and Eliza thought you couldn't tell us about— No, there I go again, being an idiot. You told her how we're Amish, and if she left us, we would shun her."

"I tried to get her to go home and come back when she could. She said that would hurt worse than being apart all the time."

"If you love each other as much as you just said you do, I

understand. I don't think I've ever seen Eliza as happy as when she kissed you and told you she loves you." He reached around her to pat Denver's shoulder. "You could always come back to Ohio. You'd make a fine Amish son-in-law."

"No thanks. I'm not into umbrella haircuts."

"Jon's joking is rubbing off on you. Then again, you couldn't drive or fly here to see Willow, not with the Amish bans on technology." He shook his head. "Your situation was impossible. I see why you both didn't say anything."

Eliza raised her hands. "Papa, I'm sorry for making so much trouble."

Denver translated, and Absalom said, "The time for sorry is over, Eliza. None of us can be happy if you aren't happy."

"You don't mind leaving home?" she signed. "Denver told me how you honor God by being Amish."

"When our bishop disapproved of my haircut, I'd almost decided I could honor God without being Amish. I respect the Amish order and everything it stands for, but I think I can still honor God by honoring my daughter. Besides, your mama's right about moving here to be near our grandchildren."

Denver laughed. "When Oneita told you to come back so you could make plans to move, it reminded me of a saying we have in the south. If Mama ain't happy, ain't *nobody* happy.'"

Chapter 37

Three months later.

Escaping the wedding reception at the local golf club's old manor house, Denver drove away.

Eliza waved to her family, along with Willow and Mark and his parents, Jon and his family, Akina and Dan holding hands, and several local friends gathered in front of the grand old house. Even Jan had come to mend her broken friendship with Denver, a new guy at her side.

At the stop sign at the club's entrance, Eliza signed, "I'm still mad at you."

"I know, I know, you don't like our honeymoon being a secret. I didn't tell anyone else where we're going either, if it makes you feel any better."

"We didn't pack many clothes, is it far?"

He kissed her, almost the same as the kiss that night on the dock. "That give you a hint?"

"It must be really really close because you really really want me like I really really want you."

"You think so?"

Eliza poked his ribs. "I know so."

"Can you close your eyes? It's a surprise."

"How will I know when to open them?"

"I'll kiss you."

Eliza closed her eyes and Denver hit the accelerator. The tires squealed away from the stop sign. Eliza, hanging onto the seatbelt, giggled low in her throat.

Denver could hardly believe it. Here they were, married and on their way to a great honeymoon in the perfect season for one—late October in lake country; autumn leaves blazing in red, gold, orange, and every shade between; the weather mild and the tourist crowds lessening in Occoneechee State Park. It didn't get any better than that.

He glanced at his beautiful bride. It would *definitely* get better. *And* soon.

For the reception, she'd changed into the same tie-died dress she wore to her first art show. In the two shows since then, collectors raved over her oils, earning enough money to offer to Absalom for a house nearby. He wouldn't take a dime, saying Jon had made an offer on the farm. Subsequently, he signed a contract for a house on the next street over in the same large subdivision as Denver and Willow's house, which all three planned to share until Willow returned to college, or until she started a life on her own or with Mark.

Denver took a right on the bypass, drove over the arching bridge, drove over another shorter bridge spanning a cove, then took another right at the park's entrance, where he checked in with the attendant who mentioned the new honeymoon cabin's amenities, including a king-sized bed, hot tub, gourmet kitchen, and gave him the key.

At the cabin, he ran around to the passenger door and helped Eliza out, faced her toward the gorgeous log structure and kissed her.

"It's beautiful," she signed. "I remember what you said about renting a cabin." She ran to the rear of the cabin, where a deck faced the lake. From a nearby oak, red and gold leaves fell around her, and she raised her nose into the breeze. "I love the smell of the leaves. My river's nice, but I love your lake."

"Don't forget how much you love me." Denver gave her the key. "Check out the inside while I get our luggage."

With the two suitcases in the living room, he returned to his pickup for the new laptop he had bought for work. Eliza stopped looking around the kitchen. "No, sir, no work on our honeymoon. When did you sneak your new laptop into the pickup?"

"I didn't tell you, but Jon was so impressed with my design for his solar system, he wants one for your parent's house when he makes it into a sign language school."

"As much as I care about the house being a sign language school, this week is about us, not work." Eliza went to him, took the laptop case, and set it by the television. "This goes by the big-screen TV you're not watching either."

Denver took the luggage to the master suite. Eliza left his side and went to the bed to pull the covers back. She slipped the straps of the dress from her shoulders and let it fall to the floor.

Denver was speechless, thoughtless, and completely dumbfounded. No painting in the world compared to Eliza.

She wore the same nearly-nothing panties and matching bra she'd worn on the night they had slept on the pontoon boat. She also wore the same silver clasp in her hair, which, like that night, held two lengths of her long, shining hair away from her face. She pulled the clasp free and placed it on the nightstand, lifted her hair and let it fall, turning around as she did. Denver held his hand to his chest. A good pain—an excellent pain even—nothing like the day she broke his heart.

He undressed to his underwear and started toward her, but she ran past him to the sliding glass doors that led to the deck. He caught up and tapped her shoulder. "Hey, I'm right here."

"Look."

A pulsing, shimmering ball of molten red, the sun hovered above the autumn foliage across the lake, the same scene he'd imagined showing her. Behind her, he slipped his hands around her waist and held the warmth of her tight against him, his cheek next to hers. His eyelashes fluttered in her hair, soft and sweet with her favorite shampoo.

Eliza turned in his arms and pressed against him. Warm and smooth skin. Intense gray eyes. Noble nose. Full lips defined as if an artist had sculpted them in rose quartz. She kissed him feather-soft, sharing their taste, the tingling hint of desire, until she took his hand and led him to the bed.

Eliza turned the lamp on.

Denver's chest rose and fell slowly, like the waves on their lake at sunset. She raised on elbow to study his nose, his lips, the small cleft in his clean-shaven chin.

Dreams of love. Prayers to the Creator for love. Her heart filled. Her soul sang. Her colors bloomed into rainbow brilliance.

Tears wet her cheeks.

Thank you.

She eased from the bed and took the new silk nightgown from her suitcase. A tie-dyed gown would've been perfect, but when Willow had translated the clerk's words, that she never had seen one, Eliza's frown changed to a smile. She signed to Willow to ask if the clerk had a nightgown in blue. The clerk answered with a nod, then took her to a rack with several shimmering silk nightgowns in the deepest blue Eliza had ever seen. The clerk took one out. A robe fell to the floor and Eliza picked it up. The clerk reached for the robe, and Eliza signed to Willow to ask if the robe was for men. The clerk replied that it was, including how it would make a fine present. Eliza added the robe to her purchases, happier than ever because the robe and gown matched Denver's blue eyes.

She slipped the gown over her head, and cool silk caressed her skin. At the glass doors, she slid them open and stepped out onto the deck, shivering immediately at the cold touch of the boards beneath her feet.

The moon had risen, huge and bright, like the night she and Denver swam in the lake. Slight waves dappled the bank with foam. A sudden breeze tousled her hair. Golden leaves tinged with red fell from the tree beside the deck.

An owl swooped by to land on a naked limb hanging over the water. Twisting its head almost in a circle, it stopped and stared at her with huge blinking eyes. The curved beak opened and closed, opened and closed.

The owl flew away. A suggestion of brown on silent wings, it glided low across the shimmering water.

The waves, the leaves, the owl's call—all silent. What did each of these wonderful things sound like? Was she destined to never know Denver's laugh? Their child's "I love you?" Life's countless wonders out of reach like Denver had been a few short months ago?

His hands slipped around her waist. His touch, his warmth, the solid feel of the strength within him would see her through life's challenges.

She turned around, and he signed, "I love the gown. Do I get one?"

"Silly you." She took the robe from the bed and held it open.

"Wow," he signed, "we match."

He slipped the robe on, and she tied the belt. "I bought this when I bought the gown. I love them both because they're blue, like your eyes."

"I love you" —he kissed the tip of her nose— "even when you're naked and not in this gown."

"Like this?" The gown fell to the floor.

"Definitely." The robe fell to the floor.

At the bed, he climbed in beside her and kissed her, kissed her again and again until she rolled him over.

His throat vibrated beneath her lips. His chest rose and fell beneath her caresses.

Afterward, she snuggled into his shoulder, sleep taking them.

"I love you, Deevrr."

Chapter 38

Two years later.

In the back yard of Eliza's former home, not far from the rusted well pump, now shiny with a new coat of green paint, she waited while Denver inspected the batteries inside the barn, which also housed the electronics of the newly installed electrical system. To one side of the barn, on a black tripod, a huge solar panel gleamed in the midday sun. Perspiration slickened her underarms. Denver said it was hound-dog hot, meaning all a hound dog did on a day like this was stretch out in the shade and pant, and she completely agreed.

He closed the door, wiped sweat from his forehead, and said something she couldn't catch on his lips. Eliza turned the volume on her hearing aids up. "What did you say? And don't forget to sign."

"I said it was too hot for work," Denver said, signing also. "I also said the workers did a great job with the installation."

"Can we try it now?"

"See if Ethan and Timothy are ready."

The grass swished against Eliza's ankles. Her brother, ever the bookworm, had surprised her with his choice to learn sign language over the past two years and teach here instead of staying in Virginia, but he promised Papa and Mama he'd return to finish high school and go to college. Tess surprised Eliza, too—well, not really—using a smart phone and playing games on the internet. Still, she made sure to study, and she earned honor roll grades her first year in junior high school.

The surprises didn't end there. Papa got his driver's license and a job at the golf course as a greenskeeper in training, as well as building a shop at home to make rocking chairs. Between household work and tending Ivy, Mama learned from Willow how to grow vegetables in containers. Ivy was still Ivy—cute, dark-haired, endlessly talkative and, because she was potty trained, a joy to keep when Mama, Papa, and Tess were all busy at the same time.

Something else surprised Eliza. Willow and Mark broke up when she told him she wanted to go back to college full time. He said he couldn't handle a long-distance relationship, but he understood how important she took her education. Willow told Denver all she wanted for her part in the lake house was a welcome-home hug and her bedroom whenever she needed it.

When Papa went back home and told Bishop Marley he was leaving the Amish, including how Jon was buying the farm, he also told him how Ethan was thinking about teaching sign language there. Bishop Marley didn't mind as long as Ethan didn't interact with anyone personally, because officially, the family was going to be shunned. Bishop Marley didn't mind Timothy teaching either, as long as he went home after class so it wouldn't look like he was interacting personally with Ethan. This upset the two young men, who wanted to fish on the weekends. Vernon spoke to Bishop Marley, who finally conceded the point of how fishing together shouldn't cause any problems.

Eliza closed the kitchen door, signed and said, "Ethan, are you and Timothy ready to try the lights?"

Sitting at the table with a book, Timothy raised his head. "I'll be happy when I don't have to study sign language by a kerosene lamp."

"Don't worry, you'll learn enough to help Ethan when the classes start."

"I'll tell Denver we're ready." Ethan left the schoolhouse.

"Timothy," Eliza signed and said, "I haven't seen—"

"Eliza?" Timothy looked up from the book. "You can talk?"

"Ethan didn't tell you about my hearing aids?" She pulled her hair back. "I got them a few months after my wedding. They're not perfect, but they help. My words are kind of mushy in my mouth, but I see a speech therapist and practice all the time." Eliza smiled to let Timothy know her next sentence was a joke. "Denver says I practice *too* much when he's working."

Timothy grinned. "I shouldn't say this, but I bet Hannes wishes he was deaf."

"What do you mean?" She sat beside Timothy.

"I was always sorry for how we teased you." Timothy's hands faltered. "I'll try to sign while I talk. I've learned a lot in a year, but I get mixed up sometimes."

"That's all right. Do the best you can."

"I was especially sorry that day at the river."

Eliza neither signed nor said anything in reply. Those days were long gone and never would return. "Is something wrong?"

"For Hanne's it is. He got married last month, and his wife bosses him worse than he ever bossed me. That's why I bet he wishes we was deaf."

Eliza covered a grin. "Well, maybe things will get better for him."

"At least I can say if it weren't for him, you might not have met Denver and learned sign language."

"Why is that?"

"I thought you hit him that day at the river. The next time he and Papa went to town, he heard about the sign language school. He told Papa to tell your papa as soon as they got back."

"I'm sorry, but it's hard to believe he wanted to help me."

"He told me he did it to get rid of you for however long you'd be gone. At least he did something nice for you, even if he didn't mean to."

Ethan came inside, breathing hard. "I've been yelling to ask if you're ready for the lights."

"Timothy told me about Hannes."

Timothy got up from the table. "Let's see if we have lights." At the open door he waved, and six overhead LED fixtures lit the room.

"All right!" Ethan said, pumping his fist. "That's what *I'm* talkin' 'bout."

"I see you brought that southern saying back here," Eliza signed.

"Come on, sis, be cool. Now we can get air conditioning and running water and bathrooms and a dryer and a stove and—"

Eliza grabbed his hands and let go. "Slow down your signs and your words. You'll confuse your students if you teach like that."

"Sorry. Tell Denver the lights are great. We'll have lunch in about an hour."

Eliza met Denver at the shed and told him about the lights and lunch. "Do you need to do anything else?"

"I need to show Ethan and Timothy how to check the propane level for the generator and how to fill the batteries with distilled water before we go."

"We can do that later. I never showed you my river."

Eliza took Denver's hand and led him along the path. Leaves from last fall, dried and brown, crunched beneath their shoes to release their spicy aroma. Two squirrels chased each other across the path and zipped up a hickory tree, gray blurs in the branches, flared tails trailing them.

At the river, Eliza expected Denver to sign or say something.

She waited, then signed, "You're quiet."

"I'm thinking about how we're both drawn to water. Your river is as beautiful as my lake."

"It's not as wide, but it was wide to me when I was little." She leaned over and gathered a bit of mud on her fingertip, studied it, flicked it away, and stood.

"Is this where you got the idea to paint with what you call your colors?" Denver signed.

"You could say that. I was standing in the water when I got the idea. I was sad because I didn't have any friends. I was sad because Mama slapped me at the well. I rubbed mud on my arms because I felt like I belonged at the bottom of the river."

Looking at the river again, Denver glanced at her. "Well, at least we don't have to worry about *that* anymore."

"I can't tell you how happy that makes me." She faced him. "I have you and I have our colors." She patted her tummy, which Willow said would soon be big enough to call a baby-bump. "And our colors are in our baby."

"It didn't look like it for a while, but everything worked out." Denver kissed her forehead. "What do you think would've happened if your family hadn't come to Virginia?"

Eliza looked away, ashamed of how she'd considered killing herself. She poked Denver's stomach. "I'd have married some hot Amish guy and had a dozen kids. What about you? Would you have married Jan?"

"Are you kidding? I would've drowned myself first."

Denver laughed. Eliza slipped her arms around him and held him close. This was what she was made for, to share her life, her love, and her colors with the one man who loved her as much as she loved him.

She smacked his butt. "Race you back for lunch."

Eliza ran into the path, laughing as Denver ran behind her. Leaves crunched beneath their feet. Their breaths came in quick bursts. She slowed to let him pass. He stopped and she ran to him.

"Lunch can wait, my hot Virginia guy." She smacked his butt again. "If you know what I mean."

She took Denver's hand and led him off the path, to a clearing where she'd spread a blanket while he was busy with his work. No words or signs were necessary. They kissed, slowly undressed each other, and lay on the blanket, their bodies melting together with their familiar joining … loving, passionate, and as always, filled with their colors.

Book Club Questions

1. Eliza lost her hearing from the measles between the ages of two and three. In the first chapter, it's mentioned how people treated her when she tried to speak later in life. How did they treat her, and how did it affect her?

2. Do you think Eliza turned to the natural world, along with painting, as an escape from how people treated her for being deaf?

3. As described in the first chapter, what does she hope for most in life?

4. Discuss Eliza's memory of what happened at the well pump when her mother slapped her.

5. In the second chapter, we meet Denver, Willow, and Jan. Are there any hints as to how Jan and Denver aren't a good match?

6. In the same chapter, Denver mentions what influenced him to get a minor degree in sign language, which was an African documentary about deaf kids in remote villages not being exposed to sign language. Discuss how it would feel to live without being able to communicate with anyone, except with gestures.

7. In chapter eight, Eliza secretly dressed in Becca's clothes. This, along with other hints, foreshadowed her family's exit from the Amish community by the end of the book. What do you think they were, and in what order?

8. Some readers may disapprove of Denver's relationship with Akina. However, understanding why it happened could add insight into Denver's personality and his relationship with Jan. Why do you think his and Akina's relationship became physical if he cared about Eliza like he thought he might?

9. In what ways did Denver fight his growing feelings for Eliza, and why did he fight them instead of giving in to them?

10. The scene when the reader discovers why Eliza's mother slapped her at the well is tense and revealing. Did you empathize with her, or were you angry with her, like Eliza was angry with her?

11. Why did Eliza sabotage Jan's ski belt? Although it was wrong, was it understandable?

12. Willow doesn't think Jan and Denver are a good match. For the reader, more is revealed during the story to strengthen this belief. What are those things?

13. After the internet chat with Eliza's father, Denver admits he loves her. Why did she leave him when the one thing she wanted most was to know he loved her?

14. Before the chapters where Eliza and Denver were considering suicide, there were hints concerning this. What were they?

15. After Denver took Eliza to the airport, he saw Jan. What did she see to make her confront him about his feelings toward Eliza?

16. When Eliza's father attacked Denver and told him Eliza was "dead and buried," how did you feel?

17. Did you expect Eliza's family to leave the Amish order to be with her?

18. During Denver and Eliza's honeymoon, when she goes to the cabin balcony in the middle of the night, what is she thinking about when she sees the owl?

19. In the last chapter, did it surprise you to discover how Timothy and Ethan were going to teach sign language in Eliza's old home? What were some hints that this might happen?

20. At the river, Eliza told Denver what gave her the idea to paint with things from nature. What was that? Are you happy about Eliza and Denver expecting a baby? Did the story end as you hoped it would?

AUTHOR'S NOTE

One of the settings in this novel is Clarksville, Virginia, including their annual lake festival called Lakefest. Clarksville is the only town on Kerr Lake, affectionately known to locals as Buggs Island Lake.

It's a wonderful town, quiet and charming, and one of the nicest places for a lake vacation a person will ever visit, with boating, fishing, and camping opportunities galore, including nearby Occoneechee State Park.

Visit clarksvilleva.com for more information.

I would be remiss to not mention how my research has given me a newfound respect for the Deaf and the Amish. Both lifestyles are challenging. However, in their own ways, both are rewarding. Be that as it may, some Amish schools do teach their children sign language, while some of the stricter groups do not, and I am using the latter for this novel.

A huge thanks to those who helped critique and beta read this book, especially a deaf writer I know online. It would not be what it is without you. And a special thanks to my barber for allowing me to use his name. After he read his dialogue, he smiled and said, "That sounds just like me!"

To follow my work, find me on Facebook under J. Willis Sanders and at jwillissanders.wixsite.com/writer.

J. Willis Sanders lives in southern Virginia, with his wife, banjos, resonator guitars, and one acoustic guitar.

With ten novels completed and more on the way, he enjoys crafting intriguing characters with equally intriguing conflicts to overcome. He also loves the natural world and, more often than not, his stories include those settings. Most also utilize intense love relationships and layered themes.

His first novel (not this one, but he plans to publish it) is a ghostly World War II era historical that takes place mostly in the midwestern United States, which utilizes some little-known facts about German POW camps there at the time. It's the first of a three-book series, in which characters from the first continue their lives.

Although he loves history, he has written several contemporary novels as well, and some include interesting paranormal twists, both with and without religious themes.

He also loves the Outer Banks of North Carolina, and he has written three novels within different time frames based on the area, what he calls his Outer Banks of North Carolina Series. (Yes, they'll be published too, and he has more idea about the area.)

Other hobbies include reading (of course), vegetable gardening, playing music with friends, and songwriting, some of which are in a few of his novels.

For readers who didn't want *The Colors of Eliza Gray* to end, his banjo-picking muse thought of a sequel right before publishing, so stay tuned.

Readers: to help those considering a purchase, please leave a review on Amazon.com, or wherever you buy this book.